STRANGELY PARTED.

CHAPTER I.

"SURELY these words must have been written by a madman! What connection could Dick have with such a mystery? And yet—how vividly it is all explained! No, no! It is too horrible! I will destroy this paper before he returns."

This speech was uttered in a woman's horrified voice, and a fair trembling hand thrust a letter over the flames of a spirit-lamp—too eagerly. The paper, instead of catching fire, extinguished the flame, and the words remained as distinct as before.

A man had entered the room just in time to witness the action, and he gave a short cynical laugh as he noted the feverish despair with which the scorched paper was held at sound of his step.

"Secrets, Florence!" he exclaimed in a half-bantering, half suspicious tone, "Come, tell me—what it is you are hiding from me?"

The woman turned swiftly to him, her beautiful face white and panic-stricken.

"What is it you are hiding from me?" she asked, echoing his words with chill desperation. Oh, Dick, Dick! what does it mean?"

"What does what mean?"

NOTICE.—With this Number is Given Away a Coloured Picture for binding with the Work. Other Coloured Pictures will follow.

"This strange letter I found between the leaves of the book you gave me to read. Dick, why—why are these words addressed to you. Surely there must be some mistake."

She hastily smoothed out the paper, her lips growing paler as her gaze rested on her husband's name:

"Richard Garth."

The letter was signed "C. C."

With a sudden movement, Richard Garth tore the paper from her grasp.

"How dare you pry into my secrets!" he muttered through his teeth, his anger betraying himself. "What right had you——"

The words were checked on his lips by the accusing light in Florence's eyes.

"Such a secret Richard," she said scornfully, "all the world should know. Oh, Dick!" breaking into a passionate entreaty, "say it is not true—say so, for pity's sake!"

He folded his arms, and watched her with a dark smile.

"Would you have me lie?" he asked, bending his face closer to hers.

She shuddered, and clasped her hands over her eyes.

"I cannot believe it, Dick—I cannot!"

He gave a cold cruel laugh.

"You do believe it, Florence," he said with a calmness that made her recoil as though the tongue of an asp had pierced her heart.

"It is true then?" she moaned. "And I thought you loved me, Dick."

"I did love you; what I have done was for your sake. I thought you would not be a beggar's bride."

She looked at him as though she could not grasp his meaning, a dull anguish freezing the warmth in her eyes—blue eyes that only a day ago had been as happy and as bright as a ch ld's.

"A beggar's bride—a beggar's bride!" she repeated drearily. "And what fate did you choose for me—what have you made me? A felon's wife! My baby a felon's son!   Oh, Dick! oh, Dick! why have you sinned like this?"

"I have told you—for your sake."

"Then it is I who must give you your reward—betrayal!" she said with passionate contempt. "I could not burden my soul with the secret of such a crime"

"Do as you like" he muttered, "only remember, when you denounce me, you will denounce your child's father."

"He should never know.   Better for him to be reared apart from you, and in ignorance of your existence, than he should live daily under your influence, trusting you and loving you, knowing nothing of the guilt hidden in your heart!   Your sin is greater to him than to me, and I can never forgive you, Dick—never!"

"What can you do, pretty vixen, here in Cairo, where you have not one friend to help you when you have cast me off?"

"You forget there are English officers here," she said quietly;   "I claim their protection."

"From me?"

"From you!   I would rather see you dead, or die myself, than share your sin."

"Nonsense, you are in no way responsible for my actions.   All that is required of you is silence."

"You mean a life of dumb misery with you?   No—no Dick, I could not!   I think my baby's lips would cry out against me if I became a partner in your guilt, and if I kept secret my knowledge I should be that."

"You would not dare carry out your threat!" he hissed, his dark eyes gleaming dangerously under his knit brow.

"I would dare anything to free myself and my child from you," she returned unflinchingly; "only what I do will be done in justice."

She spoke with bitter resolution, her fair young face as white as the snowy robe she wore, her eyes as fearless and as pure as the eyes of an accusing angel.

Richard Garth's gaze drooped before hers, and, muttering a curse, he strode fiercely from the room.

"So this is her code of truth," he thought.   "A deadly weapon to turn against me just now—in her present mood.   What a fool I was ever to have married!"

He walked out into the hot close streets, the sultry desert-air sweeping over him seeming to fan to greater heat the angry fire burning in his soul.

He had a conviction that to reason with Florence would be useless, and he was perplexed as to what course of action he had best choose.

There was little time to be lost, and he hurried on with bent head, trying to devise a plan by which he could escape Florence's threat.

"Only eighteen months married," he muttered, kicking a stone savagely out of his path, "and yet how completely all is changed! It was a mistake—a big mistake; I ought always to have been a free man."

He had been walking at a swift pace, heedless of what direction he took, and he did not realise how far he had gone until he found himself in a balmy rich-budding garden, in the centre of which a young Arab chief—Osman Omar—had pitched his silken tent.

The Arab was one of his most constant companions, but Richard Garth was in no humour to meet him to-day, and he swung round to go in an opposite direction.

Too late. A dark stealthy hand was laid softly on his shoulder, and Garth was forced to turn and face the man he had tried to shun.

"You look as if you were in a cloud," Osman said, drawing him farther into the garden. "Is it ill with the English Lily?"

Garth knew his allusion was to his wife, and his brow lowered.

"Ill? Yes, very ill," he exclaimed, with his eyes fixed on the ground; "she ought never to have been my wife; our lives clash."

"Aye, good and evil always struggle one against the other," the Arab remarked with a sinister laugh; "she is as beautiful as paradise, this white lily you have brought amongst us. Would I could claim her!"

"I wish you could, too, so that I had never seen her; I'm sick to death of her, and she's in my way."

"What if I snatched her from you?"

"I would kill you," Garth said, turning fiercely on him.

Osmam laughed.

"I meant nothing; I could not give love where it is returned with loathing, for, mark you, your wife hates me as much as she fears you."

Garth caught at some scarlet blossoms drooping in his way, and ground them savagely in his hand.

I am more in fear of her than she is of me," he exclaimed bitterly; she is my worst enemy—a traitress who will not hesitate to betray!"

The Arab looked at the red flowers clenched in Garth's hand, and drew back from them.

"We have taken a wrong path," he said, motioning his companion to follow him; "I should not have brought you here. Drop those blossoms; you are playing with death!"

Richard Garth opened his hand and let them fall.

"How do you mean? What is in these flowers?" he asked, drawing back from them as Osman had done.

"Poison! I call this the Garden of Death; the odour of every flower blooming here is deadly.

There is a fountain just outside this grove—you had better go there and cleanse your hands; that powder contains deadly poison."

Garth did as he was advised, then returned to the Arab's side, fascinated by the awful beauty of the deadly garden.

"Those little white buds up there," he said, drawing Osman's attention to some blossoms that were almost like English snowdrops, "are they as fatal as the rest?"

"Not quite; the poison is in the very heart of the flower, and does not evaporate till the berry is broken, then there is little chance for any who inhale the odour. Ten minutes, and there comes a sleep which lasts for ever."

"I can't admire your taste in cultivating these poisonous flowers," Garth observed with a slight shudder, toying with the buds he knew were harmless until they should be broken.

"It is my fancy," the Arab replied. "I hold the key of the gates myself, so there is no danger of anyone coming here, unless by my guidance. Come; the odour is so powerful, we are best farther away."

Osman opened the gate, and led the way to another part of the grounds, passing through many gates, and locking each one after him; but not before Garth had secured some of the deadly white blossoms—not before the Arab's stealthy eyes had caught the action of his hand, as he plucked the buds whose fatal power he had just learned.

When Richard Garth returned to his home that evening, he found Florence sitting in a low chair, with a pale little baby cradled on her breast, one dark-skinned woman fanning her with a huge palm-leaf, another arranging a gorgeous gold-fringed shawl over a swing-cot that was placed in the coolest part of the room.

A quiver passed over the young wife's face as Garth entered, and she held her child closer.

"Have you formed your plans yet?" he asked, standing before her with folded arms.

She met his gaze unflinchingly.

"Yes."

"What are they?"

"That one man shall not bear the curse of another's crime."

"You intend, then, to work against me—to make use of the power you think you have gained?"

"I intend to do what is right," she said briefly, a slight waver in her sweet voice. "With God's help I may be able to undo your sin."

"You will repent your decision bitterly."

"I should have greater cause for repentance if I chose to act otherwise," she answered gravely; "nothing shall tempt me to forego my first resolution. The wrong must be righted—if not by your hand, by mine. You can go away and hide yourself from the world, before your guilt is known; but, if any earthly power can prevent such cruel injustice, an innocent man shall not bear the dishonour and the degradation that to him must be worse than death."

"Have your own way," Garth muttered between his teeth; "I say again you will repent it!"

All this had been spoken in English, and the two waiting-women knew nothing of what was passing between Richard Garth and his wife.

As soon as he had left the nursery, Florence dismissed them both.

You need not come up again to-night," she said to them in their own language; "I will take care of baby."

They looked surprised, but they obeyed in silence, awed by something in the manner of their beloved mistress—something that made them feel ill at ease, and left them no peace in sleep.

Florence was relieved to be alone with her child, and more than one heart-wrung tear fell on to the tiny golden head, as she paced restlessly up and down.

"Oh Dick, Dick!" she exclaimed over and over again, the same helpless cry always coming to her lips, "how hard it is to do right; and yet, I dare not shrink!"

Hour after hour she remained in the dimly-lighted room, sometimes sitting down with her burden from sheer fatigue, then starting up again and hurrying aimlessly to-and-fro.

Her restless mood seemed to have affected the child. It turned its head feebly on her breast, and commenced to wail piteously.

Florence tried to soothe it. but the baby would not rest in her arms, and she began to wish she had not sent the women away.

"I will call nurse," she thought, laying the child tenderly in its cot, "she will know, perhaps, how to soothe him."

She hurried from the room, looking back and calling softly to the baby, that the little one might not miss her.

As the last sound of her voice faded, Richard Garth entered the room she had just left—not by the same door, but through a curtained archway at the back of the cradle.

"Where will she go?   What will she touch first?" he muttered, giving a stealthy glance round.

Attracted by the baby's fretful moaning, he paused, crept nearer, and bent over it.

His face had a terrible darkness upon it, and the child, looking up into his evil eyes, silenced its cry.

"This will be the surest magnet," he exclaimed under his breath. "Here, you wailing atom of humanity—sleep! None shall complain again that you are too wakeful."

He laid his hand for a moment on the tiny embroidered robe. Then, with a furtive glance round, he stepped swiftly back, and thrust his way silently through the curtains into another apartment.

A bronze statuette, accidentally struck by his arm as he hastened out, fell from a bracket placed near the *portiere* to the floor with a resounding crash, and, fearing her baby might be in danger, Florence rushed back into the room.

A silence, a stillness, struck on her senses as she entered, and with a strange shapeless foreboding, she leaned over the cot and peered breathlessly into her child's face.

What change had taken place in her absence?

The sweet blue eyes of her darling gazed fixedly up at her, without recognition, without sight, it seemed to her, and there was a stony pallor on the little face that filled her with terror.

"He has been frightened—he is dying!" she gasped, snatching the child wildly from the cot. "Baby—baby! Dick! Oh, will no one come? My darling is dead!"

The last word came from her in an agonised shriek, and, with the tiny form clasped to her heart, she rushed towards the door, and tried to utter a cry for help.

Tried—but without avail.

No sound came from her white lips, and her gaze grew blind.

Frantic with despair, she tried to shake off the numbness creeping over her—to alarm someone before this heavy faintness should drag her down.

Locking her arms closer round her baby, she staggered forward—swayed helplessly, then her head dropped back, and she fell heavily to the ground.

* * * * *

"This is the poison of the white flowers," Osman Omar said, when, alarmed by the shrieks of the women, he went into the house, near which he had been hovering, and found Garth bending over the lifeless forms of Florence and her child. "Your work, Richard Garth. You have put death upon them both. Poor, pale lily! Even now—even now her cold arms are linked round her child, clasping in death that which she loved best in life! Richard Garth, you, who are a devil, have murdered a saint!"

Garth's brow grew damp, and he looked at the Arab half fiercely, half pleadingly.

"You will be silent?" he muttered hoarsely. "Remember, she may have done this herself."

Osman turned his glittering eyes upon him without moving his head.

"Tell that to the world, Richard Garth—not to me."

"And you will be silent?" Garth repeated with clenched teeth.

The Arab laughed, his gaze resting on the golden hair streaming at his feet.

"Yes. What is it to me? She was your wife—not mine. It's a sad sight, Richard Garth," Osman added, shivering. "I wish it had never met my eyes! I would give half my wealth if I could awaken them!"

It was too late.

The sleep that no earthly power could rouse them from had come over them.

CHAPTER II.

HILE poor pale Florence and her baby lay dead, a young girl far away from that cruel desert-land was listening to the old, old story that might mean as much sorrow to her as it had meant for the wife of Richard Garth.

"I love you Gladys—I love you!"

Gladys trembled and glanced up with large frightened eyes into the eager face bent above her own.

"Why do you love me?" she asked faintly, scarcely heeding what she said.

"Why do you love the sunshine, the birds, the flowers?" replied her companion.

"Because they are beautiful, and make life glad."

"And you, too, are beautiful, Gladys—I must call you Gladys; do you mind?"

"It is my name, Sir Edmund."

"I know it is, you little moss-rose; but all the same, I want you to share mine as well; will you?"

Gladys looked up at him in shy bewilderment, her grey-blue eyes growing darker under their silken lashes.

"I don't quite understand," she faltered, her heart throbbing so wildly that she could hear its beat. "Are you asking me to be your wife?"

"Of course; or what would be the good of loving you?"

Gladys was silent.

"Come, sweet, have you no answer for me?"

She cast him a look of despairing appeal.

"I cannot be your wife, Sir Edmund."

"Not my wife!" he repeated slowly, a blank disappointment coming over his face. "You mean you do not love me, Gladys."

"It is not that," she exclaimed quickly, distressed by the pain in his voice. "But I cannot forget I am only your ward's governess."

"Only a pure-hearted, golden-haired fairy, who has made this old home seem a paradise to me?" he interrupted, taking her little trembling hands, and drawing her nearer to himself. "My darling, life now without you would be like the summer without its sunshine. I shouldn't care to live if I could not have you always near me. Come, Gladys, I'm sure you like me a little; look up and say you do, for I won't let go your hands till you have given me the promise I want."

"But Lady Etheridge—she will be so displeased! Oh, I cannot! Please—please let me go."

"I never break my word, Gladys, and I have told you I will not release you till you have said what I want you to say."

"But——"

"But nothing at all, moss-rose. I will not listen to a word from you till you have given me the one I am waiting for—a truthful 'Yes.'"

"Yes," she whispered, her cheeks flushing hotly as she obeyed. "Now let me go."

He held her hands in a closer clasp, and his face brightened.

"Yes—what, Gladys? You must speak plainly—and the truth."

"As if I should ever speak anything but the truth," she exclaimed indignantly. I wish you would let go my hands, Sir Edmund."

"I have not the slightest intention of doing so till we have come to a settled understanding. You have said yes; but I forced the word from you. I want you to promise of your own free will, sincerely and steadfastly, to be my wife."

Gladys gave a swift upward glance into his half-teasing, half-earnest eyes.

"Are you sure," very wistfully, "quite sure that you love me?"

"As sure as I am that I will have no wife but you. My darling, if you knew how dearly I hold you in my heart, you would not be so slow to give your life into my keeping. Promise, Gladys, for my love's sake.

The girl's lips moved with a slight tremor, a faint shadowy smile, and her clear bright glance was lifted steadily to meet Sir Edmund's gaze.

"I promise," she said softly, "not only for the sake of your love, but because I too love."

"Do you love me, Gladys?"

"You know I do."

"Thank you, darling," he said gravely, his voice full of tender pride. "You have made me the happiest man on earth. My own sweet Gladys!"

Her name seemed to quiver on his lips like a caress.

A new warmth melted in his eyes, and, slipping his arm round her, he kissed her brow once, and then her lips.

No one saw them.

They were at the extreme end of a long conservatory, softly lighted with coloured lanterns, for there was unusual excitement on at the Towers to-night, in honour of the birthday of Beatrice Etheridge, Sir Edmund's half-sister.

There had been much uncertainty on the part of Lady Etheridge and her daughter as to whether Gladys should take her place amongst the guests, or remain up in the nursery with her young charge.

Sir Edmund had unconsciously decided the question at breakfast, by presenting Gladys with a great bunch of moss-roses, and telling her, in tones loud enough for everyone in the room to hear, that "he hoped he should see her wearing some of them to-night."

Of course she had done as he wished, and her white muslin dress, with the pink buds nestling in the soft folds, looked pretty enough to please the most exacting taste.

"Miss Clifton seems so very quiet and unaffected," Beatrice had observed to her mother, when Gladys, looking like a fresh spring-flower, had entered the drawing-room. "Who would have thought she could be coquette enough to get herself up like that? She certainly has a knack of wearing the simplest thing to advantage."

"GLADYS, ARE YOU TRYING TO BREAK MY HEART?"

"What pretty girl has not?" Lady Etheridge said, as she gazed at Gladys' small graceful form, with its fluttering white drapery. "And Miss Clifton, if she were anyone but Miss Clifton, would be a decided beauty."

"I dare say," Beatrice responded with a slight uplifting of her arched eyebrows, "though, for myself, I never admire women with those fair baby-faces. It may be prejudice, but I have no faith in them."

"Well, as yet, she is hardly more than a child," Lady Etheridge said reflectively; "too young, I fancy, for the duties she has undertaken. I am rather sorry little Amy has become so attached to her. I expect it will be a trouble to part them now."

It was strange neither Lady Etheridge nor her daughter had once thought it probable Sir Edmund might feel more than an ordinary interest in Gladys.

He was so proud and cold—so reserved; it seemed impossible he could ever give a thought beyond that of simplest friendship to this penniless orphaned girl who had come to live beneath his roof.

It was a shock to them when he announced that Gladys was to be his wife.

"Wish me a long life, *belle mère*," he exclaimed later that night, when he found Lady Etheridge standing alone. "I am so happy—so intensely in love with life, I feel as if I could stay on in this world for ever!"

Lady Etheridge smiled up at her handsome stepson.

"My dear boy, I am so glad to see you in such good spirits. What has pleased you?"

"Much. I have true cause to be grateful for, having won the bonniest little girl in the world for my wife."

"Your wife? I do not understand."

"My future wife—the sweetest wife that was ever given to man," he said, catching Gladys' hand as she was passing, and drawing her towards Lady Etheridge. "Don't you think I have shown great taste in my choice?"

"I cannot say. You—you have surprised me."

She looked coldly at the girl's pale startled face—angrily at Sir Edmund.

Then with an impatient gesture which, for the present, dismissed the subject, she swept into the midst of her guests.

"Don't mind, my darling," he whispered, turning to Gladys; "I chose a wrong time to tell my news. Come out on the terrace, so that I can talk to you alone."

She let him lead her in silence through one of the open casements.

Then, as soon as they were alone, she turned piteously to him, and held out both her hands, as though imploring him to leave her.

"I have made a mistake," she whispered, the hot tears starting to her eyes; "it must not be. Oh, Sir Edmund, why—why did you ask me to be your wife?"

"Because I want to have you always near me. Come, sweet, your promise is binding, and I haven't the slightest intention of letting you off. I would rather give up my life than let you take back the word you gave me such a little while ago. The idea of your hinting at such a thing! You deserve to be punished severely!"

He did punish her, though the chastisement was not very hard to bear—only to be enfolded in his arms, and to have her head pressed gently against his breast, while his lips sought hers in a passionate caress.

"Remember, darling, you are my promised wife," he said, holding her for a moment longer against his heart. "Be true to me—true to my love, and to your dear self; and nothing shall ever come between us to mar our happiness."

"How can I be truest to you but by giving you up?" she exclaimed helplessly. "To marry you would be, perhaps, to bring sorrow into your life. Don't tempt me any more; what I am saying now I know is right; I know I ought not to be your wife. I should feel like a thief for having come here to steal your love—I should indeed."

"Nonsense! it's a free gift, little one; and I hope you will never forget how completely you possess it. When I leave you to-night, all the happiness of my future will be in your keeping."

"And is there nothing else that I can do—is there no other way?"

"Certainly no other way of making me happy than by giving your sweet little self to me. If you cared for my love, you would not pain me by showing so little happiness. This seems a very unwilling betrothal, Gladys."

"I cannot help it. I am unwilling, because I shrink from doing you a wrong—because I feel that in some way your marriage with me will destroy the peace of your life. Lady Etheridge would have chosen a different wife for you."

"If that's the case, I'm glad I saved her the trouble. I prefer my own choice. I want none but a wife whom I could love, and who would love me in return. I thought you cared a little for me, Gladys!"

"Not a little. I love you with my whole heart and soul—with all my life. I have said so, and it is true. Oh, Sir Edmund! guide me, and what you say is for your happiness, I will do!"

Sir Edmund gazed tenderly at the sweet impassioned face—the face that looked so purely fair in the soft clear starlight.

"My darling," he said, laying his hand gently on her golden head, and drawing it once more down on his breast, "whatever happens—whatever remarks are made when I am not near you, be faithful to your promise. Remember in your love is all the hope of my life. I would give up everyone in the world for your sake; but no earthly power should take you from me. You are dearer to me than all else in life. I wish you never to forget that."

"I never will," Gladys murmured, looking up at him with wistful eyes; "only this happiness seems too great—too wonderful; I am afraid to face the future with my heart so full of joy—it is too sweet to last!"

"I share none of your fears on that point, moss-rose!" he exclaimed. "While I have you, I shall not care what befalls."

They stayed out there in the fragrant starry night, till their absence was noticed in the drawing-room, and Beatrice went out to look for them.

"One would imagine it was Miss Clifton's birthday instead of mine," she remarked dryly as she saw Sir Edmund's displeasure at the interruption; "you seem to be giving her all your attention to-night. Is she to be considered before a daughter of the house?"

"Before the whole world," he answered steadily, a cold gleam coming into his eyes as they rested on his half-sister. "Allow me, Beatrice, to introduce you to my promised wife—the future mistress of my home."

Beatrice turned proudly away.

"The introduction was not necessary," she said disdainfully; "I know her, perhaps, better than you do."

"I envy you that privilege," he returned quietly.

Then, without another word, he took Gladys' little trembling hand in a close clasp, and turned to lead her back to the drawing-room.

"You are shivering, darling," he said, putting his arm lightly round her shoulder, and drawing her to his side; "I ought not to have kept you out so long in that thin muslin thing. Come in, and let me get you a glass of wine."

"No, thanks; I would rather go up to my room; I could not bear anyone to look at me now. Good-night, Sir Edmund."

"Say 'good-night, Edmund!'"

"Good-night, dear, dear Edmund!"

"God bless you, Gladys!"

There was a clinging, yearning hand-clasp; a lingering glance exchanged.

Then the girl hurried away, and left Sir Edmund standing alone.

After the guests had left, he sought a quiet interview with Lady Etheridge.

"I want you, *belle mère*, to impress upon Beatrice's mind that Gladys is to receive no slight, in word or in deed, while she is under your care," he said almost sternly. "Whatever position she has held in this house, she now holds the place of my future wife—let her be treated as such."

"I think you are mad," Lady Etheridge exclaimed, her lips quivering with anger. "Are women so scarce in your own circle, that you must choose for a wife a girl of whom we know nothing?"

"Nothing, at least, but what is sweet and good," he put in firmly. "Pray do not let any worldly thought blind you to that."

"I have no fault against the child," Lady Etheridge admitted reluctantly. "She is not to blame; the folly is yours. You should have left her to go her own way. I hope to-morrow you will have decided more wisely."

"How?"

"By giving up all idea of a marriage with Miss Clifton."

"Impossible! I have given her my word of honour, and my heart is the pledge! I would sooner part with my life than with her love!"

"Well, of course I have no right to interfere, only I feel sure you will repent this folly. I cannot wish you happiness; something tells me disappointment will come of it."

CHAPTER III.

A T breakfast, the next morning, Gladys looked at Lady Etheridge with such great yearning eyes it was impossible for her to harden her heart against her.

"I hope you have thought well of the step you are taking," she observed gravely when the others, with the exception of little Amy, had left the room. "You are very young. Are you sure you are acting wisely?"

A soft dreamy smile stole to the girl's lips, and she gazed wistfully through the open window out into the garden, where she had last seen Sir Edmund's tall form.

"I love Sir Edmund," she said, her heart giving a quick throb as she uttered the words, "and he has asked me to be his wife. Was it wise to say 'Yes'? Because that is how I have answered. And he wished me to keep true to my promise."

Lady Etheridge smiled; this simple, unaffected way of speaking pleased her, and as she looked at the girl's eloquent face, she could not blame Sir Edmund for his choice.

"I trust all will come right in the end," she said rather vaguely. "You told me once, I think, that you have no living relative. Do I remember aright?"

"Yes; I have no one belonging to me in the whole world. When my aunt died, I lost all, and then I came to you."

"Had you no brother or sister?"

"I had a brother until three years ago; a fever seized him out in Australia, and news was sent me of his death."

Gladys' voice trembled a little, and her hand wandered out to clasp Amy's.

The child, a pretty dark-eyed waif, who had been left to the guardianship of Sir Edmund by a distant connexion on his mother's side, nestled close to Gladys' side, and gazed wonderingly up at her.

"Haven't you anyone to love you?" she asked, with a child's ready pity.

Glady's bent and kissed the tiny face.

"My pet! I lost much, but I have found more, and I owe it all to you, dear."

The child glanced up with bright laughing eyes, as she laid her warm cheek against Gladys' hand.

Is it true you are going to marry Sir Edmund?" she questioned eagerly. "I heard Mary tell nurse so when I was being dressed. Are you?"

"Ask him," Gladys whispered, flushing hotly, and trying to disengage herself from the child; "I am not quite sure. Shall we go to the stables and see how your new pony looks this morning?"

"Yes; I wish Sir Edmund would buy you a pony, too. Shall I ask him?"

"I do not want one, dear."

"By-the-bye," Lady Etheridge remarked, laying aside a book she had taken up, "Racer would just suit you if you are anything of a horsewoman. Are you fond of riding?"

"Very." Then, with quiet dignity, as she saw Lady Etheridge's quick look of enquiry: "I was not reared in such poverty as I have been thrown in since my aunt's death. Her wealth passed to strangers."

"Well, for the present, then, I suppose you will remain my guest? As for the riding, I will see that you are provided with a proper mount."

Things went on more smoothly than Sir Edmund had anticipated, and the summer passed pleasantly to the lovers.

Everyone in Deepwood who had been attracted by Gladys' sweet young face heard the news of her engagement to Sir Edmund with little surprise.

"He has won a pearl," they told each other, "and he deserves her, too. The first time we saw them together, we prophesied how it would be."

Three months of intense dream-like happiness, and then to Gladys there came a shock that seemed to wreck all the joy of her life.

She was wandering along the outskirts of the forest one evening, rather later than was usual for her to be out alone, when a heavy rustling in the foliage startled her, and made her turn swiftly in the direction of the sound.

"Gladys!"

The one word—her name—came from the darkness in a husky whisper, and the next moment two sun-browned hands were thrust through the leaves to draw her into the gloom.

Gladys uttered a low cry, and a sickly faintness came over her, as though she had heard a voice which had long been dead calling to her.

The stranger looked at her with a wild haggard gladness in his eyes, and his breast heaved with a deep hard breath, like a sob.

"Gladys, don't you know me?" he muttered brokenly. "How can I wonder," with sharp bitter pain, "when I know how I am changed? You haven't forgotten me, Gladys, have you? I'm changed, and you have believed me dead, but you have remembered me—I'm sure you have remembered me, dear?"

There was a weary aching wistfulness in his voice that stirred every fibre of the girl's nature.

"Speak—speak!" she whispered, her blanched lips scarcely moving. Call back my memory. Oh, Frank—Frank, they told me you were dead!"

"I wish they had told you the truth—not now that I am free," with a wistful glance at the broad open country fading in dim outline. "Free, Gladys; do you understand the word? You would if you knew what my life has been—tortured, starved, driven, kicked down into the dust as something viler than the vilest reptile—something lower than the lowest creature that grovels on this earth."

Gladys trembled as she looked at the sunken pallid face, and the thought flickered across her mind:

"Is this madness—is he mad?"

She had got over the shock his sudden appearance had caused her, and her heart ached as she saw in the wreck of manhood before her the once careless handsome brother she had lost long ago.

"You are so white and so worn, Frank," she said, stroking the thin hand that grasped hers. "You must have been very—very ill to make you like this—you are ill still, and so tired. Come with me to the Towers, and you can rest while you tell me all about yourself; they will be glad to see you there, Frank. Let us hurry; it is getting late."

She held his hand, and tried to lead him out of the thicket.

He drew back, and something like a groan came from his drawn lips.

"No, no, Gladys; if you must go—if you think your absence will be noticed—you must leave me. I dare not be seen with you."

Her eyes grew large.

"Why not, Frank—what cause have you for concealment? Surely—surely you do not mean that I must leave you? Oh, Frank! what has come to you—why do you look so strangely?"

She clung to him, shivering, a passion of despair and dread sending a sharp pain through her.

"Oh, Frank, why do you look so strangely?" repeated Gladys.

Frank Clifton took a step back, and covered his eyes with his hand, his whole attitude one of deep dejection.

"Frank, what is it? Why do you say you dare not face the world with me? Are you hiding some terrible secret?"

"A terrible secret, indeed! I have come back to you with a curse dragging at my heels, the very shadow of which might pollute you. I ought to have kept away from you, but I could not. You are my sister, and I am in sore need; I thought it could do you no harm to see you here—only once, Gladys—I will never let you run the risk again."

Once more he turned away, and hid his face from her.

He was dealing her pain, and he knew it; and he could not look on the bewilderment he had brought to her eyes, unmoved.

"Frank, for pity's sake explain this mystery!" she exclaimed, grasping his arm, and trying to drag his hand from before his face. "Cannot you trust me? You must—you will—I know you will! I could bear anything rather than this suspense; it makes me so afraid—afraid to think!"

He seized her hands and gazed down at her with fierce intensity, his haggard face bent low, as though in that long passionate look he showed her his soul.

When he spoke it was in a low firm voice.

"Gladys, how long is it since I left you?"

"Two years."

"To me it has seemed a lifetime. But let that pass. I want you to let your mind go back. Gladys; if within an hour of my departure, someone had told you that I had committed some foul deed, would you have believed—would you have taken the accusation as evidence against me?"

She gave a slight start, and a cold chill swept over her.

She knew he was preparing her for something—something that made her shrink closer to him, and droop her face on his arm, as though to shut out the phantom dread his words called to her vision.

"Go on," she whispered, shuddering.

He still held her hands in that fierce grasp, and he crushed the magainst his breast with unconscious force, perhaps to thrust down under control the bitter pain raking his heart.

"You have not answered me yet, Gladys."

She lifted her face, and met his gaze fully and clearly.

"If all the world had proclaimed my brother guilty, unless his own lips had echoed the cry, no proof would have been sufficient to make me believe"

An expression of gratitude gleamed for a moment in his eyes, and his mouth quivered.

"If you were put to the test now, Gladys," he said earnestly; "if some charge were brought against me,

and I pleaded innocent, would you take my word before
that of my accuser? Does the old trust—the old faith
still live?"

"Yes, Frank—yes. Whatever you told me I should
know was truth. I would believe you if the whole
world turned against you."

"The world has turned against me!" he exclaimed
bitterly. "I am guiltless of the evil put upon me, yet
I am hunted down like a thing cursed with crime, powerless to defend myself—powerless to prove my innocence!
A false charge is brought against me—remember,
Gladys, a false charge—for which I was cast into exile.
I did not endure it long, the life they condemned me to
was worse than death! I escaped and fled to England—
an outcast, a fugitive, pursued on every side by a justice
that had chained upon me the punishment of another's
sin!"

He drew a deep breath through his clenched teeth,
and releasing Gladys hands, took a few restless strides
past her.

Suddenly he stopped and faced her.

"What I have told you is the truth," he said with
fierce bitterness. "Do you believe me, Gladys, or
not?"

"I believe you, Frank," she answered steadily.
"Whatever charge is brought against you, I know you
have done no wrong."

"Bless you for those words!" he exclaimed brokenly,
taking her in his arms and kissing her. "One day I
may be able to prove that your trust is not misplaced.
Heaven help me to find the man whose guilt is put upon
me! The one aim of my life shall be to find proof of my
innocence."

He spoke with a passionate determination, and a
long silence followed his speech—a silence Gladys shrank
from breaking, because she understood the despairing
thoughts struggling through his brain.

"In the carrying out of this resolution you will want
stronger aid than I can give you," she said presently;
"the firm true friendship of a man, Frank. If you will
confide in Sir Edmund—"

THE OUTCAST SWUNG ROUND, AND HIS FACE GREW WHITE, AS HE CONFRONTED GARTH.

"I dare confide in no one, Gladys," he interrupted, a hunted look coming into his eyes, "even now my footsteps may be dogged. If discovered here, I should be dragged back into exile, and I do not want to be seen with you or with anyone to whom I might bring trouble."

He paused for a little while, as though he found difficulty in framing the words.

Then, giving his head a jerk back, as if to throw off the weakness which for a moment had conquered him, he went on as calmly as before:

"I was charged and condemned under another name; that is how it came to be reported that Frank Clifton was dead. You understand, dear?"

She shivered, and let her frightened gaze rest wistfully upon him.

"But you, under your own name, and in your own country, are safe?"

He turned sadly away. The hope he heard in her voice and read on her face only pained him.

I shall never be safe till I have proved my innocence. I should not have let you run the danger of this meeting, but—it's an unmanly excuse I have to offer, Gladys—I want you to lend me money."

"You shall have it, Frank—all I have to give—a hundred pounds; not much, yet it may help you, and I can work for more—"

He put up his hand in a pitiful gesture. Her words seemed to wound him.

"You working for me!" he exclaimed with broken pride. "Poor little sister—poor little Gladys! Pray Heaven the time may come when I shall be able to fulfil my duty to you. Can you forgive me the sorrow I have brought you."

"What is my suffering compared with yours?" she asked, clasping her hands tenderly on his arm. "Dear, we must be patient and wait. In the end, I know all will come right. If only you would trust Sir Edmund," she added regretfully, "he would help you, and be such a true friend!"

"I dare not. What I have to bear I must endure alone. It would not be a fair action towards him, and would bring nothing but danger to me. My one chance of safety lies in secrecy. If you will let me have the sum you have promised, I shall get out of England as soon as possible. The hounds may be on my track even now."

"Must you go?" she asked anxiously.

"Yes, that I may the sooner return—free from pursuit. Those who do not know me will not take my word as you have done. The world wants proof; I am going to find it."

"You will succeed, I feel sure, Frank," Gladys said hopefully. "Shall I bring you the money here to-night?"

"No; if you are seen with me unpleasant questions may arise, and I might be watched. Meet me again this day week; it will give you time to think over all I have said, and to understand why it is best that my presence should be kept secret. Go now, I am afraid I have kept you already too long. Say nothing of this meeting to anyone, Gladys; my only hope is in concealment."

"I shall be miserable till I have seen you again," she said, glancing round them at the deepening gloom, as though she feared some hidden foe might be lurking near. "Are you sure—quite sure you will be out of danger all those days? I shall be so wretchedly anxious, Frank."

"Don't think about me, Gladys, I shall be all right; I have escaped too often to have any misgiving now! I have been here sketching every day in the hope of seeing you pass alone. I shall finish my picture this day week, and shall be able to sell it, I have no doubt, for a few pounds. You remember I was always rather good at water-colours? My brush has been a faithful friend to me lately."

He was speaking quite cheerfully now, and Gladys felt the pain grow lighter at her heart as she recognised a return of his boyish spirits.

Their parting was much less sad than their meeting had been. Frank seemed suddenly to have grown so full of hope, that Gladys thought all the worst danger must be over.

She did not know how he stood there after she had left him, his form bent, his face buried in his hands; she did not know how that parting smile had been forced to his lips to hide the sharp pain he was enduring.

"This is the bitterest of all!" was the cry that seemed to ring through his brain. "Poor little Gladys! It is hard I should have brought my misery to her!"

CHAPTER IV.

FTER parting with her brother, Gladys ran swiftly towards the Towers.

She had not noticed how quickly the time had fled while she had been talking with Frank, and she became alarmed when she found how late it really was.

Sir Edmund had gone out to look for her, and she bounded against him just as she reached the foot of the steps leading to the terrace.

She started back breathlessly as she recognised him, and for the first time the words of greeting she would have uttered died confused and indistinct on her lips.

"My darling, I have been searching everywhere for you," he exclaimed, taking her hand and placing it on his arm. "Where have you been hiding?"

"Nowhere—that is—I wandered into the wood, and stayed there longer than I had meant to do—"

"Lost yourself, I suppose? That is a punishment for not asking me to go with you. Do you know, Gladys," leading her from the terrace-steps into the narrow pathways of the rose-garden, "I had made up my mind to speak to you on a very important subject to-night. I want you to name a day for our wedding."

She halted, and shrank closer to his side.

"Not now," she said quickly. "You must give me time—I must think first."

"But I have given you time, darling," he urged, trying to look into her face. "Three months—a whole summer-season—and yet my wife is not more mine than she was a year ago. Dear little love, when will you let me bind my happiness more securely to me—when will you let me claim my wife?"

Gladys did not answer.

A great fear made her tremble, and she clung to him, drooping and pale, while her heart seemed to burst itself in a low sobbing sigh.

Sir Edmund put his arms round her, and lifted her white face upward against his breast, letting his hand rest caressingly on her head.

One look showed him the change in her, and he knew she had endured some shock since he had last seen her.

"Gladys, something has happened," he said, his deep blue eyes gleaming with sudden determination. "What is it? Tell me all, and "—with a fierce glance round— "If anyone has been frightening you, I'll—I'll—"

He did not complete the threat; his lips tightened, and Gladys felt he was bracing himself to deal out punishment to whoever had been the cause of her distress.

Her thoughts flew to the lonely outcast making his way under cover of the darkness, and she feared for him, as she saw how bent Sir Edmund was on being her protector.

"It's nothing," she murmured, overcoming the weakness that had assailed her. "Let us go indoors; I am tired."

"Tired! you look half dead," he exclaimed with concern; "you must be ill, Gladys, darling. I wonder I did not notice it sooner. You are quite right not to wish to stay out: I will take you in at once!"

Silently she allowed him to lead her through the rose-arches, up the terrace-steps.

The scene she had gone through with Frank was beginning to tell upon her now, and a dull cruel thought lay like lead at her heart.

It was this:

"Must I deceive him—must I be false to one to be true to the other! Oh, Frank, you have asked a sacrifice indeed!"

Sir Edmund noted the anguish visible in her face, and wondered miserably at its cause.

He was so big and so strong, and he loved her so tenderly, he could not bear to see her suffer, and not to know how to help her.

When they had reached the last step he paused once more, and drew her away from the long French-window opening into the drawing-room.

He was selfish in his love for her; he wanted all her trust, all her confidence. He could not bear that she should go in and be cross-examined by Beatrice and Lady Etheridge; that they should find out what grieved her before he had been able to give her any comfort.

"I cannot help thinking you are hiding some trouble from me," he said abruptly; in fact, I should feel sure something had upset you, if I did not know—if I did not believe that you trust me too well to keep a secret from me."

She looked up at him with eyes full of pain, and he felt her hand quiver and grow like ice in his clasp.

"Gladys, have you nothing to say? Can you not confide in me?"

The gentle reproach in his tone stung her, and she turned away from his gaze.

"Don't ask me!" she cried, like one hard driven, pleading for mercy. "Don't ask me; for my sorrow is not mine to tell!"

He watched her for a moment in silence. Then, gently releasing her hand, and standing before her with folded arms:

"You have a secret, Gladys, and you will not trust me. I am glad I understand; I would not, for the world, force myself into your confidence."

"Don't be angry with me, Ned!"

"I am not angry, only disappointed and sorry for you. The heart that is burdened with a secret can never be made glad. I pity you, because my love will have no power to give happiness to your life. I thought my wife would have no secret from me. It will be a shadow between us, Gladys."

"I know—I know!" she moaned wildly. "You need not torture me by telling me what my heart is crying out! 'A wife should have no secret from her husband.' I understand, and I give way to the command. I must never be your wife! Take back my promise, and leave me—leave me—and let the shadow fall on my life alone!"

She flung herself on her knees, and, throwing her arms over the stone bulustrade, dropped her head upon them in a passion of despair.

A sharp spasm passed over Sir Edmund's face.

She was suffering like this, and yet could keep her sorrow from him!

He laid his hand tenderly on her shoulder.

"Gladys, are you trying to break my heart?"

He spoke so gently, and yet with so much pain, that his voice roused all the love she was trying to hush down in her soul.

His touch, light as it was, sent a thrill through her, and, half turning, she laid her cheek against his hand—her cheek, and then her lips.

"You will think of me sometimes," she pleaded, "my love—my love that I have lost!"

"If you would only trust me, Gladys!" he exclaimed, bending over her with yearning compassion. "It is bitter torture for me to see you like this."

"I will leave you soon," she said pathetically. "Say good-bye to me, Edmund. It is not my fault that I have this secret—indeed, it is not! It has come like some poisonous thing into my life, and has destroyed all my happiness. Dear, you will not think hardly of me when—when I am far away?"

This was more than Sir Edmund could endure.

He put his strong arms round her, and lifted her up to his breast.

"Gladys, you are driving me mad!" he exclaimed, crushing her to him with unconscious force. "Do you think I would let you go from me—like this? No power on earth would induce me to give you back your freedom! You are my plighted wife, and I hold you to the promise which gives me the right to guard your life!"

He paused for a few seconds, and his breathing grew thick and heavy.

Then in a lower tone, he added:

"I forgot; there is one thing which would have power to part you from me—the belief that you had ceased to love me. Is it so, Gladys? Answer me from your heart. If the truth be the worst, I would rather bear the blow now than in after years—and you might be spared the misery of a life's mistake."

She clung to him in silence, and in her wide-open eyes, in the quick tremulous throb of her heart against his own, he found his answer.

"I love you," she whispered softly, after a long pause, and it seemed to her that if he could hold her against his heart for ever, and lift her soul up with his passionate gaze, this new sorrow could never darken her life again. "Can you love me still, though you know I have one heavy thought I cannot share with you?" she asked presently.

He looked earnestly at her sweet wistful face; then bent his lip to the fair young brow.

"Of the nature of your secret I have no knowledge," he said gently. "But this I know, Gladys, the heart which holds it is true and pure as an angel's; so I trust you. When the time comes for you to tell me, you will do so without one shadow of shame in those sweet eyes. Of this I am sure; so I do not care how long I have to wait."

Her face flushed with sudden gladness.

How generous, how noble he was! If only she dared unburden her heart to him—if only Frank had been persuaded by her, and had confided in this trustful, truthful nature!

If! How often the dull echo of that one little word weighed in her thoughts in after years!

Now she dismissed all misgivings from her mind.

Sir Edmund could trust her, and she was satisfied, because she knew the proud day would come when she could prove to him that his faith had not been misplaced.

Frank was innocent—what had she to fear?

"When I see him again, I will ask him to let me tell Edmund," she told herself more than once that night as she tossed restlessly on her hot pillows. "It would be such a comfort to feel he knew my secret; and poor Frank would have a friend."

The following day brought fresh excitement, and Gladys had not much time to brood over past events.

By the morning's post there came to Lady Etheridge a letter bearing foreign marks—a letter which announced Richard Garth's return to England.

"I have had deep losses within the last few months," the missive ran. "My wife and child died in Cairo, as you doubtless know. My life is no longer what it was, and I return broken down and sick at heart. However, I am glad to say I am not without a companion; I have one friend, a young Arab, rich and accomplished, whom, on my return, I hope you will permit me to introduce to you."

The letter contained a good deal more; some passages gently recalling to Lady Etheridge's mind a fact she had almost forgotten—that Garth's mother and herself had passed their girlhood together—close friends and schoolfellows.

"I never can think of Richard Garth as poor Maggie's son," Lady Etheridge said dreamily, as she laid the letter aside, forgetful that neither Beatrice nor Sir Edmund, to whom the remark was addressed, knew anything of Maggie. It may be a wrong idea on my part, but I always fancy he must resemble the man she married, and whose cold stony heart made her sorrow till she died. Poor Maggie! for her sake I ought to think more kindly of her son."

"His letter does not sound as though it had been dictated by a 'stony heart,'" Beatrice observed, interested. "He seems in a most melancholy state of mind."

"No wonder!" Sir Edmund exlaimed, his gaze wandering over to Gladys. "If I had lost what he has lost, life would be worth nothing to me. I never liked the fellow, but 'pon my word, I am sorry for him."

"He will arrive to-morrow," Lady Etheridge announced, referring to the letter, and looking thoughtfully at Beatrice as she replaced it in the envelope. "I had better ask him down. He will be wretched in that great lonely place of his, and he evidently wishes to come to us."

"Will his friend come with him?" Beatrice asked.

"Of course, my dear. I could not ignore Richard's request."

Gladys listened with a strange sense of foreboding at her heart.

Her thoughts had flown to Frank, and she felt that her meetings with him would be attended with greater danger when those two visitors come to Deepwood.

For the rest of the day she was silent, and more than once Sir Edmund missed the light in her violet eyes, and noticed they were dark with thought.

"What is troubling you, sweet?" he asked her once when he heard her sigh deeply over a fairy-tale, she was reading to Amy. "Is the story such a sad one?"

She started and flushed as though guilty of some wrong against himself.

"I hardly know what I was reading," she said, her gaze resting miserably on the broad clear pages of the book. "It was nothing sorrowful, I think."

"But you are sorrowful, darling."

She looked at him piteously; then her head drooped again, and he saw that she was trembling.

A cloud passed over his face, and he watched her in silence.

He had been walking through the grounds enjoying a smoke, when he caught sight of her sitting under a broad chestnut-tree with the child; and he had listened to her sweet low voice without interrupting her reading, till that deep-drawn breath had struck like a chill wind on his ear.

He threw his cigar away now, and slowly seated himself by her side.

"I know what it is," he said, gently taking her hand, and trying to look into her eyes; "I shall be glad, Gladys, when the time comes for you to trust me. It pains me to see you so sad, and not to be able to help bear your sorrow."

She turned towards him, clasping his strong hand feverishly in both her own.

"If you understood what I suffer, you would pity me even more than you do," she cried passionately. "Dear love, you will have faith in me always—no matter what happens?" with wistful pleading. "My sorrow is that I cannot tell you my secret. If you knew everything

I should have no cause to fear—and I do fear, Edmund, greatly."

Her words made him feel wretched—wretched because he was powerless to lift this shadow from her life.

He could only draw her clinging hands up against his heart, and tell her over and over again how truthfully he loved her—only ask her to put all hope in that love and trust to the happiness in store.

His deep tender voice soothed her wondrously, and he talked to her till her dread was drowned in the wild warm love she bore him.

It would have been sweet, she thought, to have sat under the dense green chestnut branches for ever, his hand clasping hers, his eyes glowing with all his soul's tenderness.

But she knew the hour must end, and with this remembrance came back to her that dread of the future Sir Edmund had dispelled for so short a time.

CHAPTER V.

ICHARD GARTH availed himself of Lady Etheridge's invitation, and in a few days he and his friend arrived at the Towers.

Their coming put an end to Sir Edmund's quiet rambles with Gladys and little Amy.

The gentlemen spent a good deal of time fishing, and the girls could not join them in this as they did in nearly every other open-air pleasure.

Beatrice complained at this.

"I think mankind a horribly selfish race," she said to Gladys in a burst of confidence. "As if they couldn't give up fishing for something we could all take part in! I shall persuade mamma to get up a picnic. It would be good fun to have a gipsy-dinner in the wood."

Gladys did not make any response.

Making merry on the spot where her brother was hiding, hunted down by a pitiless and condemning law!

She shivered, and wondered how she could turn Beatrice's mind from the object it now held in view.

To say anything would only be to rouse suspicion, and to put Beatrice at once on the defensive.

There was nothing for her to do but to wait and to pray for Frank's safety.

She went about all that day with a heavy restless ache at her heart, and at dinner she grew deathly white as though she had received a sudden shock when she heard Beatrice repeat to Lady Etheridge the proposition she had made in the morning.

"Mamma, we ought to have a picnic. Mr. Garth must find it dreadfully slow down here with nothing going."

"You are quite mistaken, I assure you, Miss Etheridge," Richard replied courteously, then bending his head slightly, so that she alone could catch his next words, he added : "Living under one roof with you, it would be impossible to be dull. I could wish for no greater pleasure than what your presence gives me."

"I think you are trying to flatter me, Mr. Garth," she murmured, smiling at the compliment.

"When you say that, you accuse me of an impossibility," he returned, still speaking in an undertone, and she understood the meaning conveyed in his words.

Lady Etheridge was conversing with the young Arab, and did not notice those few murmured sentences exchanged between Beatrice and Garth.

Sir Edmund did, and flung a glance of disproval across the table at his sister.

Gladys, too, noticed, and her dreamy gaze rested reproachfully on his dark face.

How could he so soon forget the wife he had left in a grave far away, and the child that lay at rest on the pulseless heart ?

Garth seemed to feel what was passing through her mind, and, like one mesmerised, he looked up and met her gaze.

Her pale pure face, made unusually pensive by the sadness weighing on her soul, appeared to him as an accusing angel's, and in all the insolence of his strength he felt his strong frame tremble, as though the phantom of his crime had suddenly risen before him.

Perhaps it was because the eyes watching him were deep, and blue, and intense, like the ones he had made dark and sightless for ever. Perhaps this thoughtful intent gaze looking out from under soft golden hair recalled Florence to him.

Whatever it was, the silent half-formed distrust struck home to him, and he turned his face quickly away.

"She'll make me hate her if she looks at me often like that," he mused, savage with her and with himself. " I wish to goodness she were out of the house ! "

"What were you saying about a picnic, Trissie ? " Lady Etheridge asked, remembering Beatrice's remark.

"Suggesting we should get up one," that young lady replied promptly. This is just the weather for it."

"Very well, dear, I will see that everything is arranged. How soon would you like it to come off ? "

"As early as possible, unless something is to come before it, or we shall all die of *ennui*."

Lady Etheridge smiled, and the smile meant consent to whatever proposition Beatrice chose to make.

Before they rose from the table the day was fixed.

Gladys leaned forward and glanced wildly into Beatrice's face as she heard the decision.

It was the day on which she was to meet Frank.

Gladys felt as if her heart had suddenly turned to stone, and with her lips tightly closed, she sat gazing straight before her into vacancy.

She started when Sir Edmund touched her arm, and she saw that the ladies were leaving the dining-room.

She rose hastily, and moved towards the door. When she reached the hall, she found Sir Edmund had followed her.

"Good Heavens, Gladys! how ill you look!" he exclaimed, regarding her with concern. "My darling, I cannot see you like this day after day. You must have advice. I will speak to Lady Etheridge about you. I wonder she doesn't notice what a bad state of health you are in."

"No—no. Pray don't say anything to her!" Gladys pleaded. "I am not ill—only troubled, Edmund," looking at him wistfully, "could you get this picnic put off for one day ? "

"If you wish it, I'll try—and I have no doubt I shall succeed."

"I do wish it," she replied fervently.

"Then you may depend on my doing by best to please you, darling."

She thanked him silently with a look, and left him watching after her with a grave tender regard.

"Poor little Gladys!" he sighed, passing his hand lightly over his tawny moustache; "how I wish she would trust me ! "

He knew she had a reason for the request she had made, and that reason a strong one, judging from the agitation she had displayed, and he was determined to do all in his power to postpone the picnic.

He commenced by suggesting half-a-dozen little difficulties to Lady Etheridge.

He suddenly remembered he had to lunch with some friends that day, and would have to give up all idea of the picnic, unless it could be put off for a time.

"Who are your friends, Edmund—the Staceys?"

He nodded his head, searching his brain meanwhile for another excuse in case this one should not have effect.

"Have they asked anyone to meet you?"

"Oh no!" he exclaimed, off his guard. "The General has some fine old armour to show me—that is all."

"The difficulty is easily got over then. We will ask him to join our party. I had intended doing so from the first."

Sir Edmund muttered something under his breath that his stepmother did not quite catch.

"I don't at all care for the idea," he grumbled, kicking a footstool out of his way impatiently. "I think there are plenty of more enjoyable ways of eating one's meals than having everything spread on the ground as though dining-room comforts had never been invented—to say nothing of the insects one swallows with one's wine. I wish Beatrice would enjoy those kind of things by herself. She gave everyone ague last time."

"Nonsense, my dear Edmund; you know you enjoyed yourself as much as anyone else did. As to ague—there is no fear of that, considering the intense warmth of the weather. Don't disappoint Trissie by letting her see you do not appreciate her plans. She has set her heart on this picnic."

Lady Etheridge spoke kindly enough, but there was something in her tone expressive of:

"If you do not care to join the party, don't bore yourself; your absence need not prevent other people enjoying themselves though."

This seemed to leave him at a standstill, and he felt himself fairly vanquished.

The first time he came upon Beatrice alone, he tried what a little careful persuasion would do towards making her bend to his wishes.

All he said only made her think him "horribly selfish," and "slow," and she persisted in keeping to her first arrangements.

"Gladys is nearly as bad as you are!" she exclaimed pettishly. "She doesn't take a bit of interest in the picnic, and I cannot get her to help me in a single thing. I can't make out whether she is going against it to please you, or whether you are trying to upset everything to gratify her. You two are certainly in league, and I should be glad if I could discover what cause you have for acting like this."

"My dear girl, you are letting your imagination carry you away from the point! As matters stand, everything rests in your hands, and I ask you, as a particular favour, to put off this picnic for at least a day. Will you grant me this request, Triss? It is about the only thing I have ever asked of you, and it's not much."

If he had been a condemned wretch, entreating one day's reprieve, he could not have spoken more earnestly.

Beatrice gave a clear ringing laugh—a laugh that sent a flash to his eyes, and made the colour deepen in his cheeks.

"Would you do as much for me?" she exclaimed scornfully.

"Anything that I could do to serve you, Beatrice, should not be left undone."

She raised her face, and watched him curiously, the light from the chandelier falling softly over her, and imparting a sheen to her gold-satin dress.

"Are you in earnest?" she asked.

"On my soul, yes."

"Could you make a sacrifice for me?"

"So that nobody but myself suffered through it, I would."

"Then give me my birthright—half of the wealth that was my father's, and which you alone inherit."

Sir Edmund started back, and stared at her in mute amaze.

"Have you not all you wish for?" Sir Edmund said, after a long pause, recalling how Beatrice, since her childhood, had been the worshipped idol, the pampered queen of the home, where she was the daughter of a second marriage. "I never thought you envied me my wealth, Beatrice. Why, do you know, I have hardly learned its worth yet, I have given it so little consideration."

"It is that which makes me feel it so bitterly!" she urged, the words falling swiftly from her lips. "It seems so unjust for you, who don't care about riches, to have everything, while I, who think wealth the greatest blessing the world can give, have nothing I can really call my own."

"A thousand a year is sufficient pocket-money for you, I should imagine," he observed, with a touch of sarcasm.

"It is; but I should like to have more. I want to be a great heiress."

"Do you think you would be the happier for that?" he asked, contemptuously.

"I am sure I should," in low, earnest tones, "for my ambition would then be gratified."

"A selfish ambition, unworthy to hold a place in a womanly heart," her brother replied, in a voice of grave rebuke. "I am sorry you should have this greed for wealth, Beatrice; I am afraid you have been spoilt with over-indulgence."

He would have left her, but she caught his arm in a feverish grasp.

"Ned, will you give me your fortune—even half of it? What you hold so lightly would be so much to me!"

"So much that it would, perhaps, prove a loadstone," he said, gently putting her away from him. "You know the contents of our father's will. It was that his wealth should pass from me to the one who, after me, should inherit his title. Should I die without an heir, everything will pass to you. I cannot act against those wishes, Beatrice. You must bide your time."

He moved slowly towards the door as he uttered the last words, and this time she made no effort to detain him.

Sir Edmund was disappointed in his sister.

That she could covet his wealth was a revelation to him; and he could not help feeling sorry, while he blamed her for her worldliness.

He told Gladys of the ill-success his scheme had met with regarding the picnic.

"I am awfully annoyed about it," he said, regretfully. "My having spoken seems only to have made the case more hopeless. They will accept no excuse from me."

Gladys grew very pale.

"Won't they change the day, or even the place?" she asked, her eyes growing darker under their thick fringes.

"They don't seem to have the slightest intention of doing so. It is no use talking to them; if the picnic is to be put off, it can only be done by letting them make all their arrangements, and at the last moment something must happen to cause a complete wreck to their plans."

"But if nothing does happen?" Gladys faltered, sinking down in a chair, and looking at him in a bewildered way.

Sir Edmund gave a smile.

"I will manage that," he said, reassuringly. "This time my plan shall be of too practical an order not to have effect."

They were alone in an ante-chamber leading from the drawing-room, and they could hear Beatrice's clear perfect voice as it rose and fell to the soft notes of an old Scotch ballad.

She was singing to please Richard Garth; but it was the Arab who bent over her, and whose ears drank in every change in the rich voice.

Garth was seated away from them, near the velvet hangings that divided the two rooms, and he could hear what passed between Gladys and Sir Edmund.

Their conversation set him wondering, and he paid no heed to Beatrice's song.

CHAPTER VI.

HE eventful day arrived, and Gladys, worn out with anxiety and sleeplessness, looked white and wraith-like in her cream-coloured cashmere, and pretty shepherdess hat that suited her so well.

She was enduring an agony of suspense.

Everyone was ready and eager to start—Beatrice, more ready and more eager than all, standing out on the balcony, her beautiful face flushed under her scarlet sunshade, her graceful figure bright with the glow of silken poppies and fluttering ribbons.

"Ned, what are we waiting for?" she exclaimed, suddenly turning to her brother. "Everyone and everything is ready; I wish you would tell some of them to make a start."

"All right," he muttered, good-humouredly, and going out into the hall, he said something to the footman—only told him to see that the hampers were properly fastened—and everyone still found themselves waiting, without knowing why.

Gladys felt a sickly faintness creep over her, and she shrank into the darkest corner, not daring to meet the glance of any present.

Garth was watching her, but she was too agitated to heed his presence, apart from the others; and as the minutes passed, she began to fear that the "something" which was to detain the party would never happen.

It did not occur to her there might be selfishness in this wish to upset the enjoyment of so many.

What was their disappointment to her, in comparison with the suffering their pleasure might cost her brother?

Perhaps, after all, Ned had been unable to help her.

Time dragged on.

There was no further excuse for delay.

The carriages filled, and filed off one by one, and Gladys took her seat mechanically, scarcely noticing who it was had told her there was no longer need to wait.

Some of the guests were to meet them on the spot which had been arranged for the picnic, and Lady Etheridge had been anxious lest they should arrive before she was there to receive them.

She was surprised to be met by them half-way along the road, and startled by their greeting.

"Turn back!" was the frantic cry chorussed in a dozen voices; "the circus lion is loose, and has rushed into the wood! The keeper is trying to capture it, but he has warned everyone to keep as far away as possible."

Lady Etheridge turned pale with alarm.

"How dangerous!" she exclaimed; "and how fortunate we were not earlier. We had better drive back to the Towers at once."

"Perhaps the animal is secured by this," Beatrice suggested, thinking they might as well wait; "or it may be only a false alarm."

A savage, sullen roar echoing from the forest just then, dispersed all doubts as to the truth of the story, and Lady Etheridge's party started off at a furious rate towards the Towers.

Sir Edmund bent over and whispered something to Gladys.

She did not heed him.

It was as if a great whirlwind had swept about her and scattered every familiar object from around.

She was deaf to her lover's voice, deaf to little Amy's terrified cries. The fierce roar of the lion seemed to have dulled her senses.

She dared not think of Frank—Frank waiting for her in the darkest depths of the woods—a prey to the ravenous beast that might trace him out!

A wild, piercing shriek broke from her lips, and, while the carriage whirled along, she stood up and leaped into the road.

The movement was so sudden, the danger so unexpected, that no one was able to realise what had
happened.

She stood for a second, with the dust clouding her
sight and stifling her breath, the horses' swift hoofs
clattering around her, the wheels driving by her in
bewildering succession.

She put her hand to her head and gazed round
wildly, confused by the noise and the dust.

Then, before any check could be placed on the
tearing horses, she was knocked down by a spirited
mare a lady was riding, herself trembling and half
fainting with fear, as the lion continued its savage
roaring.

Guided by its own instinct more than the check
placed on it by its terrified mistress, the mare halted,
quivering, and strained in every sinew.

The lady, completely overcome, loosened her grasp
on the bridle, and the animal let its splendid head droop
against the half-lifted hoof that might have trampled
out Gladys' life.

Sir Edmund sprang amidst the rearing horses, and,
snatching the white-clad form in his arms, bore it to
the footpath.

Gladys opened her eyes and gazed up at his drawn
face, as he held her supported against his breast.

"Is this how you meant to scare everyone away from
the woods?" she asked, in a dry, aching voice. "Oh,
Ned! how could you have had such a cruel thought?"

She looked at him with wild horror, and struggled
to free herself from his encircling arm, faint, bruised,
and sorely in need of strength as she was.

He held her fast, his heart beating hard against her,
his pulses quickened by the agony he had endured in
those past few moments.

"Hush, Gladys! I should have prepared you," he
said, huskily, thinking of the danger she had escaped.
"The lion is not at large. I bribed the showman to let
it be chained somewhere in the woods for a few hours.
I thought there could be no surer way of fulfilling the
task you had given me. As to the lion, he is as

harmless now as he is in his cage at the show, and I never saw a tamer beast in all my life."

Gladys gave a heavy sigh of relief.

"Are you sure there is no chance of his getting loose —of his harming anybody?" she asked, not quite recovered from her terror.

"Quite sure, dearest. Do you think I would have entered into such a scheme without first guarding against every possible danger? I would take you to the den and let you see for yourself, only, if I did, all the others would get suspicious, and we should have to tell them everything. Come, sweet, they are all waiting and wondering. Let me put you in the carriage."

Now that he had set her fears at rest she submitted herself to his guidance, and allowed him to lead her back to Lady Etheridge.

She felt very miserable, and, as she saw all the white, frightened faces turned towards her, she could not help thinking it might, perhaps, have been best if she had let things take their own course, and have trusted to Frank's discretion to keep out of sight.

It seemed to her almost a crime, and every kindly glance—every kindly word bestowed upon her, cut into her soul with bitterest reproach.

Sir Edmund watched her gravely throughout the homeward drive, and once, when he was arranging her more comfortably in her seat, she felt his clasp close for a single second on her hand.

He knew she was suffering, and felt for her.

Yet, instead of this being a consolation to Gladys, it only added to her distress, and she inwardly asked herself:

"What must be his thoughts? What reason does he think I have for acting thus?"

Her conscience was not eased of its burden until she saw everybody enjoying a magnificent luncheon in the grand old dining-room, and knew they had forgotten their disappointment.

"We can enjoy our tennis and our boating all the same," Beatrice observed, content now that she had half-a-dozen admirers hovering round her. "After all,

I don't very much regret the change in our day's programme, do you, Mr. Mortimer?"

The gentleman to whom her remark was addressed, glanced half unconsciously towards Gladys.

"I'm not sure," he answered, doubtfully. "I am afraid Miss Clifton has been the sufferer; she is so awfully pale that I am certain she must have been hurt by her fall more than she will allow us to believe."

Gladys grew still paler when she found herself the object of everyone's gaze, and repeated that she felt scarcely any pain from the fall.

"It was certainly a miraculous escape," Lady Etheridge said, awed, as she recalled the incident.

Nobody suspected but that Gladys had been thrown from the carriage through the wheel passing over a hillock, or some other obstacle on the road.

At the moment, when she stood out amid the dust and foam, the scene had been one of such wild confusion that nothing was noticed beyond the simple fact of Gladys having been plunged under the horse's feet.

How she had flung herself into this danger was not guessed even by those who had been nearest her, and she was thankful her mad impulse had not been recognised.

She tried to shake off the miserable feeling clinging to her, and to give her mind to what was going on around.

But it was not possible for her to assume a light-heartedness she could not feel.

When luncheon was over, news was brought them of the capture of the lion.

"It is too late now," Beatrice said, turning laughingly to Mortimer; "I hardly imagine any of us will venture near the woods to-day."

Gladys heard this with an inward thanksgiving, and, later on, she watched them depart for the river.

"You are coming, Gladys?" Sir Edmund asked her, going over to where she sat on the deep cushioned window-seat.

"My head aches," she murmured, wearily; "please don't mind me, I would rather remain at home."

He took his seat quietly by her side.

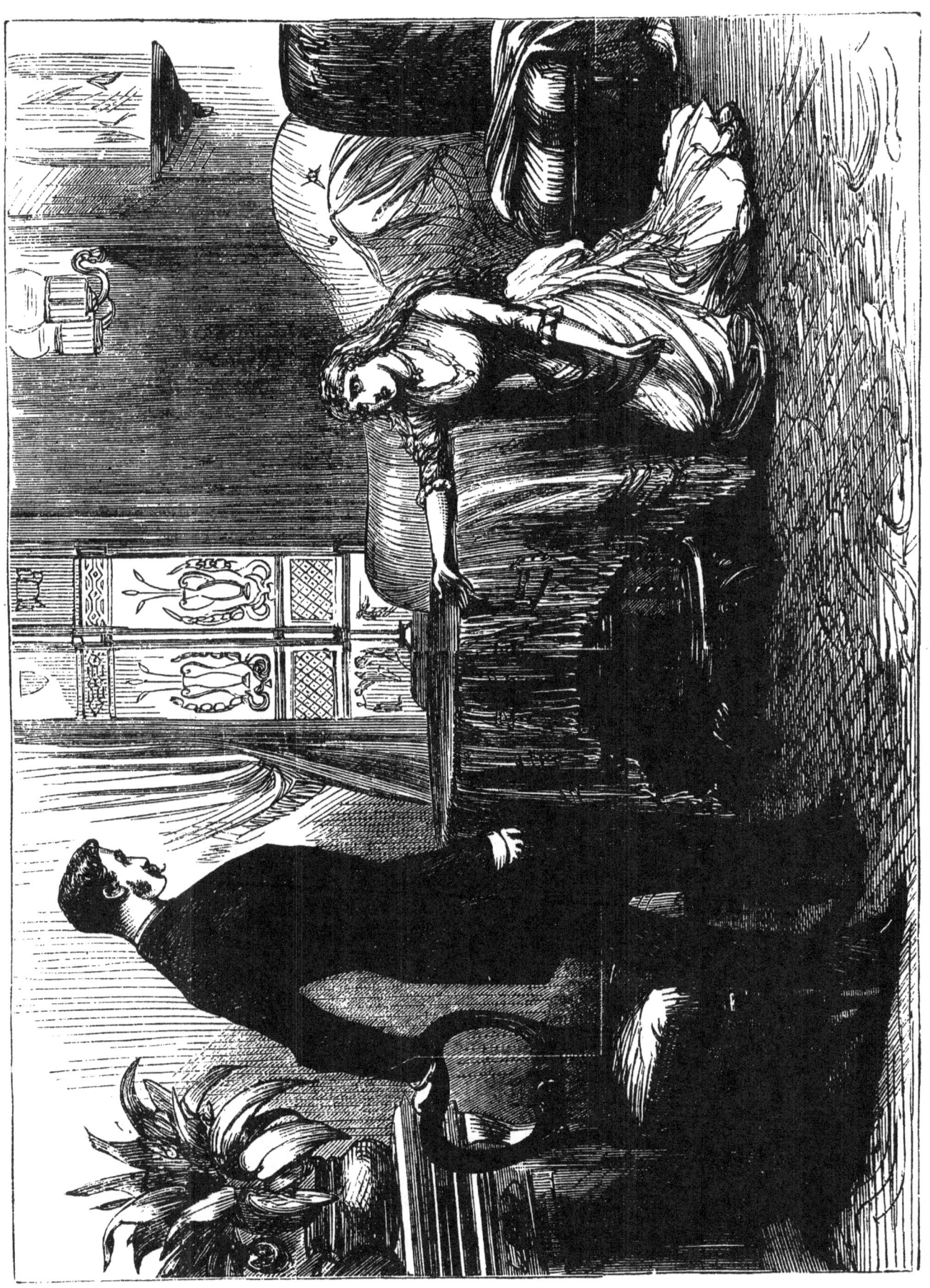

"MY DARLING, I AM KNEELING TO YOU, PRAYING YOU TO TAKE ME BACK."

No. 3.

NOTICE.—With this Number is Given Away a Coloured Picture for binding with the Work.

"If you stay, I shall too," Sir Edmund declared, glad of an excuse to be alone with Gladys. "Perhaps you will be well enough to follow them by-and-by."

"I would rather be left to myself," she replied quickly; "I do not feel fit for any enjoyment, and I should be happier up in my own room."

"But not for the rest of the day!" he exclaimed, disappointed. "After you have had a little quiet, you will be yourself again. I shall come back in an hour or two, and I'm sure by that time you will have changed your mind."

She turned her troubled face entreatingly towards him.

"Will you still go on helping me?" she asked, her voice very low and earnest. "You have done so much for me already, and my manner must seem so strange, yet, in spite of this, can you render me even further service?"

"If you need it, Gladys."

"I do," fervently; "I want to be free all this evening. I told you my secret was another's; to-night I have to fulfil a promise made to that other—a promise which, if broken, will wreck a strong brave life. Perhaps to-morrow I may tell you more—now, I cannot."

It was not so much the words as the look accompanying them that pleaded to his generous heart.

This mystery puzzled him a good deal. Yet he felt he could refuse her nothing; and he told himself he was not worthy her confidence, if his faith could not stand this test.

"I understand," he said; "your actions are still governed by that secret."

"Yes; I must be alone all this evening; and," with a gleam of love in her eyes, "I know no one but you will miss me. Unless you call attention to the fact, my absence will not be noticed."

"Are you sure this is the only way in which I can serve you?"

"The only way; and it is the greatest service you can ever render me."

"Is it? My darling, I shall be glad when this mystery ends. I don't like having to give you up, even for one evening."

"Amongst so many, you will scarcely miss me, Ned."

"Does your heart tell you that, Gladys?"

"Not quite that," she answered, smiling tenderly up at him. "Leave me now, Ned; they are waiting for you."

"Promise just to give yourself a rest."

"I will try; but don't let me be again the subject of everybody's conversation; I cannot bear to listen to their remarks."

"Very well, darling; for to-day, at least, your wish shall be my law."

He pressed her hand gently for one moment, and then moved from her side.

She would have slipped quietly from the room at once, had not Lady Etheridge, followed by Richard Garth, gone over to where she was seated.

"So you have made up your mind to remain at home?" Lady Etheridge remarked, in a carelessly indulgent manner. "I hope you are not suffering from your fall."

"My head aches a little—that is all," Glady's faltered, as though she was committing a crime by this prevarication. "I do not feel quite up to boating this afternoon."

"I will tell Murray to look after you then. You have eaten no lunch, my dear; she must get you something directly we are gone."

Lady Etheridge, having fulfilled her duty to Gladys, swept away, and Garth stood alone before her.

The girl trembled as she met his sinister gaze, and shrank farther into the shadow of the heavy curtain.

"You and Sir Edmund have served us a bad trick, Miss Clifton," he muttered with a dark smile; "it was rather a severe joke to practise upon us. Was it simply to gratify a caprice that you prevented our picnicking in the woods?"

Gladys was silent; her form drooped and seemed so motionless, that Garth thought she had fainted.

With a rapid stride he went over to the table, and pouring some wine into a glass, returned with it in his hand.

"Drink this, Miss Clifton," he said, bending over her; "it will give you fresh strength."

Acting from the instinctive desire to ward off the weakness fast creeping over her, she roused herself, and taking the glass from him drained it feverishly.

"Thank you," she murmured, conquering the fear his words had called up in her; "if you will leave me now you will grant me a favour; I am not well enough to talk."

He bowed as he took the empty glass from her.

"You leave me no choice but to obey," he replied; "I hope when we meet again you will have recovered from this morning's shock."

He gave her a long piercing look, and then left her—left her with the mockery of his voice haunting her ears, and with the strange knowledge that she had in Richard Garth an enemy who, if she were ever in his power, would show her no mercy.

CHAPTER VII.

GLADYS remained in her room all the afternoon, her door locked, and the curtains drawn closely over the open window.

Mrs. Murray, the housekeeper, had taken her up some cold chicken and a cup of tea; then, after persuading her to eat and drink, had left her to lie down and sleep away her pain.

Strangely enough, the girl did sleep, though for the last few nights she had lain awake, tortured with the dread of what would happen on this day.

She was so full of anxiety for Frank, it had seemed to her a mockery to lay her head on the cool soft pillows.

Yet, just to please the good-natured woman, she threw herself outside her little white bed, and, in spite of herself, fell asleep.

When she awoke it was twilight, and she had almost forgotten the terror she had undergone during the morning.

The sound of voices and laughter under her window roused her recollection, and, with a weary sigh, she got up and bathed her face.

When she drew aside the window-curtains, the voices had gone beyond hearing distance.

"Has Lady Etheridge returned?" she asked of a maid who came in answer to a summons from her.

"Yes, miss; but they have all gone off again to see some ruins that's supposed to be haunted at this hour. Everybody was anxious to know if you could join them, but her ladyship heard you were sleeping, and would not have you disturbed. If you would let Loid drive you down, there's plenty of time to overtake them, miss."

"Thank you; I have had enough of horses and wheels to-day," Gladys answered, feeling stiff and sore in every limb. "I think I will take a little walk, and meet them coming back."

"Alone, miss?" looking wonderingly at the fair sweet face, with its large fever-bright eyes.

"Bruce can come with me"—Bruce was a splendid collie, whose obedience she could rely upon. "I shall not go very far. I left my hat downstairs; I wish you would get it for me, Mary."

Mary went rather reluctantly.

She had an idea that Gladys did not look fit to go out by herself; there was something about her appearance which seemed to belong to one who had just recovered from a long illness, and Mary, who knew nothing about sickness of the heart, only thought some devouring disease must be working its way into the "poor young lady's" life.

She fell to thinking so deeply over this while she searched for the hat, that it gave her quite a start when she turned and saw Gladys standing in the doorway.

"There it is, Mary; it must have fallen behind that chair. Thanks," as she took the hat from her. "I shall be back soon, if I do not meet anyone."

Those last few words conveyed a dangerous meaning.

Gladys thought nothing of the suspicion they might rouse as she hurried through the dim hall out into the twilight.

The money she had promised Frank was safe in her pocket, and, keeping in the shadow of the trees, she made her way swiftly towards the spot where she knew he was waiting.

Her heart was beating very fast, and she glanced back again and again to assure herself that nobody was following.

She was glad to have the dog with her on this account. If he had caught scent of anyone from the Towers, he would have given some sign that would have put her on her guard.

Nothing happened to alarm her on the way, and when she saw Frank coming towards her from a dense screen of foliage, she felt within her only the gladness of meeting him once more.

"Poor little girl, how good of you to come !" he murmured, taking her hand and kissing her pale cheek. "I waited, but I did not expect to see you. I have been painting while the daylight lasted, and I know all about your accident. Were you hurt, Gladys ? My heart stood still when I saw what had happened, but I dared not show myself."

"I thought you were near," she cried faintly. "I am so sorry for you, Frank. How lonely your life must be in this concealment ! "

"Lonely while I breathe free English air !" he exclaimed, drawing a deep breath. "Lonely with the shelter of these grand old trees, and the sound of the birds ! I knew the word in its bitterest meaning once, Gladys, but it was on foreign soil."

She understood to what he referred, and she clasped his hand closer, as she walked with him farther into the wood.

After all these months of separation they had a good deal to tell each other ; and, seated on the root of a giant oak, where Frank had been working at his sketch, they exchanged long confidences, as they had done in days gone by, when they had sat together, boy and girl.

"So you are going to be Sir Edmund's wife," he said thoughtfully, when they had come to this subject. "Is the marriage to take place soon ? "

"I wanted to put it off till all this secrecy is over, but Sir Edmund wishes otherwise. He does not mind that I am keeping something from him."

"He knows, then ? "

"He knows I have a secret, yet he is so generous he does not even try to find out what it is. Do let me tell him, Frank. He deserves my trust and yours, for it is only through his help that I have been able to see you to-day."

The outcast knit his haggard brow ; not with anger, but with pain, as though some inward struggle tortured him.

He put out his hand as if thrusting some thought away from him.

"No—no!" he muttered hurriedly; "don't tempt me, dear. Men who do not know me might not take my word as my own sister has. Let us talk of something else; only remember, Gladys," he added, turning his clear open gaze full upon her, "you are in every way worthy to be Sir Edmund's wife, for I swear to you most solemnly that I am not guilty of any wrong done against God or against man. How this curse has fastened itself upon me I know not; but that I have suffered so long, makes the fault of the guilty a double crime."

The earnestness with which he spoke impressed Gladys, and a sudden longing to rise up and help him in his search for the guilty man filled her.

"I think I will give up everyone and follow you, Frank," she said, this new resolve forming itself in her mind. "Together we might find the man."

He smiled a little sadly.

"No, dear; I shall make my search better alone. There's no need for two of us to bear this burden. Your fate rests with the man you love. I hope you will be happy, Gladys."

"I can never be happy till I know that justice is done you," she answered sorrowfully.

A short silence followed, and for a time both were lost in thought.

A restless movement on the part of Bruce who, like a faithful sentinel, was keeping watch, warned Gladys not to linger longer.

"I had almost forgotten this," she whispered, slipping her little purse into his hand. "It is all I have, and for your sake I wish it were more; I am afraid it will not buy you many comforts, Frank."

"As many as I shall want," he replied cheerfully. "I am not half as badly off as you imagine. You know I always had a good eye for colours, and my pictures sell well; I shall send two or three up to London to-morrow, and as soon as I get the cheque for them, I shall start on a tour."

"You will let me see you again, Frank, before you go?"

"It would be safer not, dear. Nobody about here knows me, and the coming and going of a strolling artist cannot rouse curiosity; only if you were seen with me it might prove dangerous to both of us."

"But only once more!" she pleaded.

"I am afraid to promise. You had better go, Gladys; I am getting anxious."

"I shall come here as often as I can and chance meeting you," she said, without heeding his last words. "I know if you are near you will not hide from me."

"Hardly," he replied assuringly. "Say good-bye, Gladys—for the present, at least—and whatever happens, always remember what I have told you to-day—I am not guilty."

"As if anything could ever make me believe otherwise!" she exclaimed, gazing up at him with eyes full of faith. "Why do you say these things to me, Frank?"

He laid his thin white hands on her shoulders, and bent down and kissed her.

"All the world is against me," he said with sad bitterness. "It is difficult to understand how one gentle little heart can keep true to me."

"Not when you think I am your own sister," she put in softly. "I know you too well to be able to believe ill against you."

"God bless you for those words!" he exclaimed gratefully. "You are my comforting angel, Gladys."

"Yet you will not even be advised by me," she said wistfully.

"Not when you ask me to do what would betray myself," he answered, guessing what her mind was dwelling upon. "Before we part to-night, I want you to give me your solemn word that you will never repeat the secret I have trusted you with. I have escaped from a felon's dock. Who, knowing this, and having no proof of my guiltlessness, would spare me?"

Gladys could have answered easily enough, but she saw that to persist on this subject only distressed him, so she gave him the promise he had asked for, and meant to abide faithfully by it.

"Poor Gladys!" he exclaimed with a heavy sigh, when she had left him, and he stood watching the white gleam of her dress fade away in the gloom. "I had not the heart to tell her this must be our last meeting. The risk is too great—for her, as well as for me."

"I agree with you," muttered a voice close to his ear. "You are not too cautious, Frank Clifton."

The outcast swung round, and his face grew white almost to ghastliness as he confronted Richard Garth.

"You here?" he whispered hoarsely.

"Assuredly. But it is I who should evince most surprise at this unexpected meeting. Till now I believed you were in Australia or Siberia——"

"Hush, for Heaven's sake! Do you want to betray me?"

Garth lifted his dark brows in feigned astonishment.

"You speak like a madman. What fear is upon you?"

"You know!" Frank answered fiercely, folding his arms on his breast, and watching Garth steadily. "Why pretend this ignorance?"

Garth's eyes fell before Frank's gaze.

"You have escaped?"

"I have."

"I'm not sorry to hear it. I am one of the few who have never believed you guilty of the charge brought against you. It was lucky that you dropped your real name while you were out in the diggings; it has been the one chance which has saved you."

"I have to thank you for my escape, then," Frank said, taking Garth's extended hand in a firm grip. "It was through your advice that I kept my identity a secret during the trial."

"Was it? I don't remember," carelessly. "So Gladys Clifton is your sister? Strange that her name should not have struck me as being the same as yours. I had no idea of the relationship till I saw you together just now."

"You know her, then?"

"I am staying at the Towers."

Frank lips tightened with a twinge of pain.

He still grasped Garth's hand, for Richard had said he believed him innocent, and the words had filled him with gratitude.

In this man who knew his secret, he had unexpectedly found a friend.

"You will not speak of me to her?" he asked huskily. "She would be frightened, poor child, if she thought others knew her secret. You are man enough, Garth, to spare her this humiliation?"

"Certainly, my dear fellow; I should be the last one in the world to mention the subject, either to her or to anyone else."

"Thanks; I feel safer now. Nobody but you and the wretch who committed the deed could have suspected that I was not what I seemed to be. When I find him, it will go hard with one of us!"

The threat was uttered fiercely, and Frank clenched his hands and glanced round him, his pulses beating hot and feverishly with the longing to have within his reach the coward who had betrayed him.

"Do you think you will ever find him?" Garth asked, shrugging his shoulders.

"I have taken an oath that I will never rest till I have tracked him down. This is the use I shall make of my freedom."

Garth gave a short laugh.

"I advise you to give up the idea, and make more profitable use of your time."

"And be a fugitive all my life? The slur hangs too heavily on me for me to rest till I have got rid of it. Besides, it would fit better on the one who created it."

There was a sarcasm in the words that jarred on Garth, and the vengeful bitterness in Frank's eyes seemed to burn him.

He turned away.

"I suppose you want to get money?" he muttered, treading some of the last year's leaves under his heel. "Shall I lend you money?"

The boyish face flushed up to the tawny waves of hair clinging to the broad honest brow.

"Thanks; I do not require it. Poor little Gladys has been my banker."

"Then I suppose we shall not see you again?"

"Not at present. I have to be continually on the move, and I have been here a good time."

"Well, don't forget, if you ever want a friend, come to me. I have stood by you from the first, and if there is anything I can do for you, I'll do it."

"I shall not forget," Frank said, his haggard eyes brightening. "Be kind to little Gladys; I know she is full of sorrow."

Garth brooded over those words as he walked homeward.

"Be kind to little Gladys!" he muttered with a sneering laugh. "What a fool the fellow is! He deserves to be somebody's dupe!"

Somebody's dupe!

Poor Frank! he was that, and he knew it, but did not know his duper—did not know he had grasped in friendship the hand of the man he could have slain.

He had blindly put his trust in a traitor, and had parted in peace with the enemy he was searching for.

"My wife is dead," he said, turning his hollow, aching eyes from those around him.

CHAPTER VIII.

LADYS knew nothing of the meeting which had taken place after she had left her brother, and a load was lifted off her mind now the money was safe in his keeping.

"If any danger overtakes him he can leave Deepwood at once," she thought. "I have not half so much fear about him now."

She managed to go every day to the woods.

She was anxious to know if he had gone away yet, or if he wanted her to do anything more for him.

Once or twice she saw him working with his brush in the fair bright daylight.

But he would not let her stay with him more than for a few measured moments; yet short as those interviews were, they were long enough to work her misery.

Rumours uprose that made Lady Etheridge watch Gladys with cold suspicion.

Her changed manner—her indifference to things that had pleased her before—and her desire to be left always to herself, all helped to increase this dark mistrust which had risen against her.

She had been seen with a stranger—a pale, sad-eyed artist, whom several of the keepers had noticed wandering through the woods.

"I always thought you had been mistaken in her," Beatrice observed dryly, when the matter was being discussed before Sir Edmund. "I think it is time her visit ended; it is a pity she ever became a guest in a house where she was only governess."

Sir Edmund flushed hotly.

"You will oblige me, Beatrice, by not repeating this nonsense. Gladys is too far above such suspicion for it to be coupled with her name. The charge against her is simply to be laughed at."

"Why don't you laugh then?" she asked, mockingly. "You seem tremendously put out about it."

"The remarks I hear annoy me."

"Do you not believe them?"

"I do not," with stern emphasis.

"But, my dear Edmund, she denies nothing," Lady Etheridge interrupted. "Her very silence is proof against her."

"She shows her courage by treating this scandal as it deserves to be treated—only with contempt."

"Do you mean to say she ought not to give an explanation?" Lady Etheridge exclaimed, indignantly.

"I would not insult her by asking her for one," he replied, decisively.

"At least you will give up the thought of marrying her till this mystery is cleared?"

"Not for a single second! All the evil the world could say of her would not turn me from her. On the contrary, I would make her my wife the sooner, that I might give her the protection she so sorely needs."

With this he left them standing by themselves in the dim old library, where they had gathered for this conference, and Beatrice, as she watched him go, gave a strange little laugh.

"One day he will find he has been deceived," she said, toying nervously with the jewelled bangles on her soft white arm. "I wish Gladys Clifton had never come into this house! It will be hard if I have to lose everything through her."

"Your brother is his own master," Lady Etheridge sighed. 'If he is so headstrong, he must go his own way and suffer the consequences."

"Others will suffer besides himself," the girl murmured, and the old discontent rose afresh in her heart.

Meanwhile Sir Edmund went to look for Gladys.

She had gone with Amy to feed the gold-fish that flashed like light in the fountains, but once out in the grounds, she had left the child to amuse herself, and, going into a summer-house almost hidden by purple passion flowers, she became absorbed in her own thoughts.

Such dreary reflections they were, too!

She bowed her head on her hand, and sighed heavily as the sadness of her life smote upon her.

What was she to do—accused of deceit, of stealing meetings with a man who in secret was her lover?

This, then, was the danger Frank had tried to guard her against.

The rumour was too evil.

Who could believe her so utterly false?

"Not Edmund—not Edmund!" she moaned in answer to this last thought. "Oh, he surely will not believe!"

"He will believe only what you tell him," Sir Edmund said, stooping under the passion flowers, and gently raising her face. "My dearest one, what is making you so unhappy?"

She started when she heard his deep tender voice, and linked her hands feverishly in his as she let him draw her head against his breast.

"Do you believe what they are saying about me?" she asked, wistfully, looking up into the manly face bent over her.

"That I have a rival? No, Gladys."

He answered her with a smile on his lips, yet it faded almost instantly, his eyes clouding as some sudden thought passed through his mind.

After all, what did he know of her secret?

She seemed alone in the world.

There was no one to say what her past had been.

Surely beauty such as hers could not have blossomed unnoticed.

What proof had he that no man save himself had loved her?

These reflections, filled him with jealousy, and slowly unclasping her hands from his own, he folded his arms on the back of the seat, putting himself in a position that would enable him to watch the change in her face.

"Gladys, I want to ask you something," he said, after a short pause, "something that I have never thought of asking you till now. Have you ever—a long time ago,

I mean; before you came to the Towers—loved somebody else?"

She looked at him wonderingly, the soft bright colour flickering in her pale cheeks.

"You are my first love, Edmund," meeting his gaze half shyly, yet with a depth of earnestness in her pure eyes; "and I love you with my whole heart.

He could not resist this sweet reply—the tender light on the child-face.

Once more his arm stole over her shoulder, once more their hands met and clasped, and her head went back to its old resting-place.

"No other man has ever spoken to you of love," he said, still jealous lest another should have won a thought that should have been saved for him, "or had you near him as you are to me now?"

"Of course not. Why do you put such strange questions to me, Edmund?"

"I won't any more—only," drawing his arm more firmly round her, "you cannot blame me for being inquisitive—just now."

She drooped her head for a moment, and a quiver passed over her lips. Then she looked up at him and clung to him passionately.

"Do you trust me?" she asked, with wild pathos. "Do you believe that my heart is true to you?"

"Yes, Gladys," he answered, firmly, and gazing into her violet eyes, he knew that he spoke truly.

Presently he said, thoughtfully:

"I am going away for a little while, Gladys, to Scotland, and when I come back it will be to fetch you —you will be ready, dear?"

"If you wish, Edmund," very softly.

"I do wish; and I have a fancy for you to meet me at the church-door—all in white with orange-blossoms, and a bridal-veil—do you understand, wild-rose?"

"I think so, Ned," she whispered, her face tremulous with shy gladness. Then after a short pause, "Must you start at once?"

"It will be better, darling, for I shall return all the sooner. I have a quaint little place in the Highlands

that I think would please you, and I want to make it fit
to be your home for a time."

"Will you stay away long?" she asked, wistfully, remembering how lonely she would be when he was gone.

"Three weeks. I shall return on the very day; and,
remember, I shall go straight to the church. My
darling, there will be no drawing back then," he added,
the deep love he bore her shining in his eyes. "You
will be mine, and nothing will take you from me."

"Not even the secret?" she said, with a touch of
sadness. "You are sure that in after days, whatever
comes of it, you will not reproach me?"

"Never, Gladys," he answered, gently kissing away
the shadow that had come to her brow; "I have so
much faith in you that I shouldn't care if I knew your
whole life were a mystery. Cheer up, little love, or I
shall imagine I am leaving a sad heart behind me."

"I shall be sad while you are away—the weeks will
seem so long. Don't you think, Edmund"—faltering
slightly over the words, and letting her gaze wander towards the child with the gold-fish—"don't you think it
would be better to put off the marriage for a time, and
to go on just as we are now? It seems such a bright
beautiful happiness to have all your love and all your
confidence. I almost dread a change, lest that perfect
faith you have in me should be disturbed"

"Nonsense, Gladys!" he laughed, determined not to
encourage gloomy forebodings. "It would take very
powerful proofs to make me believe you were not worthy
of more trust than any one man could give. As to letting
you off now you have once consented to be guided by
me—the idea is quite out of the question! I have
made up my mind that you shall be my wife on the
very day of my return to Deepwood, and I shall stick
fast to my resolution."

Notwithstanding the careless happiness with which
he warded off all misgivings on her part, Gladys could
not quite shake herself clear of the secret anxiety prey-
ing on her mind.

Yet, when the time drew near for Sir Edmund to take
his departure, her first sorrow sank down under this

new pain of parting, and she clung to him, and asked him not to leave her, in case some storm should come to ruffle the smooth flow of their lives.

"This will be our last parting," he whispered, when he bade her farewell. "After this, nothing shall take me from your side."

He had made arrangements with Lady Etheridge to hasten the preparations for the marriage, and had told his little ward to "make Gladys very happy" during his absence, which Amy readily promised to do.

Even Beatrice seemed inclined to show more tenderness towards the girl who was so soon to be her brother's wife, notwithstanding that his marriage would do away with the possibility of her inheriting his fortune.

Garth and the Arab had gone up to London for the end of the season, and were to return on the day arranged for the wedding.

"You already seem quite to belong to us," Lady Etheridge said to Gladys, when the bride's trousseau was being discussed. "Have you no friend or relative whom you would care to have near you during the ceremony?"

"Nobody," the girl answered, her eyes filling with a strange dreamy pain.

"Well, Gladys, you will not feel the want of friends when you are Edmund's wife. You are lucky to have won such a love as his. He will be everything to you. Have you made up your mind which of these dresses you will have?"

Gladys looked wearily at the pile of costly satins that had been sent for her selection, and then turned away her gaze with a short quick sigh.

Lady Etheridge gave her a searching glance.

"One would think you were scarcely interested in this marriage," she observed, watching the girl with proud surprise. "Had you hoped to make a better match?"

Gladys grew pale—pale as the dead-white robe spread out before her.

Lady Etheridge had summoned her to her dressing-room directly the silks had arrived, and Gladys felt while they were alone there was no need for her to disguise her thoughts.

"You hurt me when you talk like that," she said, a dull ache in her voice; "you do not read my heart aright. I love Sir Edmund dearly and faithfully, but if he had left me the choice to say yes or no to this marriage, I would have answered 'No.'"

"For what reason—if you love him?"

"I do love him," she repeated, her eyes dark with intense feeling; "but I would rather never see him again, than that he should one day repent having made me his wife."

"Have you told him this?" Lady Etheridge asked, her keen glance resting on the troubled young face.

"I have told him over and over again, yet he will not even listen. If I could only see into the future!" she broke off passionately; "if I could only feel sure that he will always trust me. It would be so much easier to put his love from me now, than that my heart should break afterwards!"

The very thought of what might come seemed to break down the barrier of restraint, and she could not repress the sob that quivered up to her lips, or shut that deep strange pain out of her eyes.

Lady Etheridge, with all her worship for her beautiful daughter, could not see this poor motherless shivering bride fretting her heart out without trying to comfort her.

She laid her hand kindly on her shoulder.

"Edmund will think we have not taken good care of you in his absence if you give way to these fits of sadness, Gladys; you must do whatever he says will please him most, and he would not like to know you are making yourself miserable because you are to be his wife. He would imagine you capricious, and would think you do not care about him."

"He knows I care for him," Gladys said mournfully. "It is my love for him that makes me half afraid of binding my life for ever to his."

"Quite a groundless fear, my dear," Lady Etheridge responded, her eyes softening as their gaze rested on the pale sensitive face. "About this dress," she added cheerfully, "I suppose as it is to be my present, I had better choose what I think will suit you best. But you must get rid of all these strange fancies before Ned comes back."

Gladys had no cause for any doubts as to the truth of Sir Edmund's love.

Every day brought her a letter full of tender, earnest thought, and when the last week drew to its close, a velvet case containing a magnificent set of pearls was placed in her hands.

"They are too costly," she said, and she put them aside, and treasured up a little bunch of white heather she had found amongst them.

The morning following the one on which she had received the pearls, when she drew back the curtains and opened the rose-hung casement, she found lying on the window-sill a large cluster of wild heartsease and forget-me-nots.

It was her wedding-day. Who but Sir Edmund could have thought of sending her this sweet message?

She had the bouquet placed near her while she was being robed in her bridal-dress, and the wreath of starry orange-blossoms was placed on her golden head.

When her toilet was completed, she took a few of the flowers she had found outside her window, and fastened them at her breast, close over her heart, and the sun shone down on a bride fairer than the day.

Little Amy flitted round her, looking like a fairy in her pretty lace frock, her small arms weighed down with a mass of creamy roses, that were to make a fragrant carpet for the bride.

Two pages, in white velvet, were waiting to lift the sweeping train, and when Gladys was led to her carriage, a thrill ran through the knot of villagers who had gathered to see her.

"Its an angel-princess," they murmured, straining to get a glimpse of the pure downcast face. "She'll be a blessing to the one who loves her."

Gladys heard, and a soft flush wavered in her pale cheeks.

It was much to feel that these good people thought her worthy to be the wife of the master they worshipped, and a sweet happiness stole into her heart.

Beatrice had gone on to meet the rest of the party at the church, and Gladys as yet had exchanged no word with her or with Richard Garth.

How could their coldness affect her when she was going to meet her lover, and to give her life to him?

She glanced at the heartsease nestling in her breast —his message—and smiled softly as she read their meaning.

The old shadowy dread had vanished, and she thought only of the love awaiting her.

CHAPTER IX.

SIR EDMUND was waiting to hand her out of the carriage, and he looked at her with tender pride as she stepped on to the rose-leaves strewn in her path.

"My white pure Gladys," he murmured, clasping both her hands; "you have made me the happiest man in the whole wide world!"

He looked very handsome—this tall broad-shouldered fellow, with his fair manly face—handsomer with the sun-bronze on his cheeks, Gladys thought, than when he had left her three weeks ago.

"Did you reach Deepwood only this morning?" she asked, letting her hands rest within his clasp.

"An hour ago," he replied, smiling. "I kept away, as I said I should—till the time came for me to make you my wife;" then, noticing that she did not wear his last gift: "What has become of the pearl necklace, Gladys? Didn't you like it, darling?"

"Yes; the pearls were of great price, but, to-day, I do not value them so much as I do this little cluster of wild flowers."

She touched the velvety blossoms caressingly, too happy to note the disappointment in Sir Edmund's face.

"I thought the pearls would please you," he said, with just the slightest tinge of reproach in his rich voice. "I wished I had known what flowers to send you."

"You sent me the very sweetest——"

"You did like my roses, then!" he exclaimed, flushing with pleasure at her words.

"Not better than these," she said softly, and he noticed the tenderness with which she again touched the wild-flowers she prized more highly than his pearls.

"I did not send you those Gladys," he muttered abruptly. "Why do you wear them in place of mine?"

She started, and gave a half frightened look into his face.

For the first time the truth rushed into her brain.

They had been sent by Frank, the outcast who could make her no other offering.

Sir Edmund saw the sudden surprise that flushed her cheeks, and he felt inclined to snatch the poor little blossoms from their resting-place.

"You know the sender of those flowers," he said jealously; "Your manner shows me that you do. Gladys, I don't like to see you treasuring them up in this way. Tell me who gave them, and then give them to me to mind."

She drew them gently from her dress, and handed them to him in silence.

"You won't tell me, Gladys?"

She met his keen glance unflinchingly, her eyes shining with love.

"One day I will," she answered gently; "I cannot now, Edmund. Please do not ask me any more."

"But I don't like to see you wearing somebody else's flowers instead of mine."

She looked at him reproachfully.

"I thought these were yours, Edmund."

"Not since I told you I knew nothing about them."

"No."

"And they are still as dear to you?"

"I should not like to discard them, Edmund."

"Because you know who the sender is?"

"That is why."

Sir Edmund knew she was not playing with him.

Her voice was earnest almost to sadness, and she seemed to shrink from the subject, speaking only when he forced an answer from her.

A sudden jealousy took possession of him, and before he entered the church he dropped the flowers into the dust, and trod them under his foot.

"If she be true to me, she will not care what becomes of them," he thought; and he watched her closely.

Before anyone could see what had happened, Gladys stooped and picked up the broken flowers, as though they could feel the hurt.

"That was most unkind!" she exclaimed, angry because poor Frank's flowers had met with this fate. "I didn't think you could do anything so mean. "Is this a proof of the faith you have in me?"

He called himself a brute for having chased the gladness from her tender eyes.

"When you talk like that, you make me think you do not love me," he said.

"You can never think that—not seriously," she answered in a firm low voice, "for you know my love for you is greater and stronger than my life."

After this, there was peace between them, and Gladys laid her hand trustfully in his while the words were spoken that gave all her life to him.

She heard the deep proud love that vibrated in his voice as he repeated each binding sentence, and a thrill of happiness ran through her when she knew herself his wife.

The grand strains of the "Wedding March" pealed through the church, and the rich swell of music seemed to lift her soul to almost too great a joy.

"God bless my wife!" Sir Edmund said fervently, pressing the trembling little hand that clasped his arm, as he led her into the vestry. "Surely no man has ever won so sweet a fate."

The register was laid open on the table, and a look of pleasure crossed Sir Edmund's face as he saw two white packets, daintily tied with satin-ribbon, placed on the open pages.

"What have we here?" he asked, carelessly taking up one of the packets, when everybody had finished signing. "Hallo! both for me! That's hardly fair. Let's see what is in them, darling."

He placed one in her hands, and untied the other himself.

Then suddenly all the colour left his face, and he looked at her with eyes that were filled with a mad horror.

GLADYS CLUNG TO FRANK WITH A LOW, FRIGHTENED CRY.

No. 4.

"What does this mean—a joke? Gladys, speak—tell me you knew of this—that it means nothing!"

He seized her arm with convulsive force, and thrust before her gaze the thing that had been placed on the register for him—the photograph of a girl, with her arms twined round the neck of a man.

The girl was Gladys, but a branch of drooping leaves screened the face of the man, and the likeness only showed a tall figure full of refined ease.

Before Gladys could understand what the photograph revealed Sir Edmund had drawn it away from her, and was looking at it again, his hand clenched on his brow, as though he felt his senses leaving him.

He could not mistake what he saw.

The pose of the child-like head, the clustering hair—even the dress he recognised; it was a faithful likeness of Gladys—and yet of the man who was bending over her he knew nothing!

Across the picture, in an unknown hand, were traced the words:

"Taken in the woods, one month before the marriage of Sir Edmund Etheridge with Gladys Clifton."

"What does it mean?" he whispered, hoarsely, his voice scarcely recognisable. "Gladys, is this your secret?"

She leaned nearer to him—paler than the dead-white silk falling round her; trembling as though some sudden storm had shaken her delicate frame.

The truth dawned into her stricken mind: there had been treachery.

She had been discovered in the woods with Frank, and this plot had been laid against her.

With a bitter moan of despair she hid her face in her hands.

An awful silence followed, and a tremor ran through the little group gathered in the vestry, as Sir Edmund seized her hands, and once more thrust the fatal picture before her gaze.

"Gladys, is this your secret?" he repeated, with despairing bitterness. "Look at me, Gladys, and say that I am wronging you—that this proof against you is false!"

She raised her pure eyes to his.

"You are wronging me, Edmund," she said, pitifully; "I have never been but true to you."

"This thing is a lie, then!" he exclaimed, with a strange laugh; "oh, accursed thing, that has made me believe my darling false!"

He flung the picture fiercely to the ground, and trampled it under his heel, just as he had trampled into the dust the flowers Frank had sent her.

The action recalled to his memory the little knot of heartsease and forget-me-nots she had prized above his roses, and the jealous mistrust grew stronger within him.

"I see it all," he muttered with pallid lips. "I have been deceived—blindly and madly deceived! It was for this I left you on the day of the picnic—for this I kept away from the woods. I believe everybody lied when they told me you were false, and I trusted you— you who disarmed me with soft excuses while you stole out to meet your lover! Gladys, your guilt is greater than my love. Go—I never wish to meet you in this world again!"

His accusing words seemed to strike a chill to her soul. She shuddered and sank on her knees at his feet.

"Oh, Edmund! cannot you trust me a little longer?" she cried, trying to clasp his clenched hand. "You are wronging me most cruelly! On my knees in this sacred place, with my lips on this holy book, I swear I have never uttered one false word to you, or had one false thought against you! Edmund, listen to me. Look into my eyes and read the truth there! This horrible suspicion is killing me!"

He flung her touch off almost roughly, and held the contents of the second packet towards her— another photograph in which the same figures were faithfully reflected, the face of the man turned away in this as in the first.

"When you can explain this in words that will prove your innocence, I shall believe you," he said with unrelenting bitterness, and he waited for her to speak.

She wrung her hands, and lifted her white face in utter despair.

"Edmund, Edmund, hear me and believe me! This is all a dark mistake! I have loved no man but yourself! One day you will understand, and pity me for the wrong you are doing me to-day!"

"I could never have pity for a woman who has betrayed my trust as you have. The only regret I have is that I had not believed this sooner—before this miserable marriage had brought dishonour on my name. It ends here. Your sin has parted us; I can never look upon you as my wife!"

There was a stony ring in Sir Edmund's calm voice, a stony pallor on his face, and his eyes were sunken and dark as though they had no recognition of anything around.

Gladys looked up at him, and the pleading words died on her lips.

What power had she to move this cold, pitiless man before her? This was not her lover—the steel-blue eyes were strange to her.

The heart that had gone out to her full of tenderness was frozen and dead.

She shrank from the sight of him as from some ghastly thing. She could not plead with this man; could not cling to the clenched hands. She did not know him—he was not the same.

She gave a faint, startled cry, as though she had suddenly found herself face to face with death. Then her head sunk on to his feet.

Sir Edmund recoiled.

The photograph—the convicting evidence of her guilt—was still grasped in his hand, and as he glanced from it to the white drooping form, a thin streak of blood oozed from his lips.

"My wife is dead," he said, turning his hollow, aching eyes on those around him. "I shall leave her, and tell my soul that she is dead."

He left, and Lady Etheridge and Beatrice followed him; they were frightened of what might come to him in this ghastly mood.

The children clung to each other shivering, and Richard Garth, seeing they were forgotten, took them under his protection.

The startled children let him lead them passively, but before they had reached the door, little Amy broke away from him and threw herself beside the motionless form of the poor bride.

"Sir Edmund is cruel—and you are all cruel!" she exclaimed with a child's impetuous indignation.

"You saw her fall down crying, and you are leaving her because she is hurt. You are wicked, and I won't go with any of you. I shall stay with her the same as she stayed with me when I was ill."

Without a word Garth took Amy up in his arms, and paying no heed to her struggles, carried her out into the sunlight, and placed her in the carriage.

Of all the guests only the Arab remained.

The minister had lifted the bride's white face, and Osman moistened the parted lips with a few drops of water.

"Is it true?" he asked abruptly.

"It is true that she is Sir Edmund's wife," the minister replied gravely.

Osman looked long and earnestly at the fair face, so like a sleeping angel's now that the knowledge of life had left it.

"They have misjudged her," he muttered, "She is not guilty."

The minister lifted one of the cold hands and let it rest in his palm—the hand which, only a few moments ago, he had joined in holy wedlock.

"God help her!" he said, his calm voice grown unsteady. "Her soul seemed as pure as heaven's own light. I can only believe her innocent."

"Have they all cast her off? Won't they take her back to the Towers?"

"Not at present, I think; but she will not be left friendless. My wife has a tender heart, and will give her a mother's care. Poor child! she will need that, whether the charge brought against her be false or true."

*   *   *   *   *

When Gladys recovered consciousness she was lying in a pretty white bed, with the clergyman's wife bending over her.

The Rev. Joshua Heath had himself brought the girl to the vicarage, and Mrs. Heath had taken a tender interest in the beautiful young wife who was never to know a husband's love.

When, after long delirious days, reason returned to her, the memory of that strange wedding seemed only the impression of some horrible dream.

The sight of the heavy gold ring Sir Edmund had placed on her hand was the first thing that recalled to her mind the sad truth, and she turned on her pillows with a piteous cry.

"How long ago was it?" she asked, for it seemed to her that ages must have elapsed since Sir Edmund had loved her.

Mrs. Heath lifted the tangled hair gently away from the hot brow.

"You have been very ill, dear; try to sleep a little; you will feel stronger and better able to talk by-and-by."

"I cannot sleep. I want you to tell me everything now," Gladys said feverishly. "Does anyone think of me up at the Towers?"

"They all think of you, my dear."

But—I mean do they miss me? Are they sorry?"

Mrs. Heath sighed.

"They are very sorry, and it is not you alone they miss."

"Who else?" with a faint breathless dread in the tired voice.

"Lady Etheridge."

Gladys breathed more calmly.

"Will she come back soon?"

"She will never come back, She has left this world."

" Dead ! "

" Yes. Her heart has been affected for years, but no one was prepared to meet the last shock. They thought she only slept when they took up her breakfast yesterday morning. It was the sleep of death."

Gladys was silent after hearing this news, and her mind grew full of mournful memories.

The thought that others were bearing a grief apart from her own filled her with a different pain, and she roused herself to new life.

" They must be in need of comfort," she said, raising herself in her bed. " I might be able to help them in many things. Will you please help me dress ? "

" My dear, I am afraid you are not strong enough Wait till to-morrow."

Gladys dragged herself out of bed, and looked round for some sign of a bell.

" Can you expect me to lie there ? " she exclaimed with a touch of scorn, " now I know what has happened ? "

Mrs. Heath saw that to reason with her would only agitate her, and expose her to fresh danger, so she offered no further remonstrance to this mad scheme.

To rise from a bed of sickness and go out when consciousness had only just returned, seemed like challenging death.

Yet might not this step hasten a reconciliation between Sir Edmund and his disowned wife?

CHAPTER X.

RS. HEATH clung to the hope, as she helped Gladys dress, that her visit might lead to a reconciliation between her and Sir Edmund, though she said nothing to the girl, and her kind voice had a pleased ring in it when she ordered the old-fashioned brougham to be brought round to the door.

"I would rather go alone," Gladys faltered, a sudden flush wavering in her face as she remembered how Sir Edmund had flung her off from him. "Perhaps I should be troubling you for nothing."

"Nonsense, dear; I couldn't think of letting you go by yourself—Joshua would never forgive me."

Gladys shivered with a chill sense of awe when they came within sight of the Towers.

The deserted terraces and drawn blinds gave token of the sadness resting within, and there was no sign of life in the dreary aspect.

"Sir Edmund will see no one," they were told, when the pondrous door was opened to them.

"And Miss Etheridge—is she not well enough to receive a friend?"

"She has kept her room since Lady Etheridge's death, and is too ill to be disturbed."

Mrs. Heath was not to be rebuffed.

She murmured a few solemn words to the footman, and the housekeeper came forward, and led the way slowly to the chamber of death.

Gladys shrank from the sight of the white passionless face.

She felt, in some vague way, that she had been the cause of this awful change, and a great sob broke from her heart as she left the room, with its snowy flowers and chill white draperies.

Had she come only to gaze on this pale face that could give her back no recognition?

She looked down at her wedding-ring, and asked again to see Sir Edmund.

"He is in the library, my lady," the housekeeper said, glancing compassionately at Gladys. "He will give me no answer if I go to him, but perhaps——"

The woman hesitated, hardly knowing how to express her thoughts without paining the wistful-eyed wife Sir Edmund had discarded.

Gladys caught quickly at her meaning, and, on an impulse, she went swiftly downstairs, and paused at the library door.

She knocked softly on the carved panels.

There was no response.

Gently turning the handle, she pushed open the door and entered.

Sir Edmund did not notice her presence.

The daylight was shut out from the room, and she could only just distinguish his dark form where he sat by the table, his elbow resting on the massive bar of his chair, his hand shading his eyes.

One glance at the bowed figure, and Gladys glided to his side, and, kneeling down, crept close up against his heart.

She did not speak. She only drew nearer to him, and hid her face on his breast, and closed her aching eyes, as though her soul sought its rest there.

She was never certain whether Sir Edmund was conscious that she was near him.

His senses seemed wrapped in a dull dreamlike apathy, and he remained in the same motionless attitude she had found him in.

She felt his chest heave with a great sigh, and his heart throbbed hard.

Some strange breathless spell seemed to hold them in thrall.

Presently she raised her piteous face, and saw that he was watching her—watching her with a yearning passionate pain which seemed to have dragged his soul into his eyes.

Still no word.

Gladys, weak from recent illness, let her head droop once more wearily on his breast.

In the dim light she looked dead. With a sudden passionate movement, he crushed her against him, and kissed her with hot lips.

"I am mad!" he muttered. "You have sinned against me, and against yourself, and yet I love you! False, cruel love! Why have you come to mock me again?"

She clasped her wan arms round his neck.

"Edmund, believe me—only believe me!" she cried. "I am true to your love, as the stars are true to heaven. Let me come back to your heart, Edmund. You love me, and I am your wife. If you send me away I shall die!"

The spell was broken.

The passion in his eyes grew fierce, and he seized her wrists in a vice-like grip.

"Do you know that I could kill you while you kneel here?" he exclaimed wildly; "in coming to me you peril your life and my soul. Go: if the parting kill you, so much the better."

He thrust her away from him, and walked to the other end of the room.

He hated her for having brought back a rush of the old love to his heart.

She had sinned against him. What had come to his pride that he could look on her with anything but loathing?

He crushed down the momentary tenderness which had crept, unbidden, into his breast.

"You thought to find me unmanned in this time of mourning," he muttered bitterly; "I wish to Heaven you were lying in place of the dead! Your life is my curse!"

"Then I shall pray for death," Gladys said, with a strange calm in her voice.

"Do you think your prayers will avail you anything?" he asked mockingly; "be dead to me; that is all I want."

"Oh, Edmund, if I could only clear your eyes—if you could only see the mad miserable mistake you are making. For your own sake, Edmund, do not shut your heart against me; you are wronging yourself as much as you are wronging me; for one day you will repay this passion with a bitter repentance, and wonder how you could have been so cruelly blind. Edmund, do be pitiful—be your true dear self. I cannot die, Edmund; love is stronger than life, and it will not leave my heart. My darling, I am kneeling to you, praying you to take me back, to end the pain that is parting us—that is breaking both our hearts. Will you clasp my hand in the old sweet way, and let your soul come near to me? I am so desolate, Edmund, without your love."

She had dragged herself to where he stood, and she stretched her yearning hands towards him, her pale face uplifted in an agony of pleading.

He did not look at her. A convulsive thrill ran through him as he heard her calling to him for mercy, and his colourless lips drew together in a close rigid line.

She clasped his hand, and laid her face against it in passionate tenderness.

"Edmund, send this trouble from us; let me be your comforter—let me make peace between you and your love. I will try so hard to please you, and to bring back the old happiness! Don't turn away from me—don't shut me right out from your heart, Edmund."

He shook off her clasp, and clenched his hand as though he would strike her.

"Gladys—Gladys! How can you, who are so young, deceive so vilely? Go; hide yourself from me and from the world, and try to atone for the curse you have created. I shall forget I ever met you."

"But I love you, Edmund," she moaned despairingly, "and I am your wife!"

His brow grew dark.

"You have betrayed me," he muttered; "this is all I know."

"Oh, how can I prove to you that you are wrong? Edmund, it is all a horrible mistake—this suspicion—

this accusation! I cannot bear it any longer—you must hear the truth——"

He silenced her with a quick gesture of scorn.

"I have heard it already," he said briefly.

"Everything?" she asked, looking up at him in frightened wonder.

"Everything," he responded icily.

"Yet you do not pity me?"

He turned his hot eyes towards her with an expression of mingled contempt and compassion.

"I pity you," he said slowly; "I pity you because I cannot show you mercy, and because one day your sin will come home to you. Who will help you then, you poor slave?—not the one for whose sake you have borne such deep disgrace!"

Gladys shuddered.

He was so calm, so chill in his bitterness; no word of hers could move him.

A sudden dread came to her that Frank might suffer —that if Sir Edmund discovered his hiding-place, he would have him thrust back into exile.

While he condemned her, it was not probable he would believe in the innocence of her brother—an escaped convict.

Frank had suffered so much already. Not even to clear herself would she have him hunted down to that living death from which he had broken loose, and the old resolve came back to her to bear the injustice that would fall on him with such crushing force.

She rose from her knees, and stood silent for a little while, her brave eyes looking strangely large and bright in contrast with the paleness of her face.

"Good-bye, Edmund."

There was a quiver in her sweet voice, and she waited wistfully.

She meant to leave him, yet somehow she could not turn away, and one frail hand wandered pleadingly towards his.

He folded his arms on his breast, and made himself deaf to her voice.

"Good-bye, Edmund. Edmund, won't you forgive me before I go? I had no right to marry you while I had that secret. It was wrong—I knew it from the first; but I loved you so wildly, and I believed you would trust me. When I can prove to you that there is no real shame on my name, shall I come back to you, Edmund?"

"The proof would be a lie!" he muttered huskily. "You need never place it before me."

"And you will never let me come back to you?"

"Never!"

A short silence.

Then Gladys said wearily:

"May I see little Amy? She must be very lonely now."

"Possibly; for she is amongst strangers. I felt no longer fit to be her guardian. You need not fear for her welfare; she is under the care of good women who will give her the training her childhood needs."

Another silence, longer than the first.

Sir Edmund felt a soft touch on his sleeve as though quivering lips had rested for a moment against it.

"If you would only forgive me, Edmund, as I forgive you!" Gladys cried in a heart-broken voice. "You are not purposely cruel, dear—your heart is blind, and you cannot see into my soul."

His heart was blind! That was her only reproach, and he had broken up all the peace of her young life!

The words haunted him—he still felt the thrill of that tremulous touch on his arm, and it filled him with a hungering pain.

He passed his hand over his haggard eyes; then he lifted his restless head and found himself alone.

Gladys had glided through the gloom like a white spirit, and he knew he had lost all that he loved on earth.

CHAPTER XI.

GLADYS did not ask to see Beatrice. She longed to be able to say some kind word to the girl who must be so sorely grieved.

But she knew she had no power to give comfort in this dreary house where her presence was looked upon as a curse, and she went silently away.

Mrs. Heath was waiting to take her back to the Vicarage.

One glance at the sweet white face told her their mission had been useless, and she wondered if Sir Edmund would have shown more gentleness if he had known Gladys, after lying for days between life and death, had risen in the first hour of consciousness to go to him.

"He must have seen how frightfully changed and weak she is," she thought, looking anxiously at her patient. "Poor child, he is killing her!"

She feared Gladys would break down after this; but the girl kept her strength bravely, and when the blinds were again lifted at the Towers she was able to take her walks unaccompanied.

The first use she made of her liberty was to wander to the spots where she would most likely find some trace of her brother.

More than a week passed before she met him.

He had been obliged to leave Deepwood on the morning of her wedding, and had only just returned.

He looked more wretched than Gladys had ever seen him look, when she told him what had happened.

"We have a spy—there's treachery somewhere," he muttered thickly; "and the enemy has been a close one, too. How you must hate me, Gladys, for bringing this misery upon you! Do you mean to say you suffered all their brutal insults rather than let them suspect me?"

"There was not the same danger to me there would have been to you," she answered simply. "The punishment rested between us, and it fell less lightly on me."

"I don't know so much about that," he replied resentfully. "Do you think I am going to let my sister be thrown aside and trampled under foot like dirt? Not likely. I have brought this upon you, and I shall clear you from it. I have endured enough for both, and I will not have you persecuted with this odious suspicion."

"But, Frank, who could have seen us—who could have caused all this mischief?"

"Heaven knows! A strolling photographer would not have done such a thing on his own account. Cannot you think of anyone who is likely to have watched you?"

Gladys thought of Richard Garth, and almost unconsciously she uttered his name.

Frank laughed.

"That's a bad guess, Gladys," he said decisively. "Garth is really a good fellow; he is the last to be remembered as an enemy."

"Why?" she asked, looking bewildered. "Do you know him?"

"He knows me," Frank replied, with a touch of pride, recalling the words Garth had uttered in that unexpected meeting. "He knows what I am, and he does not believe me guilty. I met him out in Australia, and he has proved one of my best friends. With his help I have been enabled to enlist, and the regiment I have joined being on the point of starting for Cairo, I stand a fair chance of getting clear of detection."

The girl's lips grew a shade paler.

"I wish you had told me this before."

"I was afraid it might make you feel under some obligation to him. I made him promise not to let you know he knew anything about me. Has he kept his word?"

"So well," Gladys answered with a touch of scorn, "that he stood by while Sir Edmund accused me of such dark sin. He was right, perhaps," she added, ashamed of the bitterness which had come over her. "It was your secret he was keeping—not mine."

Frank knit his brow angrily.

"It was my fault," he muttered. "I should not have bound him over. I might have known one of us would have to suffer the sacrifice. It shall not be you, though, Gladys. I can, at least, prove that you are innocent."

"Not without betraying yourself, Frank. Sir Edmund is so changed—he would not believe me; perhaps, in his present mood, he would give you up to what he thought justice—"

"Let him!" Frank interrupted, recklessly. "What I have escaped once I can escape again. I will have you righted at any cost."

Gladys implored him to study his own safety first; but his mind was fully made up as to how he would act, and as soon as it was dark enough for him to walk along the road unobserved, he left the woods, and made his way towards the Towers.

In his hot indignation at the shame brought against her, he wanted to take Gladys with him, and to make Sir Edmund ask her forgiveness for his harshness towards her.

The girl shrank from the ordeal.

"I wish you would not go, Frank," she said, miserably. "You don't know what harm you may be doing yourself. Put it off, at least till you have had time to think."

He tossed back his head impatiently.

"It would be time lost," he muttered. "I could not be coward enough to leave my burden on your shoulders. Go to your friends, dear. Perhaps it will be best. When Sir Edmund wants you he shall fetch you."

She drew a deep breath.

· "He will never fetch me."

"Yes, he will," Frank replied, firmly. "If not, you are better apart from him. He is not worthy your love or your regret."

He watched her go slowly in the direction of the vicarage.

Then he made his way towards the Towers.

He had gone too late.

Sir Edmund was no longer at Deepwood.

No one knew where he had gone.

He wanted to "knock about" for a year or two, was all the explanation he had given, and Frank turned away disappointed.

He scarcely knew how to act.

If he could have had an interview with Sir Edmund he would have told him everything.

He could not confide his secret to hirelings, who would repeat it from one to another.

To have done that would have been to set them on the watch, and information would have been given against him.

"It is with him I must speak," he told himself. "I must wait till I meet him."

He met Gladys again on the following day.

She was waiting for him at the spot where she had been accustomed to find him, and one glance into her face showed him she had news for him.

"You have heard something of Sir Edmund?" he asked, anxiously.

She looked at him with pained eyes.

"Of him, but not from him," she answered, sadly. "His lawyer has written to say he is directed by Sir Edmund to forward me a sum of money every month. Oh, Frank," she broke off, a sudden shamed flush sweeping over her pale face, "he thinks I married him for his wealth, and in bitterness he has put nearly all his fortune at my disposal. How bad he must think me, Frank!"

"Don't fret about it, Gladys. It will all come right in time. It isn't likely this kind of thing can go on for ever. You won't take the money, will you?"

"I would rather starve."

"That's spoken like a brave girl! though, now I come to think of it, I don't think you need suffer for your pride. Quite by accident I heard that the young fellow to whom Aunt Jo's money went, had been thrown from his horse and fatally injured. So, if he did not leave any heirs—and I think it is hardly probable that he would have married at such a young age—the property comes back to us; but, as I am dead to the world, everything must belong to you till I can show myself alive again."

He told her where to write for further information, and a prompt reply told her what Frank had said was true.

Searches had already been made for them, and the executors were beginning to give up hope of tracing either brother or sister.

They had little trouble in proving Sir Edmund's disowned wife to be the Gladys Clifton named in the will; and, before Frank started for Cairo, she was mistress of his fortune as well as her own.

It was a strong temptation for him to sell out.

Yet he felt he could not do this in safety.

Having enlisted under an assumed name he could not, without creating suspicion, reveal his identity.

"Plenty of time to go in for pleasure when I have found my enemy," he said, cheerfully, when Gladys hinted at the privations he would have to endure. "Another three or four months and I shall be able to go anywhere without fear. If you should meet Sir Edmund before I do tell him the truth and I will risk the consequences."

He could not bear leaving her in the forlorn position she was placed in.

But he could no nothing now.

His regiment was ordered out, and he had to start at the time appointed.

Gladys stayed on at the vicarage.

She felt in no mood to make a new home for herself.

She was Sir Edmund's wife; the world held her as such, though he disclaimed her, and she lingered in the hope that he would come back and trample down the estrangement which had risen up between them.

Beatrice's dislike for her increased when she heard of the change which had taken place in her fortune, and she determined, if ever there should be any possibility of a reconciliation between her half-brother and this girl he had loved so passionately, she would do all in her power to widen the breach that parted them.

Beatrice thought the misery that had attended Sir Edmund's wedding was a just reproach to him.

Since her mother's death the Towers had been a dreary home, and she wished she had been born a boy, that she could have followed Sir Edmund's example and set out on some wild venturesome journey.

"Shut up in a place like this life is hardly worth living," she thought, her proud spirit fretting under the gloom placed over it. "I shall go mad if something doesn't happen to break the monotony."

She had one or two civil notes from Richard Garth, condoling with her for the loss she had sustained, but the studied sentences expressed no passionate sympathy, and she was disappointed to know his heart had not gone out more warmly towards her.

Osman Omar called often—more to hear news of Gladys, perhaps, than to see Beatrice.

He had a firm belief in the sweetness of the child-wife, and his fierce nature rose hotly against Sir Edmund.

He was getting tired of England, and began to long for the free, wandering life he had led out in the East.

"I think I shall set sail for Egypt soon," he told Beatrice, during one of his short visits to Deepwood. "But for one thing I should imagine I had made a great mistake in coming to England."

"What is that?" she asked, languidly.

"My becoming acquainted with you."

She gave a soft laugh.

"You are not going to pretend you care anything about me?"

"It will be no pretence; you are so beautiful—like a young queen."

"But you only admire fair women—foreigners always do."

"You are fair," he answered, looking at the pure dazzling complexion; "you are not like the women of our race."

"I am thankful for that," she replied, with a touch of sarcasm in her voice; "so you really do admire me?"

"I love you," he murmured, a quick fire leaping into his dusky eyes. "Now that I am come to say farewell to you, my heart tells me to take you away with me. I would have you for my wife, but I dare not ask you to follow me."

Almost slave-like in his humility he knelt at her feet, and gazed up at her with worshipping admiration.

In her present lonely condition Beatrice was glad to have this attention, even from a man she cared little about, and life began to have fresh interest for her.

"I believed no one thought of me," she said, gently; "I am glad to find I have been mistaken."

"You are not glad that I love you?" he asked, with strange uncertain happiness.

"I am—very. It is wretched to be left quite outside of all affection. I do not think I can endure this kind of existence much longer."

The Arab seized one of her hands, and covered it with burning kisses.

"If I thought you would let my love change your life—if I dared hope you would leave this cold England and come with me, I would do so much to make you happy. My beautiful one, do I ask too much?—is it a mad hope to wish that you will be my wife?"

He loved her.

Looking into his passionate eyes she could not doubt the sincerity of his words, and she found herself wondering how it was she had never foreseen what would happen.

If it had been Richard Garth, the surprise would not have been so great; but this wild, wandering chief— why had he, till now, given no sign of the adoration burning in his heart?

"It is very sudden," she faltered, letting her hand rest in his warm clasp. "I have never thought of what my life might be as your wife. What would you do with me—if I consented?"

"I would make you a queen," he replied, watching her with rapt worship. "My wealth is not in coined gold, but you should have dresses made of precious stones, and live in a silken palace, and all the men and the women of my tribe should be your servants—even I would be your slave. I offer you all that is mine. My paradise-bird, will you make your home with me?"

Beatrice hesitated.

"You must give me time to consider," she said, slowly; "I cannot decide my fate in a moment. Come to me in a week; I shall have judged my heart by then."

Some of the eagerness left his face.

"I cannot take an unwilling wife," he replied, proudly. "If it is too much I ask—if you would choose the love of a better man, I will not urge you from your choice."

"You must not think because I cannot give you a decided answer to-day I let you go from me without hope," Beatrice explained, sorry his pride should have been touched to pain. "Your kindness has pleased me greatly, and if at the end of the week I give you my hand, I promise you it will not be bestowed unwillingly."

The hot colour rushed again to his brow, and he murmured a few low words of gratitude.

Then, with a sudden passion, he caught a fold of her dress, and pressed it against his lips.

"You are lovely, and I love you!" he exclaimed, his voice sounding singularly rich in its new intensity. "What better could you do than go away with me? When I come again you will tell me so, for you have given me hope."

"Perhaps," Beatrice sighed, looking down at him in a perplexed kind of way. "But I cannot give you your answer yet. Don't give up thinking of me, Osman;

the greater your love, the greater your hope of winning me."

He gave a short contented laugh as he rose to his feet.

"Then I shall not fail," he said, assuringly; "my love is so deep that it must reach right down to your soul. I cannot but win you, Beatrice."

CHAPTER XII.

SMAN OMAR waited impatiently for the time to come when he was to have his answer, and at the end of the week he presented himself again to Beatrice.

She welcomed him with a smile that made his pulses thrill, and it needed no word from her to convince him he had been successful in his hasty wooing.

"Am I to take my bride away with me?" he asked, clasping her to his heart, and imprinting a long kiss on her soft brow.

She gave an instinctive glance at her heavy black dress, and shook her head a little sadly.

"Not yet, Osman."

"Why do you care to stay here by yourself?" he urged, wishing, in his impetuosity, to carry her off at once. "Is it not better that I should watch over you and bear you company? My beautiful Beatrice, you have said you will be my wife; why must you make this delay?"

"I want Sir Edmund to advise me," she replied, gently disengaging herself from his arms. "I feel I ought not to take this step without first consulting him.

However, when this point was further argued, nobody knew where to send word to Sir Edmund; and the Arab persuaded Beatrice that it would be madness to wait for his return.

"He may wander about for years in the wild restless mood he started in. When he comes back to Deepwood he will probably come back an old man."

Beatrice shuddered.

She did not like this way of reasoning.

She dreaded a buried life in this dreary home, and in her eagerness to escape it she allowed herself to be guided by her lover.

It was arranged that he should go to Cairo and make what preparations were needed for their marriage, and in a month's time she would follow him.

"I may hear something of Sir Edmund before I leave England," she said at parting. "I should like him to be present when the ceremony takes place."

"Yet there must be no delay on his account," Osman returned, and a passionate glance came into his eyes.

Soon after this conversation he left England, anxious to hurry on events.

Still hoping to hear news of Sir Edmund, Beatrice kept up a close correspondence with his lawyer, and her perseverance was at length rewarded.

Her stepbrother could not return to Deepwood, but he would meet her in Cairo, though he considered the step she was about to take simply madness.

"He is right—it is madness," Beatrice reflected, when she read his message. "Yet what choice have I? Anything is better than the monotonous existence I am forced to endure."

She had a restless longing for change, and she looked forward eagerly to the long journey she was about to take.

She was too independent to need more than the company of her maid during the voyage.

She would place herself under the care of the captain, and so avoid further obligation.

Joshua Heath had called several times, yet, since his roof sheltered Gladys, she considered his visits almost an insult, and refused to see him or to receive any message from him.

Had she been less obstinate in her pride, she might have had some warning of what was in store for her.

She was not prepared for the surprise that came upon her one night when she lay on deck, with the sultry sweep of the Mediterranean lulling her into a drowsy wakefulness.

NOTICE.—This Work will be published every Wednesday.   Orders should be given to your Bookseller early.

No. 5.

HE SEIZED HER WRIST IN A CONVULSIVE GRASP.

The day had been intensely warm and, glad to breathe the night air, she had stayed up on deck, preferring to get what sleep she could on a pile of soft rugs to going into the close cabin.

Her eyes were wide open, and she was gazing up at the starry skies, fancifully tracing scenes in the wide, blue expanse.

The salt sea air was refreshing, and the languor which had oppressed her throughout the day lost some of its heaviness.

She had never stayed on deck so late before, and she was a little surprised to find she was not the only lady who had not gone down into the cabin.

Someone with light, quick steps was pacing up and down, and presently, when the footfalls had ceased, she heard a deep long sigh quite close to where she was lying.

Beatrice looked idly in the direction of the sound, and saw a slight, girlish figure dimly outlined in the starlight.

It might have been a pale spirit standing against the rough bulwarks; there was a white sheen on the fluttering drapery, on the soft hair, and on the sweet face turned seaward.

"Strange," Beatrice thought, "I have not seen this passenger before. I suppose she has been too ill to leave her berth I wonder why she has come up alone?"

Beatrice was curious about this fair stranger, because she had little else to occupy her mind, and she watched her musingly, just as she had watched the sparkle of the stars and the break of the waves.

Suddenly a hot flush burned in her cheeks, and with a low exclamation of anger she rose to her feet.

In the vision-like figure she had recognised Gladys.

How had she come there?

What scheme had been laid that this annoyance should be thrust upon her?

Beatrice grew bitterly indignant.

Why had she not been warned?

Was it mere chance that had thrown them together? or had the outrage been previously arranged?

Beatrice's suspicion rose hotly against Sir Edmund's wife, and in that moment of recognition a wild hatred filled her.

She would have been glad to have seen her hurled overboard, and swept under the seas—this pale girl, who might one day have power to separate her from her brother's wealth.

Her hands clenched, and her eyes grew bright with a fearful bitterness — a bitterness which seemed to penetrate into the innocence it accused.

Gladys turned and met the scornful gaze fixed upon her, and she drew back with a slight shudder.

" Miss Etheridge ! " she gasped, faintly. " I did not know you were to sail with me ! "

Beatrice gave a cynical smile, and without a word passed her and went down to her berth.

During the rest of the voyage she did not come on deck again.

If she had there would have been little chance of her meeting Gladys, who, startled by that first recognition, hid herself away from everybody.

She had no thought that Sir Edmund might cross her path in this strange land.

She knew Beatrice was to be the young chief's wife, but no one had told her Sir Edmund had promised to join them in Cairo.

There were no home-ties to link her to the old life, and she had followed her brother, thinking she might be able to help him with the money he had placed at her disposal.

Nobody welcomed her to the sultry city.

She crossed the bridge, and made her way to the hotel alone, closely veiled, and with her head bowed, feeling sorely the need of a companion on this strange shore.

Beatrice had been almost the last to leave the boat, and she was a little surprised that the first one to greet her should be her half-brother, Sir Edmund.

" Have you seen her ? " she asked, her eyes glittering at the remembrance of that meeting with Gladys.

" Whom ? " he enquired.

"The girl you so madly married."

His brows contracted with a sudden frown.

"I have forgotten her. To me she is dead! Never again let me hear her name."

Sir Edmund's words were almost a command, and not wishing to break peace with him, Beatrice resolved to speak no more about Gladys.

It never occurred to her he might not have comprehended the meaning of her first question.

She thought he had recognised Gladys, and had passed her by as a stranger, and she was glad his heart had closed so firmly against her.

He looked haggard and hollow-eyed, as though health and spirit had been crushed in some great struggle.

Yet his manner was carelessly courteous as ever, and she felt he had worked on the determination to wrench that great disappointment from his soul rather than let it wreck his life.

"You have forgotten to congratulate me, Edmund," she said, a slight hesitation in her proud voice. "You know why I am here."

"I believe so," icily.

"Are you pleased?"

"I am never pleased. Don't worry me, Triss, with any foolish sentiment. I have met you simply because you asked me: not from any wish of my own."

"You think I am not a fit wife for Osman?" she murmured, quick to note the displeasure in his tones.

"I think Osman Omar is not a fit husband for you," he corrected quietly. "You might have chosen better."

"And worse," she replied irritably. "The choice was his, it could never have been mine, even had I waited for a better chance. I shall marry Osman," decisively.

He gave a short laugh.

"I suppose you will. I thought you had made up your mind on that point before you left England."

"I wanted you to advise me," she said, unmoved by his sarcasm; "you are never near when I want you."

"And you never want me when I am near," he muttered dryly. "I shall stay out your caprice this time, though, Triss. Do you think it at all probable you will change your mind?"

"Not in the least," earnestly. "I have thought well over this marriage, and I don't think it is wholly an unwise one. It will be an improvement on the Deepwood solitude."

If Sir Edmund detected the subdued bitterness in her voice, he did not openly observe it, and finding he was inclined to treat the subject lightly, she began to think there was really some hope of happiness in the looming future.

The ceremony, which took place at the English church, was very quiet.

Beatrice laid aside her black dress, and veiled herself from head to foot in white clinging drapery; and Sir Edmund gave her to the Arab "for better, for worse."

Then followed the more elaborate Mohammedan service, and Osman took off his bride in triumph.

"At least the fellow has given her a true love," Sir Edmund reflected as he watched them depart from Cairo. "I have no doubt he will be content in becoming a slave to her happiness. And she—well, she is an Etheridge."

He gave a strange smile, half bitter, half proud, and the thought of his own unhappy marriage hardened in his breast.

He said he had forgotten Gladys.

Yet there was a desolate void in his life—a void that had been made when he cast away his wife, and he felt himself forsaken by the world's humblest solace.

Walking in the mid-day heat, he clenched his hand on his brow to crush back the maddening memory of that love which had betrayed him.

"Pray God, I may never meet her!" he muttered, not trusting himself to penetrate into his closed heart. "She is dead to me. If I found my sweet dead living, could I pass her without recognition?"

He wandered restlessly through the hot streets, weary with the loneliness of a broken love, yearning for the gaze of those tender eyes, that he would have turned fiercely from, if unexpectedly they had been raised to his face.

In condemning her, he spared himself nothing. Not even to appease the pain in his soul would he let one weak thought stray towards her.

She was no longer penniless. She had inherited a wealth which enabled her to spurn the unrestricted income he had settled upon her.

He was glad of this, since it lessened her claim upon him, though even at this moment, had she demanded the whole of his fortune, it would have been hers during his lifetime.

He could never forget or forgive the secret which had estranged them: but if she had been in need of help, and it had been in his power to help her, he would not have shrunk from any sacrifice.

Alone in her great suite of apartments, Gladys had no suspicion of the struggle going on in that strong passionate nature.

She was thinking of him—thinking of him as she always was, but her thoughts were far away.

It never occurred to her he might be near. She tried to draw her mind away from him, and to set out some plans for the future.

She had not spoken to Frank yet. Once she had passed the barracks, and had caught sight of the pale handsome face.

But she had been accompanied by a waiting-woman— and he was in the ranks. No gleam of recognition had passed between them.

She had not gone by unnoticed.

Two grey eyes sought the child-face with admiring scrutiny, and Frank's captain pulled his moustache reflectively as he looked after the slight figure.

"Jove!" he exclaimed in a long breath, "what a face! Wonder who she is? Perhaps some of the fellows know her."

A group of officers were lounging near, idly smoking.

He turned impulsively towards them.

"Did you notice that girl in white who passed just now ?"

"Rather."

"Any of you know her ? "

"No such luck. Think she has only lately arrived in Cairo. Hallo! that man over there looks as if he could tell us something. Say, Royce, do you know who the lady is who passed just now ? "

The question was addressed to Frank with startling abruptness.

He bit his lip as he looked after the retreating form of his sister, marvelling that he could have been so off his guard as to let his face reveal the pleasure he felt at sight of her.

"Her name has not been mentioned by anyone in my presence," he said coldly, and not wishing to prolong the conversation, he moved from the spot.

The officers exchanged glances.

"'Pon my word," laughed the young captain, "Royce is the surliest fellow I ever came across. It is time he was taught a lesson in civility. I would bet my sword that he knows something about the little violet-eyed stranger. I am half inclined to call him back—only he is so confoundedly thoroughbred in his insolence. He has fallen to the ranks. It is evident he is out of his element."

"You're right, Dudley," one of his companions observed thoughtfully. "I heard Colonel Deroy remark the same thing yesterday. A gentleman always knows a gentleman, and Royce is that."

"One who knows the art of prevarication, too," Dudley smiled, remembering the polite snub he had just received ; "I expect we shall meet the little lady somewhere before long. I would go to Lady Linton's to-night if I thought I should see her there."

He did go to Lady Linton's; but Gladys was not there, and, considering he had only gone on the chance of getting an introduction to her, it was not surprising that he went home disappointed.

Nor was he the only one in whom her sweet pale beauty had excited interest.

Nearly everyone in Cairo had noticed her, and had wondered to see her driving or walking, accompanied only by servants.

Nobody could tell her name. All they knew was that she was rich and beautiful, and some thought they saw in her a young princess.

"The thing that surprises me most is the strange way in which she holds aloof from everyone," Dudley remarked as she passed him, with her train of servants, a week after he had put that question to Frank. "She doesn't seem to know a single being, and it must be precious lonely for her here. I wish I knew how to present myself favourably."

"Get in her way when she is driving," someone suggested with a good-natured smile, and Dudley, with the vision of that sweet face before him, pondered seriously over the joke.

He had bored himself with languid calls, with afternoon-teas and heavy dances, hoping to find out more about her, and failing, he had wasted hours at the theatre, scanning diligently the faces of actresses and audience.

Still no success, and he had almost persuaded himself to let matters remain as they were, when he met her at a time and in a way that he least expected.

CHAPTER XIII.

T happened thus.

He was riding along a deserted track on some hurried errand when an arrow came whizzing through the trees beneath which he was passing, and, whether it was by accident or hurled purposely against his life, it flew with fatal directness, and pierced sharply into his shoulder.

His hand dropped heavily on the horse's neck, and with a shiver of pain he threw himself from the saddle and sank to the ground.

He tried to rise, but a sharp agony reached his frame and he lay back helpless.

The sun scorched down on him, burning his lips to fever heat; the hot dust was in his eyes, and a draught of water tendered him then would have seemed a blessing.

He had taken an unfrequented track; there was little chance that aid would reach him—little chance that anyone would know his danger.

The horse, instinctively, had stopped by his side; had the animal gone back riderless, suspicion of what had happened would have been roused, and Dudley would not have been long left without attendance.

It seemed now that he must lie there and perish.

The pain grew greater as the hours passed, and he had only strength enough left to draw the arrow from his shoulder before consciousness left him.

Fate must have guided Gladys that day.

Walking out with one of her woman servants she wandered to the very spot where he had fallen, and at sight of the white face, with the dark trail of blood near it, she uttered a cry of horror.

"He is dead—he has been murdered!" she exclaimed, bending over the senseless form. "What shall we do, Galena? Who has done this?"

The woman glanced at the arrow.

"A stray shaft," she muttered, in her own language. "It has not struck into his life; there is breath on his lips, and his heart still beats."

"Thank Heaven we came before it was too late!" Gladys whispered, fervently. "Run quickly to the barracks, and send help."

The woman stood stubborn.

"There may be another stray shaft," she said, meaningly. "You will not stay? There is danger."

"Not for me, Galena. Don't lose time; I believe this poor fellow is dying."

A shudder passed over Dudley's lips, and she bent her head to catch the short, irregular breathing that followed.

Galena obeyed sullenly.

She did not like to leave her young mistress, perhaps exposed to unseen peril.

They were a long way from the barracks, and an hour, at least, must pass before she could return with the needed help.

Gladys was too startled to notice the woman's unwillingness.

All her attention was given to the wounded man, and she had no thought for herself.

She looked pitifully at the pale mouth, parched with heat and pain, and, running to a spring close by, she let some water flow into the hollow of a stone, and carried it to him.

She poured a few drops between his lips, then, dipping her handkerchief into it, she bathed his forehead, and tried to stanch the blood oozing slowly from his wounded shoulder.

When sense returned to him, the first thing his gaze rested on was the face that had grown so strangely dear to him, and, in spite of his suffering, he smiled, and closed his eyes again in dreamy contentment.

It was so sweet to have the touch of those tender hands on his fevered brow—to know those soft eyes that had looked so coldly on everyone, were full of compassionate fear for him.

In his exhausted state it seemed like a dream, and he lay back afraid to speak a word, lest he should break the spell, and drive away the girl who had roused all his heart's interest.

"Are you better?" she asked, gently. "Will you live?"

Her voice sent a quiver through him; he looked at her long and earnestly, then, with a short sigh, turned his face aside.

"Are you hurt very, very much?" she murmured, pitifully. "What can I do to ease your suffering?"

"I do not suffer," he said, faintly.

"But you are wounded."

"Yet I do not suffer—now."

He tried to raise himself. A deep pang broke his breath, and left him prostrate.

"You will kill yourself if you try to move," she exclaimed, startled by a fresh flow of blood from his shoulder. "I wish Galena would make haste!"

"Who is Galena?" he asked, as soon as he was able to speak again.

"My servant. She was with me when I found you, and I sent her for help. Shall I lift your head?" as she saw him struggle quietly to raise himself.

He hesitated, and looked at her half wistfully.

He would have been intensely grateful for the proffered help.

Yet how could he accept support from those delicate arms, that looked so unfit to bear the slightest burden?

Gladys knew that thought for her alone kept him silent, and, without a word, she raised his head and pillowed it on her lap.

"You will find more ease so," she said, pushing the damp hair away from his brow, and fanning him with a huge leaf. "Your dear old horse has never moved from you all the time. He seems to understand that you are hurt. If Galena had only been a man she could have got into the saddle, and reached the barracks in a quarter the time. She is a long while gone."

"Is the time so wearying?" he asked, with a half smile.

"For you—not for me," she replied, looking at him with her clear, large eyes. "You are bearing pain bravely, for whatever you say to the contrary I know that every moment your shoulder aches more. Who did it?"

"Did what?"

"Shot at you."

"Haven't the slightest idea. It didn't come like the act of an enemy. It was a chance hit, I think."

Gladys grew graver.

"But it might have killed you," she said, shivering as she glanced at the arrow. "Is there no guard against such accidents?"

Her words seemed to amuse him. He gave a short laugh.

"We come out here to meet danger," he replied; then, watching her seriously, "you place yourself in the same peril— Why?"

"It is my wish," she answered, flushing slightly.

"A strange wish in one so young," he remarked, impulsively. "You must have very extraordinary friends to let you come out here alone."

The flush deepened in her cheeks, deepened with surprised indignation.

"I do not care to discuss my friends," she said, coldly, and the words reminded him he was only a stranger whom she had found wounded and had succoured.

He had no right to question her mode of living.

"I beg your pardon," he muttered, penitently, "I did not think my speech would give offence. You will not think worse of me for it?"

"No."

"Thank you."

There was a short pause.

He felt he had annoyed her, and he wanted to redeem himself.

The shadow which had come over her face had set him wondering more than ever as to what her young life's history could be.

The return of Galena, accompanied by a doctor and two or three officers, filled him with an eagerness to make sure of his peace with her.

"How can I show my gratitude for the care you have given me?" he asked, raising himself on his elbow. "You have been my Samaritan. I should have died of thirst if you had not held water to my lips. If I live to be a hundred I shall never forget what you have been to me to-day; you have made me believe that angels can live with mortal life."

"I am not an angel," she said, letting her pure gaze rest on his face; "I have only done part of a woman's weak work."

"Nevertheless, you have saved my life, and I hope one day to be able to use it in your service. I should like to ask a favour of you, but the certainty of being denied keeps me from naming it. Would you say 'Yes?'"—in low, persuasive tones—"if I begged you to let me call and tell you how grateful I am?"

"I think not. All I care for you to say to me can be said in one word—'good-bye.'"

"Not even your name?" he pleaded.

"It does not matter," she said, with a touch of weariness; "we are only strangers. I have done for you no more than I should have done for anyone else who had been in the same distress. You are stronger now, and other help has arrived. I can leave you."

Her presence was no longer needed.

She left the spot with Galena; and, roused from his dream, Dudley staggered to his feet, and flung his arm over his horse to keep himself from again falling.

The wound, so long neglected, gave him deeper pain, and he was weak from loss of blood.

Yet a flash of triumph came over his drawn face as he caught something which was slipping from his shoulder—a little wet handkerchief, bearing the name of his sweet Samaritan—"Gladys."

"Gladys what?" he mused, looking at the delicate embroidery. "I shall never rest till I have found out more about her. I am more than ever mystified."

As soon as his shoulder was well enough, he went wherever he thought he might possibly meet her.

The only place where he succeeded was at church, and there she either purposely avoided him, or was too wrapt in her own thoughts to recognise him.

Once when they were leaving the church he managed to attract her attention.

She returned his bow with a slight inclination of the proud little head—absently, and with no sign of pleasure.

After the compassion she had bestowed upon him in his suffering, Dudley was at a loss to understand the reserve with which she treated him.

She never even gave him an opportunity of thanking her for the service she had rendered him.

He was almost sorry he had hurried on his recovery.

"If I had lingered on in a dying state she would perhaps have been interested in me," he thought, grimly. "There seems to be no way of melting her, except by appealing to her pity."

This was true enough.

Wherever help was needed Gladys was always ready to give aid.

Little half-clad hungry children and travel-worn women never passed her unnoticed, and those who from curiosity watched her, wondered more than ever if choice or circumstance had brought her out amongst strangers.

The want of confidence with which she treated everyone, made Dudley desperately impatient to break through the reserve surrounding her, and, unable to endure the estrangement any longer, he wrote her a brief note, and employed Frank, who was near him at the time, to be his messenger.

The name embroidered on the handkerchief with which she had bound his wound, was a link between himself and the fair young stranger, and having heard one of her servants call her "my lady," he came to the conclusion that she must be an earl's daughter, and addressed his letter to "Lady Gladys."

"Royce, I want you to take this over to the new hotel," he said, giving the missive to Frank in as careless a manner as he could assume. "Wait for a reply, and bring it to me here."

Frank took the letter with suppressed eagerness, and hastened to carry out the captain's order.

It was the first time he had had an opportunity of gaining an interview with Gladys since her arrival in Cairo, and he was all eagerness to fulfil his mission.

Arrived at the hotel, before sending the letter up to her, he pencilled across the envelope these few words—

"Bearer waits an answer."

Gladys understood the sign, and without giving a thought to Dudley told her servant to show the man who had brought the letter up to her room.

"How brave of you, Gladys, to risk so much for my sake!" he muttered, as soon as they were alone. "I am not worthy such faith."

She shook her head sadly.

"I am afraid it has been a mistake, Frank."

"I am sure it has, Gladie. I have been selfish in allowing you to share my exile. How can I make amends for all the sorrow I have caused you?"

"It's not that, Frank," the girl answered, her sweet lips slightly tremulous; "only I thought my being here would make life more pleasant for you, and I am disappointed."

She had borne up all this time, but her courage very nearly broke down now.

The tears rose in her eyes, and it was as much as she could do to suppress the sob that broke from her heart.

Frank looked at her miserably.

What consolation had he to offer her.

A fierce thought was in his brain against Sir Edmund—a fiercer thought against the man who had been the first to cast this loadstone into their lives— the man whose curse they were enduring.

"Did you see him?" he asked after a long pause.

She started, and roused herself.

"Who?"

"Your husband."

"You mean Sir Edmund," she corrected.

"I mean your husband. You know, of course, he was over here for his sister's marriage?"

"No!"

"He was. I imagined you were aware of that fact, otherwise I would have managed to let you know. I tried over and over again to get an interview with him, and each time failed. Fate seems to be working steadily against us, Gladie."

Gladys was silent.

She had sunk into a chair, and was looking straight before her with a blank stony gaze.

Sir Edmund had been within a few yards of her, and she had not known!

How strange it all seemed!

A mute anguish chilled her soul as thought crowded upon thought.

He had seen her, perhaps, or had heard that she was there, and had gone away hating her—loathing the very air she breathed.

"Is it too late?" she said, speaking slowly like one half dazed. "Is he gone?"

"Gone! Yes."

"Where?" she asked, the word coming from her lips with a hollow sound. "He has gone away from me, Frank, for he knew I was here. Beatrice and I left England together, though neither of us knew it till afterwards. She must have told him, for how could she do otherwise, knowing me and hating me? And he has purposely avoided me. Oh, Frank, when will this misery end?"

Her brother clenched his hands, and a dark look came over his face.

"When? When I can find my betrayer," he muttered; "when the right man is justly accused and justly condemned; then you and I will take our places in the world that has shut us out from its honour."

Gladys sighed.

The hour Frank spoke of seemed so far distant; how could she build on it the entire hope of her life?

Even the wealth she possessed formed one more barrier between herself and Sir Edmund, for, had she been dependent, she would have been at his mercy, and he would have been obliged to bestow on her some little care.

How could she know Beatrice had told him nothing of that unexpected meeting on board?

"If only I had seen him," she murmured, wearily, "the old love might have sprung up above this miserable unbelief, and there might have been peace between us!"

"No, Gladie—no," Frank replied with moody bitterness; "we must be able to show proof first, and peace will follow."

"Proof, proof! What proof?" a strange voice whispered—a voice so ghastly in its hollow undertone, that it sent a thrill through both its hearers. "I had it once, but I let it go, and the secret will never be known!"

Gladys clung to Frank with a low, frightened cry.

Who had spoken?

Who knew their secret?

CHAPTER XIV.

FRANK looked round, as though he expected to see some weird form lurking in the deep shadows of the room.

The day had closed into a sultry twilight, and away from the open windows, where the gloom had gathered, it was difficult to trace what the shadow concealed.

"It was a lady's voice," Frank muttered, giving his sister's cold hand a reassuring pressure. Then aloud he asked: "Who spoke?"

No answer.

There was a slight rustling sound somewhere near; then complete silence.

Gladys shivered, and shrank closer to her brother.

"Someone must be in the room," she whispered. "The voice was so near, and I could hear the breathing between each word. I will ring for a light."

She moved towards the bell, but Frank drew her back.

"I have matches," he muttered, not wishing to make a scene—a scene in which his presence would excite so much wonder. "Remain quite still, while I light the lamp."

The life he had led had accustomed him to rely always upon his own energies, and in a few seconds the oil-wick was burning brightly in its bronze cup.

The newly-kindled glow penetrated into every shadow, convincing brother and sister that they were alone.

It was certainly very mysterious.

Gladys, with one hand locked tightly in Frank's, searched behind the curtains and in every place where she thought it likely anyone might be concealed.

"I cannot make it out," Frank said in a perplexed tone, half serious, half laughing. "Have you heard the voice anywhere before?"

"Never. Do you think the words were meant for us. We may have been mistaken—"

"Not likely. A third person is in the room—or was a moment ago; but what motives she has for concealment remain to be discovered. You had better change your apartment, Gladys. I don't like leaving you in this room of mystery."

Frank did not impart his thoughts to her, but he was inclined to believe there was a mad-woman about.

Or did somebody else share his secret?

In either case, his mind was equally disturbed by the reflection cast into his brain, and he was at a loss to know how to account for this strange incident.

He would have searched further into the mystery had his time been his own.

The sight of the letter Gladys had thrown on the table reminded him of the mission he had come upon, and he felt it would be imprudent to try Dudley's patience.

"You haven't opened your letter yet," he said, tossing it towards her; "let me take back a good answer to make amends for my tardiness, or I shall not get the chance of being messenger again."

Gladys broke the seal, a slight shadow on her pure brow—brought there more from weariness than from displeasure.

A faint flush tinged her cheeks as she read the few pleading words Dudley had written, and she threw the note down almost disdainfully.

"Such nonsense, his pretending I saved his life!" she exclaimed impatiently. "Will you tell him, Frank, he owes me nothing, and that any show of gratitude from him to me will be misplaced."

"As if I could take him such a reply!" Frank laughed. "You musn't forget. I am only one of his men."

"Poor boy! How you must hate him sometimes!"

"Not a bit of it. I am afraid he has the worst of the bargain. He's a good fellow, Gladie; I only wish you bore his name instead of Sir Edmund's."

"I do not bear Sir Edmund's name," Gladys said very quietly.

"Whose then?"

"My own. I call myself simply 'Gladys.'"

"Do you allow your servants to do the same?" Frank asked, grimly.

"They could if they liked, but they are too civil. They called me 'Miss Gladys' before they saw me without my gloves; then seeing they had been mistaken, they changed their mode of address to 'my lady.' Whether they think I have a right to the title, I cannot tell. I never satisfy anyone's curiosity as to the incidents that have crossed my life."

Frank looked grave.

"I wish you had some friend out here," he said thoughtfully. "I am half sorry you left the Heaths; it must worry you to hear the remarks of those who do not know you."

"I don't mind," she answered wearily. "I seem to be apart from all the world. I can hardly think I belong to my old self. Must you take back a written reply?" she asked, changing the conversation.

"Unless you want to do away with my only chance of getting here."

"I understand."

She took some wine from a sideboard, and placed it before him, then sat down to a desk and penned a few words to Dudley.

"Give him this," she said, when she had finished her note; "and, Frank, I wish he could know—that I am married."

"I can tell him nothing concerning you. Already some of the officers suspect I am acquainted with you, and I have to beat down that suspicion. I shall seize the next opportunity of getting to you; I don't like your being here by yourself; and, Gladie, be sure if you want me at any time to make me some sign."

"I shall not forget. Good-bye, Frank."

"Good-bye."

She would have liked to go down to the door with him.

Instead, she passed into an ante-room, and ringing a bell, asked the woman who answered the summons to conduct "the man" to the hall.

Now he had left her, she felt very like giving way to a wild outbreak of grief.

Sir Edmund had been in Cairo, and neither of them had known—and now perhaps he would never cross their path again.

She went back to the room where she had parted with her brother, and shivered as the solitude struck upon her.

To-night she felt she could not bear to be alone.

The lamp Frank had kindled burned with a weird fitful glow, making the shadows shift from corner to corner.

In her present mood, complete darkness would have been less dreary, and she turned her back upon the room and looked out of the window.

There was not much to amuse her in the deserted gardens that lay beneath.

Now and then she could catch the splash of a fountain or the gleam of a lantern moving mysteriously along.

Yet even these solitary signs of life without were better than the utter loneliness within, and she stood there for a long time—a delicate flower-like form, drooping against the gold and crimson hangings.

The evening was cooler than usual, and she thought it would be better to go for a walk than to shut herself up to brood and grow melancholy.

Acting on this wise reflection, she turned to call Galena.

A startled exclamation broke from her lips as she caught sight of a woman sitting upright in a chair at the other end of the room.

How that strange figure came there Gladys never knew.

The lamplight flickered over the white face, the white hair, and the drapery clinging about her like a white mist.

Gladys recoiled as the woman rose and glided towards her.

Then, after the first shock, her pulses throbbed less wildly, and she knew that she had little cause for fear.

The eyes gazing into hers were heavy with suffering, and the hair drifted like snow over a brow soft and fair as her own.

It was the wreck of a beautiful girl—the pure mind broken by some storm of human passion, the delicate frame weakened by pain.

It was Florence Garth—a pale shadow of what she had once been; lovely still, though the tender face had lost its bloom, and the hair so brightly golden a few months since, flowed over her shoulders in soft white waves.

She was dressed in a long cashmere wrapper, with a quantity of lace about it, and this gave her an invalid look that at once roused pity in Gladys.

Gladys impulsively stepped forward and held out her hand, afraid lest her pale visitor should sink down and die in the effort to walk across the room.

Florence Garth gave a sad little smile as she leaned on Gladys, glad to accept the support of her arm.

"Thank you," she murmured, as she sank on to a divan. "I am afraid I have frightened you, but I knew you were alone, and I have come to be your friend. Do you know why?"

Gladys shook her head, and looked earnestly at her visitor.

"For the sake of this," Florence said, touching the wedding-ring Gladys wore; and on the slender finger that rested against hers for a moment, the girl saw also the symbol of wifehood.

"You are married, and you live alone; I am married, and I live alone. Your husband is not dead, neither is mine, and," with a gleam of tenderness in her sunken eyes, "we are both English. It is this that has drawn me towards you."

STRANGELY PARTED.

119

"You are very kind to have interested yourself in me," Gladys replied, still watching Florence with that wondering look. "I thought nobody knew anything about me."

"I occupy a room next to yours, and my window opens out on to the same balcony. I came thinking to find you alone, and I saw you with a stranger."

"You heard us talking, and you answered us," Gladys said, in a low eager voice. "What did your words mean?"

Florence looked at her vaguely, as though she did not understand what was asked of her.

"I do not remember," she muttered, drearily, "I do not know that I spoke to you till you held out your hand to me just now. I have been ill, and my mind wanders. I cannot remember."

Gladys knew what Florence said was true.

There was something weird in the pale face she had been gazing at, as if reason had only rested in the hollow eyes for a little while, and would flash away and leave them vacant.

Yet there seemed no cause for alarm. Her manner was so gentle and wistful that Gladys could only feel a great pity for her, and instead of summoning someone to attend on the invalid, she herself arranged a pillow behind the restless head, and after drawing the curtains back to admit what air there was, she turned the wick of the lamp up higher, and placed a huge pearl-tinted shade over the light

It was good for her to have this occupation. It left her no time to think over her own misery, and in trying to comfort Florence, she took comfort herself.

There was a volume of Tennyson's poems on the table, and Gladys, with an idea of diverting Florence's mind from the vacant abyss it might sink into if she felt herself alone, read some verses from "Elaine."

Florence followed every word. There was no sign of madness in the eyes, now so full of intense feeling.

The girl's soft voice soothed her, and she drew a deep sigh as though she had found a restfulness strange to her.

After a time she closed her eyes, and remained so still that Gladys thought she slept, and, afraid that her voice would disturb her, she left off reading aloud.

Suddenly Florence started up with a wild horror on her face, as though some ghastly thought had thrust itself into her brain, and uttering a piercing shriek, she fell face downwards on the floor.

It was a cry of an over-wrought soul, and a strange thrill ran through Gladys as she bent over the motionless form.

"What grief has made her like this?" she wondered, as she hastily summoned assistance, and the girl made up her mind that to-night's meeting should be the beginning of a true friendship.

An old woman rushed into the room, and kneeling down beside the stricken form, raised the heavy head on her arm.

"My poor mistress—my sweet mistress!" she exclaimed in broken English. "She will kill herself—she will die like this!"

"I trust not," Gladys said, softly, snatching the glass Frank had left half-full of wine, and holding it to the cold lips. "She seemed so calm a little while ago."

"A little while ago!" the woman almost wailed. "Oh, my lady, if you only knew what she was a little while ago! So young and so happy—and now her hair is white, and they call her mad."

HER HELPLESSNESS APPEALED TO THEIR STRENGTH.

No. 6.

"Grief is her madness," Gladys murmured; then, as consciousness slowly returned, she helped the nurse to raise her, and place her in a chair.

"I will go to my own room, Rano," Florence said, her voice quite calm and composed; "I am afraid I have disturbed this poor little lady."

"Not in the least," Gladys answered, eagerly. "I am only sorry that you are not well. If you will not stay, may I go with you to your room?"

Florence inclined her head ever so slightly, and glad to be of use, Gladys walked on one side of her, while Rano supported her on the other.

Gladys was not prepared for the room she was led into.

It was a tiny apartment, scarcely worthy the name of more than cabinet. It was lofty, and had a large window, otherwise the air must have been suffocating.

On the floor, close up against the wall, there was a narrow bed, with a coverlet of pale blue satin fringed with gold, and as far from it as space would admit, was a mattress with a scarlet shawl thrown over it—evidently this last was occupied by the old nurse; and after seeing this room with its air of refined poverty, Gladys was not surprised to discover that it was Rano who toiled for this shelter, and Rano who shared with her unhappy young mistress every coin she earned.

"If it had not been for her, I should have been dead long ago," Florence told Gladys when she was in one of her pathetic moods. "She has nearly starved herself for me, and I believe she would not hesitate to give her life for my sake. I had rather she had left me; there is no comfort in life for me."

Gladys would not encourage this melancholy.

She had heard Florence's story from Rano. How she had once been a tender wife—how a little child had come to make her life prouder. How one night they had found her lying on the ground, with her baby crushed in her arms—smothered beneath her weight.

The baby was dead; but after lying for days in a kind of trance, Florence recovered.

The first conscious word she uttered was her child's name, and when she cried out for him, they told her he had gone away from her, and from the world for ever.

She understood, and when she heard how they had unclasped her arms from his little lifeless form, she gave a terrible scream that seemed to rend her brain, and make all her nature wild.

She had never been herself since, and what seemed strangest of all was that her husband from that time disappeared.

"I sent him away," she told Rano. "I hated him, and I do not want to think of him. I hope he will never come near me, for if I see him, I shall want to make him suffer for the great wrong he has done."

Rano could make no meaning out of these words, and fearing the overwrought mind would give way altogether, she kept her peace, and patiently waited for health to come back to her beloved mistress—for the fevered mind to regain the high standing from which it had tottered.

And now Gladys had come to rouse interest in her, and to wean her from herself.

CHAPTER XV.

HEN Gladys knew Florence's story, she was still more determined to watch over her, and do what she could to win her from the madness that always threatened her.

All kinds of luxuries were taken to the little bare room, and the invalid was persuaded to dress herself sometimes in outdoor attirement, to take long drives with her new friend.

Those fits of frenzy did not visit her so often now, and Rano began to hope that her young mistress would forget her grief, and find fresh interest in life.

One visit was made to a tiny grave that Gladys covered with white flowers, while Florence knelt down with her brow pressed to the marble cross.

"Of such is the kingdom of Heaven."
Those were the only words that had been inscribed to the memory of her lost darling. In life his father's name would have dishonoured him; in death the burden of shame should not be breathed against his angel soul.

Gladys wondered why the little grave bore no name, but she made no remark, fearing to disturb Florence's peace.

"I used to wish that I had been laid here with my baby," Florence said, with a strange aching calm in her voice; "but now, I think it is best as it is. Since my child is dead, I owe nothing to his father, and perhaps my life is spared for a purpose."

"It is spared that you may serve God for a little while longer," Gladys answered, softly.

Florence looked at her as though she only half comprehended her meaning. Her thoughts were strained and disconnected, and her mind dwelt most on the letter which had worked the first wreck in her life.

"Do you know what drove my husband away?" she asked, abruptly.

"He believed you dead."

"He did, because he thought he had killed me," Florence replied, bitterly. "My baby was poisoned, and the same swift drug made me blind and mad. They all thought I had killed the child in my fall. It may even have been so, but nobody discovered what had stricken me down. I have kept this secret, because I alone am the sufferer; but there is another crime that shall be atoned for, and when I hold the proof of his guilt I will denounce him."

Gladys listened in horrified wonder. Was this the feverish raving of delirium? Had she deceived herself into the belief that Florence was better?

She gazed into the hopeless eyes, and, in spite of herself, believed this wild story—a story which seemed the more horrible when she remembered that Florence was called Mrs. Garth.

"What was his name?" she asked, in a strained whisper, scarcely conscious she had given utterance to the terrible thought whirling through her brain.

"Richard Garth."

Gladys was prepared for the answer, yet she could not repress the shudder that ran through her, as she heard the name of the man she had hated almost without a cause.

"Have you seen him?" Florence asked, clinging convulsively to the cross which marked her little one's grave.

"Yes," in a tone that came like a breath of ice through the pale lips.

"Where?"

"In England."

"As a widower?" his wife whispered, her voice hushed in a terrible bitterness.

"As a widower and a mourner."

"Not as a murderer, then?"

Gladys shivered as she looked at the wreck of fair womanhood before her, the great eyes, a few moments ago so pathetic, now steeled in chilliest bitterness.

"No, no, Florence," she muttered, trembling with agitation; "let us hope we are both mistaken. We will not talk of this any more—not to-day, at least, for the subject is as terrible to me as it is to you, and I could not bear to hear more."

Gladys was thinking of the faith Frank had in Richard Garth's friendship, and wondered if those two fatal photographs had been the fruit of his evil plans.

If he were capable of such a cowardly murder as Florence had described, he might be guilty of any lesser crime, and with this thought disturbing her mind Gladys was all anxiety to discuss the matter with her brother.

She longed to give Florence confidence for confidence, and to tell her about Frank; but she dared not obey the instinct that prompted her to speak, though, in some vague way, she felt Garth's wife could point out to them a clue to the mystery which held their lives in thrall.

That same evening Dudley rendered her an unconscious service by sending her a huge bunch of the choicest flowers, by Frank, and Gladys related to her brother the strange things she had heard.

"Richard Garth cannot be your friend," she said earnestly; "when you trust to him, you trust to a traitor. He has told you that he knows you are innocent. I believe he could tell you who is guilty."

Frank started, and looked at her with keen interest.

"By Jove, Gladys, if I thought he were such a villian, I would settle accounts heavily with him! If he could make his own wife his dupe, would he spare me?"

"I think not, Frank. From the first I always mistrusted him—from the first I looked upon him as an enemy."

"I wonder where I can drop down on him? It was an unlucky move my coming out here, and tying myself to a set life."

"By whose advice was it that you came?" Gladys asked, an undefined suspicion in her voice.

"His."

"Can you sell out of the army—or get sick-leave?"

"Sick-leave would be the safest, and I could easily get that. I know what you think I ought to do: follow Richard Garth, and keep a watch over all his movements."

"Yes; but don't let him have an idea that you suspect him, or he may do you some injury, Frank."

"Trust me, Gladys; if he has fooled me, in the end he shall find himself his own dupe."

A few days after this Frank fell ill, and, with the understanding that the climate endangered his life, was ordered back to England.

His plan, however, was not so successful as he had hoped. In quitting Cairo on these conditions, he found himself still under the control of the army, and he came to the conclusion that it would be better to sell out altogether.

He could still go on with his painting, and Gladys had arranged for him to draw the money whenever he wanted any.

She would have gone with him, but she felt that she would be in his way while he made this fresh search, and she did not care to leave Florence.

"I am tired of all this concealment and misunderstanding, Gladie," he told her when he went to say good-bye. "A whole lifetime might be wasted like this, and, in the end, nothing gained. If I come across Sir Edmund, I shall tell him just how matters stand, and risk the consequences; if you should be the first to meet him, he must hear the truth from your lips. There must be no more deception. Give me a fair promise that you will seize the first opportunity to right yourself, and regain the respect you forfeited to such a miserable purpose."

He spoke recklessly.

Yet there was a depth of earnestness in his voice, and Gladys knew what he had said had been well thought over.

The discovery that he had placed his trust in a traitor had made him very bitter, and he felt he was no nearer gaining his object now than when he had first found Gladys and told her his secret.

"I wish you had let me tell Sir Edmund at first," Gladys said, sadly. "Perhaps now it may be too late."

"How too late?"

"I may never meet him."

"Then I shall, and he will be forced to hear everything from beginning to end, and if he is not man enough to ask your pardon for the insult he has given you, I hope you will never call yourself his wife."

Gladys smiled at her brother's impetuous way of expressing his feelings, though there was a heavy ache in her heart, for she felt that there was little chance of a reconciliation between Sir Edmund and herself ever taking place.

After Frank had left her, she seemed to seek more after pleasure than she had done during her first weeks at Cairo.

Two or three times Dudley caught sight of her riding in the calm of the evening, and a soft smile shone in her eyes as she bowed her graceful little head in recognition.

One sweet glance, and she had flashed past him, and although he longed with all his heart to follow, a gentlemanly instinct kept him from urging his horse in her direction.

A day came which seemed to change the level run of his fate.

He had been playing tennis in the Esbekeeyeh Gardens, and having, for the first and only time in his life, lost the game, he flung down his racket and strolled towards a seat near one of the fountains.

A lady, almost hidden under a huge parasol, occupied one end, and, without heeding whether his presence might be an intrusion, he sat down, and stretched one arm lazily over the back.

Evidently the lady had not heard his approach.

The rustling of a page turned at regular intervals gave him the impression that her mind was wrapped in the book she was reading, and he thought, if he leaned the other way, he might indulge in a smoke without disturbing her.

With his conscience quite at ease, he took out his case and selected a choice cegar.

He would even have lighted it, only, by some careless movement, he let his fusee-box fall against the delicate foot of the lady, with sufficient force to cause her pain.

Before he could utter an apology, a white hand came from under the parasol, and picked up the little silver box.

With a bright smile, Gladys held it towards him, and when he knew who had witnessed his clumsiness he mentally cursed himself.

"I hope it is not broken," Gladys said lightly, half sorry for him because she saw how furious he was with himself. "It fell on the grass. I think it is hardly damaged."

"But your foot!" he exclaimed, ready to fling himself down and kiss the dainty shoes that had, perhaps, saved her a deep bruise. "I am sure you are hurt; the thing went down quite heavily. I am ashamed to ask you to forgive me!"

"It was nothing," Gladys answered. "So slight an accident is not worth an apology. By-the-bye, I have to thank you for the beautiful flowers I receive every day. I do not know where you find such choice bouquets, Captain Dudley."

His eyes gleamed with pleasure.

"I am glad my little offerings have pleased you," he said gratefully. "Do you know, at first I was half afraid you would reject them? You condemned me to such cruel banishment that at times I wondered why you had done so much to save a life you consider worthless."

"I consider no life worthless."

"Only mine?"

"Not even yours."

"That is a very unkind way of putting it," Dudley laughed, gazing admiringly at the winsome face shadowed under the drooping lace of the parasol. "What have I done to merit such contempt?"

"Lost at tennis just now, for one thing."

"How do you know I lost?"

"I watched the game."

"Why were you not playing, too? You do play, of course?"

"Not often; and I couldn't go in for it now, not knowing anyone."

"I would introduce everybody to you if you would let me," Dudley said, eagerly. "They are all dying to know you."

"It is very kind of them," Gladys replied, with a touch of weariness; "but I came here almost purposely for solitude. Their attention would worry me."

"I hope you do not mean me to take that speech to myself. If you knew how I envy even the servants who are privileged to be near you, you would have more compassion. I cannot understand why you treat me with such coldness.

"The reason is easily explained—you are a stranger."

She did not say the words unkindly, and there was a smile on her lips. Yet she had risen from the seat, and Dudley knew that she meant to leave him—a stranger still.

In an instant he sprang up, and was before her.

"You are not going like this?" he exclaimed, looking yearningly into the half-defiant eyes. "Give me your hand once in friendship—the hand that carried water to my lips when my life was parched and racked with pain! You were merciful then—be merciful now, for I as much need your sympathy.

Gladys paused and scanned his face anxiously.

"Are you not well yet?" she asked, thinking she had been indifferent to his suffering. "That dreadful arrow pierced so deeply into your shoulder!"

"Not so deep'y as you have sunk into my heart!" he murmured passionately. "I am sick at soul—mad, I believe, and you will not even give me your friendship!"

"Perhaps I have none to give."

"Take mine—take all my heart holds! I love you!"

Gladys started and drew back from him in proud indignation.

What right had he to offend her with tender words—this man whom she had succoured once in an hour of sore trial?

Her eyes grew brilliant with the scorn flashing in them, and, too angry to speak, she turned away from him.

He did not attempt to detain her now.

They were in a public place, exposed to the gaze of all who were in the Gardens, and he could only watch her moodily as she walked away from him.

"Some other time," he muttered. "I love you, dear proud little princess! Here me, and hate me, if you will—again, I love you!"

The impassioned whisper reached her ears, and set her heart throbbing with an angry burst.

Perhaps he did not know that on her hand there gleamed a wedding-ring.

Even if this was the case, he had no right, seeing how she had avoided him, to address her in this wild strain, and she imagined herself deeply insulted.

All the contempt she had expressed for him in that one glance, had not in the least disturbed his ardour.

He loved her, and he had made up his mind to conquer the reserve which parted him from her.

The coldness she maintained towards him, and the mystery in which she kept herself closely wrapped, only made him more eager to rouse the tenderness she had once shown him, and he watched her persistently, hoping by long patience to win her.

Wherever she went, he was always before her, his worshipping eyes following her slightest movement.

This watchful love become so distasteful to her that at last she began to wish she had left him to the mercy of others when he was lying wounded on the roadside.

One day she went out walking by herself, and did not return.

Florence thought some accident had caused her to lose her way, and searches were made day and night.

Gladys was not found!

Only one man knew how she had disappeared, and was grateful in his heart because no trace of her was seen.

Dudley had stolen her.

CHAPTER XVI.

GLADYS could hardly realise how it had all happened.

In her wanderings, she had been attracted by a curious-looking cave, a place which might once have been the basement of a vast temple.

She was fond of exploring, and she stepped under the rugged archway, never dreaming of the danger she was walking into.

It was a long low passage, with gloomy recesses hewn in the massive walls of rock, and by the few things scattered about, Gladys imagined it had some time been the hiding-place of smugglers or slave dealers.

A mysterious awful place for her to be in alone; but the barren solitude did not strike upon her till the end, through which the daylight crept, suddenly grew intensely black, and a dull rumbling sound told her that some secret door had been let down.

The light from a lantern sent a yellow ray across the darkness, and in the lurid glow she recognised the face of Ernest Dudley.

Do not let me make you afraid," he said, his voice full of gentle pain, " and forgive me the brutal way in which I have placed myself before you! You would not let me speak one word to you, and this opportunity came to have you all to myself, away from everybody— to make you hear all that I would say to you! My little ministering angel! if you knew the agony gnawing at my heart, you would be pitiful and pardon me!"

He looked miserable enough to win pity from any one he loved, and as he placed the lantern on a bench, Gladys saw how his hand trembled.

Her heart closed coldly against him.

"Captain Dudley, I beg you to unbar my passage and let me go!" she exclaimed angrily.

He knit his brows despairingly.

It went against his nature to act as he was doing now, for he loved her too well to cause her pain and not suffer himself.

"I have no wish to keep you a prisoner," he muttered, extending one hand pleadingly towards her. "Let me be your friend—let me see you sometimes in your home, and I shall have no cause to detain you now. All I want is this promise! When you have given it you shall not remain here a single moment against your will."

Gladys drew a quick breath of indignation.

"You do not know what you are saying!" she panted, her eyes flashing scornfully. "Open the door!"

"If you will let me speak to you in any other place, I will," he replied recklessly; "but if I know when I let you go I must lose you, I shall keep you here."

"You shall repent this outrage to me!" Gladys said, passionately. "If you had recalled you threat sooner, I would have looked over it; now, your cowardice shall not be kept secret!"

She was full of contempt and wrath.

She hated the love which made him forget the courtesy due to her, and whatever kindly feeling she had towards him turned to fire in her heart.

With an impetuous movement, she seized the lantern, and swept past him to the entrance of the cavern.

The daylight was shut out by a sliding panel, the secret fastenings of which she could not find, and she could only beat on it with both her hands in the hope that she might touch the spring.

The door remained firm, and fearing she would hurt herself, Dudley went up to her and gently held her wrists.

"Stop!" he muttered, brokenly; "every blow is a pain in my heart! My arm aches to thrust back this barrier—to do what is your will. But you would leave me then, and I should never have you near me again.

Only promise it shall not be so—only say you will let me try to win you, and the promise shall be your pass-word to liberty! You poor child, do you think it is not agony to me to see you in distress, and to know that I am the cause of it all?"

She turned her face to him with wild bitterness, her hands still pressed against the panels.

"If you have so much pity, why do you keep me here?" she exclaimed, wrenching her wrist from his clasp. "Oh, man, your heart is stone!"

"If it were, should I risk so much to keep you here?" he asked, looking at her with haggard eyes. "My heart is fire—my veins burn with the furnace heat, scorching up my soul! I love you—I love you—I love you!"

He spoke breathlessly, madly, his grey eyes gleaming with a strange light, his brow flushed and damp.

All the sudden reckless adoration which had rushed over his being at first sight of her, leapt up in his breast unchecked, now that she was with him, shut away from the world.

Unseen by her he had followed her to this lonely spot, and when he saw her enter the cavern, a swift impulse made him pass under the archway, and let down the door—the secret of which he had discovered some time before.

He thought if he could speak to her alone, the icy barrier between them would melt away, and she would be kinder to him—giving him the hope to win her for his wife.

It was a rash hope, and afterwards he cursed himself for letting his feelings blind his reason.

Gladys shrank from him, her lips quivering with proud scornful passion.

"I did not know there could be sin in helping a wounded man lying friendless on the wayside!" she cried bitterly. "I understand now, it would have been better to have left you to perish, than to give you the right to look to me for tenderness—tenderness!" she repeated, flinging the word at him with hot contempt. "I hate you! If I saw you dying now, and I knew that one draught of water could save you, even though I had it to give, I would dash it on these stones, far away from you, and let your lips parch dry! Not one touch from my hand—not one breath from my soul should be wasted on your suffering! You should die, and I would stand by—and watch!"

The scorn levelled against him was so unexpected— so full of hard meaning, it seemed to stun Dudley.

The lantern-light flickering on her face revealed it in its white set beauty. The snow that sheltered her heart against his love froze to ice, and Dudley looked at her with a kind of despairing agony, as though looking on a loved one dead.

He knew he had destroyed his last and only hope; his love would never have power to soften or to penetrate the scorn that had risen against him in her heart.

"What evil is there in my love that it should put poison in your words?" he exclaimed; "that you should wish me to die unsuccoured? I would give my heart's blood to save you!"

Gladys waved her hand, as though signalling away something that she loathed.

"Enough!" she said, impetuously. "If you have one throb of manhood left in you, let me go!"

"For us to part when the daylight creeps between us; for me to let you leave me with the sting of your scorn ranking in my heart! I could not—I could not! I would rather press you once against my breast and die, and let you watch my fading eyes till I could see you no longer! Why do you look at me with such horror? Am I mad, or has the despair working in me deformed my face? What is it that makes you recoil from me?"

Gladys thrust a fair trembling hand towards him— the left hand.

"This?"

The one word was full of concentrated bitterness. She had swept off an opal-ring she always wore, and close round one slender finger was her wedding-ring— bare to his gaze.

He seized her wrist in a convulsive grasp, and looked from the forlorn little hand to the childlike face above.

"Married!" he gasped, his eyes burning with mute uncertain pleading.

"Yes, married," she replied, meeting his gaze steadily. "Since you understand why I have evaded you, Captain Dudley, I hope you will set me free."

He gave a short wild laugh.

"Tell me where I can find him!" he whispered hoarsely, "and I will set you free. To have you against my heart for one sweet hour, I would wrench out my life to pay the price! to have you to myself always, do you think I should shrink from sacrificing another? Choose which shall be the forfeit of my love for you—my life or my soul?"

He spoke with such hot broken eloquence, and his eyes were so pained in their intense resolve, Gladys, a prisoner, and at his mercy, grew terrified.

The question that had rung from his lips a few seconds since cast a sharp agony into her heart—was he mad?

The desolation of this endless vault, the hollow darkness which the feeble light of the lantern seemed to mock, thrilled her with a sense of unutterable horror.

If only she could let the daylight in—if only she could escape from this impassioned reckless man who would not lose love for life!

She was haunted and at bay; she no longer had strength to defy. All her courage forsook her as she looked on the deep dreariness around—at the massive walls of rock, and falling on her knees she lifted her white face to him in breathless pleading.

"You do not know what you are doing—what you are saying!" she cried, her large frightened eyes appealing to his soul. "To-morrow, when you are calm, you will be sorry you have not listened to me! To-morrow the bitterness of your shame will almost make you call on Heaven to curse you. Oh, leave me—leave me! or let me go from this dreadful place alone!"

Her voice, piteous in its agony of prophecy and prayer, quivered through him, and his face worked with struggling emotions as he gazed down at her—at the pleading hands, at the wedding-ring that was as a barrier between her and himself.

"I love you!" he muttered, the words seeming to come to his lips with the breath drawn from his heart. "I love you! Sweet trembling hands—pure grieved eyes! make my heart calm and light my soul! I love you! and when I have kissed your lips once—once in parting, you shall go away alone. My life shall pay the cost! My blood shall wash the stain my love might leave on your pure life! While this mad love lives you could only loathe and shun me; death will exalt me—and the one kiss I shall give you will become a holy memory!"

All the fierce passion had faded into one resolve—a resolve which, awful as it was, grew to him sweeter than every worldly hope.

His eyes softened strangely, and a smile of passionate tenderness came to his lips, and stole over all his features.

Love was in his soul; it lifted him above every-day thought—above reason.

Dudley's sight did not reach farther than Gladys—Gladys crouched on the rough stones, with her face buried in her hands, and her golden hair shining like sunlight in the gloom.

There was a long gleaming knife stuck in a crevice near the lantern.

His arm threw a shadow across the light, and the next moment the knife had disappeared.

He wrote a few words on a scrap of paper, and thrust it in his breast.

"That will instruct you how to escape," he said, quietly, as Gladys, attracted by the sound of pencil and paper, glanced up.

She sprang to her feet and stretched out her hands imploringly.

"Why do you not give it me now?" she exclaimed, a wild undefinable fear shuddering through her. "You look so strange, you frighten me! Let me go now!"

"Presently," he muttered, with a deep hard breath. "You cannot leave me without one forgiving word. When you go from me my life will pass away! My darling, do you remember what you said just now? That you would stand near and watch me till my last breath had fled. I hold you to your word, love. Let my gaze rest on your dear face till my eyes grow dim in death—let me know that you are near me to the last —watching me!"

His voice had a weird triumph in it, and there was a hallowed light in his eyes, as though the spirit alone rested there.

He seemed to have forgotten the pitiless scorn in which those words had been uttered by her, and he only thought it would be sweet to die in his love—to sink into dreamless sleep with her beloved eyes lighting his soul in its dark passage to death.

He took her in his arms, and crushed her against his breast, gazing down at the fair shrinking face with passionate worship.

"Love, farewell! life, farewell!" he murmured rapturously. "My darling, good-bye—good-bye—for ever!"

He stooped his pale face, and his lips trembled against hers in long despairing kisses.

Gladys drooped within his arms, mute and unresisting, awed by the wild sweeping passion that shook the soul of this man, who was making himself a martyr to his love.

With instinctive terror she clung to his hand.

"You will let me go now?" she said, in a faint voice.

His arms tightened round her shivering form.

"Not till you can go alone," he answered in a strained unnatural whisper. "Remember your words. You saw where I put the writing—here, over my heart; when the time comes take it and go free. I will not ask you to think of me sometimes; for, leaving you like this— you can never forget me."

He was silent for a few moments, and Gladys could feel the dull heavy throb of his heart.

He was trembling from head to foot, and in the fitful glow cast on them by the lantern, she could see the damp awful pallor that had gathered on his brow.

With a sudden movement she tried to wrench herself from his arms, and then shrank quietly against him, appalled by the look of agony which for one brief second contracted his features.

"Not yet," he muttered, laying his face on her hair that she might not see the suffering he could no longer hide. "It is not time yet. Beloved, remember—to the last!"

His white lips seemed hardly to frame the words, but she understood, and a great fear thrilled through her.

"What is there to wait for?" she cried, piteously. "Open the door, and we will go out into the day together! You have grown weak. You are fainting! Oh, how can I let the light and the air in? Come—come! See, I will lead you, and we will go together—hand-in-hand. Do you understand? I forgive you?"

He looked at her with a smile which seemed to glow like a divine light over the ashen whiteness of his face, and to shine beyond the mist that was fast closing over his sight.

"It is as I had wished," he murmured vaguely. "My hand wrought it so. Dear love—"

He could not finish. The soft words were snatched back from his lips by a sharp breath of pain.

His hands tightened convulsively where they clasped her, then relaxed their hold.

He staggered, and fell on to the cold dark stones.

With a motion swift as the sweep of a bird's wing, Gladys flew to the closed entrance of the cave, and, flinging herself against the door, shrieked loudly for help.

Her desperate voice echoed far back into the gloomy recesses, and awoke a thousand other hollow sounds that seemed to drown her cry.

And above the din a broken whisper came to her.

"Your words— Watch—and we will part in peace!"

She shuddered! There was blood on her hair, and on her dress. She had cut her hand on a sharp rock.

She did not note that the wet stain was only where she had felt the hard throb of Dudley's heart, when his lips were pressed against her brow.

Had her ill-words come home to her?

Was he dying? Was she to watch the light fade out of his eyes without the power to save him—even to moisten his pained lips with a draught of pure water.

What did it all mean? What was happening?

She went to his side, and, bending down, gazed at him in silent anguish.

His eyes were closed, and only the pitiful quivering of his mouth told her that he lived—and suffered.

Her first feeble curse had come home to her!

Every word she had uttered in that passion of scorn, seemed suddenly to brand her soul in letters of flame.

She bowed her head in bitterest grief, and her eyes filled with tears—tears that seemed to burst through the floodgates of her soul, and to let loose the tide of feeling that had been too long pent up.

A cool moisture fell on Dudley's hot eyelids, and on his bloodless lips.

Some sweet balmy influence seemed to revive him.

He opened his eyes, and saw the desolate little figure bent over him.

Tears from eyes he never thought would weep for him were falling on his passive face.

With an effort, he raised one hand and laid it on her head.

"Gladys!"

He uttered her name softly—the dear name he had found on the handkerchief with which she had once bound his wound.

She leaned her face gently towards him.

"It will be time soon," he said, faintly. "Take the paper."

She obeyed him feverishly.

It might not yet be too late.

She could let the fresh air blow in upon him, and fetch water to bathe the damp dews away from his lips and brow.

She thrust a trembling hand in his breast, and then drew back with a cry of horror.

Her hand was covered with blood!

For the first time she realised the ghastly meaning of the stain on her dress.

He had stabbed himself while his kisses were warm on her lips, and he had held her against the cruel wound that she might not see until the end came!

Gladys gazed from the dying man to her blood-red hand with wild frozen agony.

"You have not taken the paper," Dudley whispered, speaking with difficulty. "Rouse yourself, beloved; in a little while you will be alone."

Alone with what?

Her stricken gaze wandered to the tomb-like walls, then back to the dying face upturned on the cold stones.

He moved his hand towards her appealingly.

The light had gone from his face, and it was full of aching misery.

"Was it a mistake?" he gasped brokenly. "Oh, God, what is this that I have done? Gladys—Gladys!"

He tried to raise himself and sank back with a deep groan, his frame shuddering with the agony that convulsed him.

Gladys watched him with dry hot eyes as she crouched beside him.

She had taken the yearning hand which had groped its way to her, and that cry to her smote heart.

"Forgive me—forgive me!" she moaned, pressing wild kisses on his face. "Oh, how unworthy I am of this great love—this terrible sacrifice! I was wrong—selfish—cruel! Why did you not kill me instead?"

"Hush!" he said softly, drawing her sweet face close to his side, "could I have had you near me so if I had lived? I love you, and death is sweet because it has brought you near to me."

There was a dreamy silence; Dudley's breathing grew more laboured; death's white wings were bearing fast down on him.

Yet he felt no pain, because Gladys was close beside him, her hand in his, her bright hair covering the dark stain on his breast.

He murmured a few broken words to her.

She did not answer. Her hand lay heavy in his clasp. She had fainted.

CHAPTER XVII.

S Dudley looked at the unconscious form, and felt the stricken strength fast ebbing out of his own frame, that terrible thought again pierced his heart:

"What is this that I have done?"

He was dying. With one thrust he had shattered the power of his manhood, and now he lay there helpless, unable to help the girl he had made the victim of his madness.

Who would come to her when he was dead?

Buried in this awful vault who would find her?

Perhaps she would die there too? Even now her driven soul might have winged its flight to a fairer world.

His hand wandered feebly over her face, and rested softly on her lips. Life fluttered under his touch, yet how could that faint breathing assure him of her safety! When consciousness returned, when her eyes opened to his lifeless gaze, how could she escape?

The pencilled writing had been washed away in the red stream that flowed from his breast, and he shuddered with more than mortal agony as he pictured the horrible doom he had brought her to.

For himself he did not fear death, but for her—was her living form to be buried side by side with his—his over which a numb chill was fast creeping?

He tried to raise his voice—to call for the help that would never come—to pronounce only her dear name.

His lips moved without sound—his voice was for ever silent.

Great pallid drops stood on his brow; darkness had fallen over his sight, and with each hard-drawn breath he felt his life sink lower.

His wild work was near its finish, and Gladys—how would it be for her?

As he gazed through the shadows closing so darkly around him, he seemed to gather all his strength, and to concentrate it in one great purpose—a purpose which leapt into his heart, and made it throb with sudden unnatural power.

He dragged himself to his feet and staggered blindly forward, one hand pressed to his head, one groping painfully along the rugged walls.

Three steps—steps that seemed to wrench his life out from his limbs, and to find footing in dark whirlpools of agony.

He reeled and swayed heavily against the rough archway of the cavern. The groping hand clutched desperately, like a drowning hand struggling for a hold on life.

Then there was a quick grating sound, and a flood of pure light fell over the man who had lost all for love.

Softly as an angel's wing the air fanned his brow, his eyes opened to a glimpse of heaven, and with a shuddering sigh he sank.

The sunset light rested on his upturned face—the lifeless lips were parted with a hushed smile.

*   *   *   *   *

When Gladys awoke to consciousness, she fled in wild horror from the spot.

One look at the dead face, and she knew the truth.

Dudley had passed beyond human help, beyond human hope, and his last thought had been for her, his last act one of unselfish atonement.

Her brain reeled, and she gave a terrible cry—a cry full of bitterest anguish.

"I have murdered him!" she moaned, shuddering as she saw the dull stain on her hand and on her dress. "And he had no fault but in loving me! Is my life accursed that I should cast such a black blight on all who wrap their happiness in me?"

The thought seemed to strike her with sudden frenzy, and she rushed away from the scene of horror like one pursued by a phantom crime.

AS THE STORM RAGED MORE FURIOUSLY SHE CLUNG TO HIM IN TERROR.

No. 7.

She did not heed where she went; a great darkness had fallen over her soul, and the world was as one vast tomb. Her eyes looked up blindly at the sunset glare; she saw no light.

When the sultry brooding night came she found no darker shadow on the face of the earth than what had crushed round her being in that first hour of terror.

She fled onward like some hunted creature, her feet scarcely touching the ground, her eyes dilated, her lips scorched as with a desert thirst.

Night waned; still she flew on with the same mad aimless speed, and she seemed to have lost sense of touch and sound when her wrist was seized in an iron grip, and a hoarse voice exclaimed:

"A woman's work! We have found her—the murderess of our poor young captain!"

They were rough, true-hearted soldiers, these men who had waylaid her, and they had sworn that justice should be done; their master's death should be avenged, and they had spent the night in pursuit of the murderer.

At last they had found the hand stained with his life-blood; it was a girl's fair hand, and on it there was a wedding-ring.

Gladys allowed them to lead her back.

She did not seem to feel their grasp upon her—to know that she was no longer alone.

Her steps grew heavier now a check had been put upon her speed, and she felt her limbs quiver and give way under her.

In the pale dawn she fell down at the feet of the men who had captured her, exhausted almost to lifelessness, her stained hair giving a death-like look to her face, her arms outstretched pitifully on the bare earth.

"It is the English stranger," they said, recognising the mysterious young beauty for the first time; "the captain loved her—and she has killed him!"

"See what is on her hand!" whispered one, pointing to the little plain gold ring; "perhaps there was some secret—perhaps she was his wife."

"We can only guess at what she was," another replied, not wishing this thought to overcome their demand for justice; "what she is now we know—his murderess. She is a sad sight—almost as sad to look upon as he is. She's run herself near to death; we must carry her, lads."

While she was at their mercy they could not touch her roughly.

Her helplessness appealed to their strength; they lifted her up and bore her between them almost gently.

"She's not much heavier than a wounded hare," muttered the one on whose arm her head rested. "I wonder what gave her strength to deal that horrible thrust? She has exhausted her life in this effort to escape her punishment. If—if it had not been our captain, I—I should wish we had not found her—eh, lads?"

His comrades looked at the dull, red blots on her dress.

"That calls out for vengeance," they said; and they turned their gaze from the fair stricken face, lest its pathetic beauty should stir too deep a pity in their hearts.

Yet in the secret depths of his soul, each man knew he would suffer death for her.

She looked too delicately frail to be cast to the doom they would condemn her to.

In their turn they felt they were murderers, for had they not hunted her until she had dropped down without strength—were they not bearing her to meet the judgment, that was to be death?

They bore her along in silence.

They had found their master lying dead—stabbed to the heart; and these slender hands were dyed with his blood.

Surely they had no right to shrink from the duty they were performing?

And yet they felt like cowards—they could not look into that sweet face and feel they were acting righteously.

Finding her so young and so unprotected, it would have been nobler to have left her.

They wished they had never found their captain's murderer. Yet, would not mercy shown to her be disloyalty to the dead?

So they thought in their blindness.

When Gladys opened her eyes she was lying on a mattress in a darkened cell.

She did not remember what had happened or who had taken her there.

When she tried to think strange burning pains darted through her head, and all kinds of wild lights seemed to whirl round her and gather into weird shapes.

She was terrified, and shrieked out aloud—shrieked for Sir Edmund to take her away from the horrors surrounding her.

It was strange his name should have been the first to come to her lips in the wildness of her despair.

Her whole soul seemed to cry out for him.

The faces that peered down at her were unknown to her, and she remembered nothing save her utter friendlessness and her love for Sir Edmund.

No one could hear that passionate and piteous voice unmoved.

The accusation of a horrible crime was cast upon her, but while she lay there delirious, her mind distracted with terror, how could they condemn her to greater suffering?

Her story ran through Cairo with the news of Dudley's death, and Florence, herself ill, went at once to the poor little prisoner.

Gladys did not know Richard Garth's wife.

"Why do all these strange people come round me?" she moaned. "It is Edmund I want. Oh, why does he not come? Cannot he hear me calling to him? Edmund—Edmund. Come! I am frightened—I am dying!"

"The deed was not of her own doing," an elderly officer who had seen her remarked to his friends. "I do not think the child is accountable for her act. She is mad, and madness is not crime."

"But if she dealt the blow, colonel?"

"Proof is strong against her," the colonel said, gravely; "yet it is hard to believe her guilty. Her eyes are full of horror, but there is no trace of sin or of shame in them."

They were lounging in the smoking-room at one of the hotels.

They did not notice the presence of a stranger who was enjoying a cigar at the nearest window.

"It was a tremendous shock," the colonel continued, suppressing the agitation that vibrated in his voice. "Poor Ernest! I can scarcely realise it, even yet."

He paced up and down for a few moments in silence.

It had been a shock—this sudden destruction of a life so full of strong vigorous manhood—and the colonel felt it deeply.

"The seclusion in which this girl has wrapped herself goes against her," he muttered, as though arguing with his own thoughts. "If only we knew more about her! I wonder whether the man she raves about could be found? He might be able to answer for her. Is Edmund the christian or the surname?"

"Whatever it is, they say it is never off her lips. Poor girl! It gives one the blues to think of her. Like you, colonel, I cannot believe her guilty."

They moved away, and the stranger was left sitting by the window alone.

He had heard every word of their conversation, and after smoking furiously for a little while, he threw his half-finished cigar out into the road.

The story he gleamed from the colonel's expressions fixed itself in his mind.

A girl arrested for some hideous offence, and likely soon to be condemned.

A girl, with fair sweet looks, who had been seized and imprisoned, and who now lay mad with fever, calling incessantly for one who was not near, and whose name was Edmund!

Earlier in the morning, he had heard that a young officer had been carried to the barracks dead, with a cruel stab in the cold breast, but he had not sought to learn more, and it was only now that a sudden hot interest grew in him.

He felt a longing to see the accused, whose history nobody knew, and, impelled by a restless curiosity, he left the hotel, and went towards the place where she was confined.

"I hear there was a lady brought here this morning," he said to the porter. "Of what is she accused?"

"Murder!" the man replied in an awed tone. "The murder of Captain Dudley!"

The stranger paled.

"Have they proof of her guilt?"

"They tracked her footprints from where they found the poor young gentleman—the only footprints. She was flying from the spot, and there were traces of blood upon her."

"Does she plead innocent?"

"Sir, she does not understand. She has a frenzy upon her, and shrieks with terror when anyone approaches."

"Can I see her?"

"You know her, perhaps, sir?" the porter said, with a slight touch of eagerness. "She is a lady of rank, but she does not reveal her full name."

"I should like to look at her," was all the stranger answered; and there was a dull weariness in his voice, as though he were performing a morbid duty.

He was surprised to find himself taking this interest in one on whom crime had set its brand—a woman, too.

His actions seemed to be governed by some inward prompting, he was too indifferent to define; and he obeyed the influence drawing him on, without reasoning why.

The name they said was ever on the lips of the girl-prisoner had attracted his attention, and he went in answer to the call.

He staggered back, as though he had been shot, when he was ushered into the bare little chamber where Gladys lay.

"Good God!" he gasped, all the blood receding from his lips. "I was not prepared for this!"

He turned towards the door, feeling his way with his outstretched hand.

"I have seen enough!" he said hoarsely; "let me leave her."

Gladys caught the sound of his voice, and her gaze rested on him with pained intensity.

"Edmund!"

He did not turn his head. His hands clenched convulsively, and he groped his way farther from where she lay.

Too late! The bend of his head, every line of his tall form, were familiar to her.

With a cry she raised herself, and sprang towards him.

"Did you not know me, Edmund?" she exclaimed, with a sudden rush from despair to joy. "I have been calling you for such a long weary time; I knew you would hear me, and come! Oh, Edmund! take me away before they kill me! They want to kill me, Edmund! Save me—save me!"

She clung to him wildly, her face uplifted against his breast, her soul burning in her sunken eyes.

He recoiled, as though a serpent had wound itself about him.

With a desperate fear of losing him, she drew him closer, and locked her arms tightly round his neck.

"Stay with me?" she moaned. "You do not know what blood is being shed. God has sent you to save me!"

A shudder went to the heart of the man to whom she clung with such frenzied appeal—the man who had known her in brighter days, and who would rather have seen her lying dead than look upon the living fragile wreck which she was now.

She seemed too frail and broken for him to build up hatred against her—for him to blight her mad faith in him with cold bitter curses.

He could not but pity her. An intense pain settled on his pale face.

Now that he had found her like this he could not leave her.

He held her firmly, and leading her back to the hard little couch, forced her to sit down.

"How long has she been in this state?" he asked huskily.

"Since she was brought here at daybreak."

"Has a doctor been consulted?"

"Not yet. It is not unnatural she should be like this, considering the circumstances."

Sir Edmund's eyes flashed.

"Is it possible you do not see her danger?" he muttered. "Whatever the charge be against her, remember nothing is proved yet. If even it were not so, she is a woman, and helpless. Get medical assistance without loss of time."

His words were a command, and there was a movement amongst those who stood in the doorway.

A firm hauteur in his manner compelled obedience, and no one questioned his authority.

Gladys still clung to him like a terrified child, and Sir Edmund looked hard at her, as though trying to search into her soul.

How she had changed since the first days of their love!

His heart ached as he met her shrinking gaze, as he saw the measureless horror and suffering on her face.

She had strayed from him, and had missed her way. Yet now, when he found her alone, sick unto death, how could he turn away, and leave her to perish?

"Gladys, can you understand me?" he said gravely. "I have a great question to ask, and you must answer me. Why are you here?"

"They want to kill me!"

"Why should they wish you harm?"

She shuddered as though she understood his words, but she made no reply.

"Who killed Captain Dudley?" he asked in the same tones—tones that called on her reason and stilled the tumult in her brain.

She trembled convulsively and shrank closer to him, hiding her face on his arm.

"He stabbed himself," she said in a hollow whisper. "It was my fault; kindness from me would have saved him; it was all he wanted, and he grew bitter, and chose to die rather than live without love. That is why they want to kill me—because he died for love of me."

"A little while ago she called herself a murderess," somebody, who overheard her, muttered, "and she will again directly. She raves; you cannot trust to her words—more's the pity."

Sir Edmund looked from the speaker to the wife he had never claimed, and who was sunk in such dire misery.

Embittered as he was against her, he could not believe her guilty of this horrible deed, and he was determined she should not suffer through the accusation till stronger evidence was brought against her.

He would have gone at once to make an active search in the matter.

But Gladys shrieked with such real terror, and clasped her poor pale hands so pleadingly on his breast, that he was not strong or cruel enough of purpose to cast her away from him.

He stayed with her until, exhausted with fever and pain, she allowed him to place her head on the pillow, and with his hand clasped in both her own, she sank into a kind of torpor.

"Poor misguided child!" Sir Edmund thought, unable to repress a sigh, as he looked at the tumbled golden hair, and sweet suffering face. "You have sinned, but you have not gone unpunished. Even I cannot see you in such misery and not pity you."

He left her in a dull heavy sleep—a sleep which seemed almost to deprive her of breath so calm and still she lay.

"This is not justice," he muttered to one of the chief officials, as he passed on his way out. "Before you sent out a charge of murder, care should have been taken to discover if the unfortunate gentleman met his death by violence, or took his life with his own hand. For my part, I consider the accusation ungrounded. If someone will show me the way, I should like to go to the spot where the dead man was found. I am interested in this case."

CHAPTER XVIII.

IR EDMUND was conducted to the cave, but he found there no proof of the condemned girl's innocence.

There was the long glittering knife, covered with a ghastly stain, lying just where it had fallen from Dudley's grasp.

Apart from this, there was nothing to tell the story of the tragedy, and Sir Edmund left the spot with his mind full of uncertainty.

Jealousy, born of a wild love, had made him quick to suspect her false to him—quick to believe the prayer on her lips a lie.

But this great cruel guilt—his heart would not accept it as truth, and he was ready to stand by her in this hour, when she was suffering a horrible injustice.

Only as he would have stood by a stranger—young, helpless, and desolate, whose piteous condition appealed to man's mercy.

He told himself this; yet he was conscious of a sense of overwhelming gratitude and thanksgiving when, half an hour later, he learned that in the dead man's clothing had been found a scrap of paper which proved Gladys innocent.

"My love, you have said I can never be. but as a stranger to you. Life without the hope of gaining you would not be worth the living. This will be the last time we shall ever part. One kiss I claim in farewell, then I shall end all. If the stroke is not swift enough, do not leave me while I have sufficient life in me to know when I am alone.

The letter broke off in a few disconnected sentences, as though the writer had been labouring under some great mental pressure.

A few directions were clearly written, telling Gladys where she would find the hidden spring, and imploring her not to leave him till all was over—indeed, he hoped she would not take this note from his breast till his heart had ceased to beat.

This paper, with the hurriedly-pencilled letters, blurred and faint, was all that was needed to save Gladys.

It told a story nearly everyone had already suspected, and the shock to those who had known Dudley, lost none of its keenness because of the different turn the tragedy had taken.

"Poor lost one, this suffering, at least, was undeserved!" Sir Edmund exclaimed to himself, as he made his way slowly back to where he had left Gladys; "no wonder it nearly drove her mad."

He was anxious to see that she received the attention due to her from those who had made her the victim of this miserable mistake.

He could not rest away from her until he knew she had been freed from the bondage this suspicion had hurled her into.

He found her just as he had left her. She had not moved. Just as he had placed her hands when he unclasped them from his own, they were now.

He halted half-way across the chamber as his glance fell on her, and a cold blank thrill passed through him.

A doctor was standing at the head of the low narrow bed, and Sir Edmund looked to him for an answer to his unasked question.

"Utter exhaustion of mind and body," the physician said gravely. "She may wake from this death-like trance, but the slightest shock then will be fatal. I can do little towards her recovery. If she has any friends, they had best be at hand. Somebody she knows must watch by her, so that, if consciousness returns, things may not seem strange to her."

Everyone looked instinctively at Sir Edmund.

Gladys had clung to him as long as she had been able to shake off the torpor weighing her down.

His voice alone had calmed her.

Who else was there to fulfil the duty?

Seeing her presence only distressed Gladys, Florence had gone home terribly upset and unnerved, leaving word with old Galena that if her young mistress should rally and ask for her, she was to be immediately summoned.

Nobody had sent for her, and now all appealed mutely to Sir Edmund.

She had taken comfort at sight of him; her last feverish effort had been to implore him to save her.

Without any knowledge of the bond between them, those looking on felt his was the presence most desired, and the doctor, sharing this impression, stepped back, and made room for him at the head of the bed.

There was nothing for Sir Edmund to do but to take the post offered him.

To have withdrawn would have been to excite the wonder of everyone to whom the story was carried—and if she should die, would not her death be on his soul?

He looked at the white face, with its closed eyes and frozen lips—so death-like in its unbroken repose; and it seemed to him she could never lift her head again—she was dying.

Silently he sank into the chair left vacant for him, and waited for the change that must soon come.

He had loved her—it had been a fierce task to wrench her life apart from his—and as he saw her before him now, hunted and driven down under her load of misery, he thought bitterly of the time, not so very long ago, when, had she been true to him, he would have started her life in such a fair bright current.

How was it she was alone?

Had the love for which she had bartered away her faith deserted her?

He pitied her in her desolation. Perhaps if he had not chanced to pass this way, she would have been left to die within these gloomy walls, with only hard-faced strangers to watch and wonder over her sufferings?

Though she had gone astray, and his curse had followed her; yet now he had found her, she clung to him with all her strength, and he knew that her trust had come back to him—love for him was still in her heart.

The doctor had left a cordial to be administered at a certain hour.

When the time came, it was Sir Edmund's hand that guided the glass to her colourless lips, and very gently and patiently he fulfilled the task.

Gladys moved slightly, a tremor ran through her frame, and the dark fringes of her eyes fluttered.

He had awakened her—but to what? Life or death, reason or madness?

The thought darted through his brain, and absorbed his mind in one great suspense.

He bent over her, scarcely drawing his breath, an intense expression coming over his face as she sighed faintly, and opened her eyes.

She gave him one long look—a look full of soft dreamy peacefulness.

Then the delicate lids trembled, and once more shut the light out from her face.

Sir Edmund watched her in high-strung uncertainty.

What was that one sweet gaze to prepare him for? Had her soul glanced heavenward in this silent awakening? Had she looked her last on this world?

A sudden dread seized him.

He laid his hand over her heart.

He felt a slight throb—or was it only the violent trembling of his own hand?

Her name broke from his lips:

"Gladys!"

The touch of his hand roused her, and she looked wonderingly up at his anguished face.

"I have had a dream" she murmured, weakly. "Hold my hands, Edmund. It has been such a strange horrible dream! It seemed to carry me on for ages and ages!"

He took her hands in a firm gentle clasp.

Her life at this moment was hanging on a thread; it rested with him on which side the balance would weigh heaviest, and he dreaded lest any new shock should shatter the strength feebly roused within her.

"Lie still now," he whispered, "and by-and-by you shall talk. I want you to shut your eyes, and try to sleep for a little while."

He was afraid her gaze might turn from his face and wander round the chamber.

It would not be well to call her back too rudely to her surroundings.

He had caused the room to be darkened still more, that she might not see the bare strange walls, and he stood like a screen between her and the rigid emptiness of the apartment.

With the unquestioning obedience born of great exhaustion, she shut her eyes, and lay quite still.

Her hands were held fast in his, and his clasp seemed to impart a sense of comfort and protection.

While he was near, what cause has she for unrest?

All past pain was as a wretched dream to her—vague and dimly remembered.

It did not seem strange Sir Edmund should be by her side. She was too weak to sift her feelings, or to indulge in any thought.

She had seen his dear eyes looking down at her, and felt the warmth of his clasp on her hands. She was content with only the consciousness of his presence.

Presently she stirred restlessly, and shuddered, as though the movement caused her pain.

"I cannot sleep," she moaned; "these pillows seem to burn my head."

"You shall have a better one soon," he said, soothingly, wondering how she could be conveyed to the hotel. "Drink some more of this, Gladys."

He moistened her lips again with the cordial, and smoothed the matted hair away from her brow.

Then something in her helplessness, something he read in her sweet wild eyes, prompted him to bend down and kiss her.

Whatever her sin against him—whatever the suffering she had caused him, he had forgiven her.

Whether she lived or died, his pardon had gone out to her; no bitterness against her would rankle in his breast; no passionate curse would he cast upon her life through him; at least she should not suffer.

While she needed help at his hand, he would not turn away from her; and afterwards—his mind was clouded as to the future.

As he looked at the small child-like face pressed close to his hand, perhaps he thought Gladys would have no part in the months and years to come.

He had avoided her, fearful lest her shadow should darken his path. What if now the cold still grave was to hold her away from him for ever?

He shuddered as the thought swept through his brain, and he watched her with the old yearning pain, that showed her how vain had been his efforts to forget her.

Bitterness had struck his heart, but the love which had been so long crushed down, lived still; no other passion had taken its place.

"Have you any friend you would have near you now?" he whispered after a prolonged silence.

His voice was husky, and a strange haggard look was on his face.

For a moment, while he awaited her answer, he released her hands from his clasp, and stood erect, his gaze cold and dark as it rested on her.

Gladys did not understand. Her hand wandered weakly in search of his.

"I want nobody but you," she murmured with dreamy tenderness. "Take my hand again. I love only you!"

Sir Edmund compressed his lips till all the colour left them.

Her words, so unconsciously spoken, had called to mind the estrangement which had risen between them on their wedding-day—the endless separation he had said could never be bridged over.

He took the little pale hand—the hand whose touch he had once flung off as though it had been a scorpion.

She had forgotten all that cruel past, and while her life depended on the quiet she had found, he dared not but forget too.

When the doctor called in again, she was sleeping quite naturally; the crisis had passed, and with great care she would recover strength.

"She has had a wonderful escape," the physician said, speaking in a low tone to Sir Edmund. "It appears to me your presence has worked the miracle. I was afraid the shock her mind had sustained would prove fatal."

"You think there is no danger of a relapse?" Sir Edmund asked.

"Not if her mind continues in its present state. She had better be removed from this place as soon as possible, in fact, she ought to leave Cairo altogether. The climate is greatly against her, and she needs change."

Sir Edmund heard in silence. It was evident he was expected to undertake the charge of this young life, and he wondered if the relationship between them had been guessed.

If he shrank from his post now, who was there to take his place.

Would not Gladys miss him, and grieve for him, as before?

He looked at her, sleeping so quietly, her lips parted with a lingering sigh, and he thought of the bitter disappointment that would rend her soul if she should wake to find him gone.

No! having saved her once, he could not hurl her back to darkness and death.

He would stay by her, till another should come who would take up his post; till he could reason with her, and gently make her understand why they must part.

Part?

When was that word again to crush down the tie between them?

CHAPTER XIX.

ENDERNESS had so long been shut out from Sir Edmund's life, that the sudden call on his sympathy gave a gentler tone to his nature, and he felt glad to be able to do good—to feel he could deal out human kindness even to the one who he believed had brought on her own sorrow.

He could not be hard to Gladys now.

She was like a child relying on his guidance, appealing to him with her great wistful eyes, when any untold suspicion leapt into his brain against her.

The was no one save himself to decide what was to become of her, and it was important she should be taken from Cairo.

She was hardly well enough yet to be consulted in the matter, so Sir Edmund secured two of the best berths on a splendid vessel, that was to set sail for Italy.

From thence he would take her through Switzerland to France, and he trusted she would be well enough then to decide herself where she would next go.

At the end of a week, Gladys, wrapped in a soft satin-lined cloak, with a white quilted hood drawn over her head, was carried on board, and laid on a pile of cushions.

It all seemed strange to her, but she was passive in the hands of those around her, and she found a sweet sense of safety and contentment in having Sir Edmund always near her.

"Why are we out at sea?" she asked him one day, when she was lying on deck with a heap of velvet pillows under her head.

Galena was sitting at her feet fanning her with a huge palm-leaf.

He relieved the servant of her duty, and motioned her away before he made any reply.

"I thought you would like to see Italy," he said gently. "I imagined you quite understood where you were going. Does the discovery please you?"

"I do not care where I go, so that I am with you," she answered, raising her eloquent eyes to his face. Then after a moment's pause: "Have I been ill?"

"Very ill."

"What else? Have I been mad, and have you been with me all the time, or——"

She broke off, and looked at him with perplexed pain.

She was struggling to pierce the darkness obscuring her memory, to weave into one clear thought the few disconnected ideas that straggled into her brain.

"I should not try to think just yet, if I were you," Sir Edmund said quickly, seeing her eyes had grown startled and wild. When you are stronger, we can say a lot to each other. How would you like me to read to you for a little while?"

Gladys did not answer.

She was gazing at him in a fixed way, that made him half afraid for her.

At last she realised what had seemed dim to her before. At last remembrance came rushing upon her, making her brain giddy and hot.

Her face became deathly pale, and she shivered icily—never taking her large deep gaze from him.

Then, with a pitiful cry, she turned her face away, and pressed her brow on her clasped hands.

She remembered everything.

Sir Edmund did not speak. It was well this understanding had come to her; sooner or later she must have known.

His glance rested gloomily upon her.

She seemed to be sobbing silently. Her slight frame was trembling, as though a great tempest had shaken her.

He could not look on calmly. Rising to his feet, he paced the length of the deck, his head bent, his brow knit with pain.

When he went back to her, her face was turned towards him, her eyes eager and resolute.

"Edmund!"

She uttered his name with earnest pathos, yet with a certain pride that commanded his attention.

"Edmund, have you forgotten the day when you put this little ring on my finger?"

He shuddered.

"Hush!" he muttered. "Do not speak to me of that."

"But the secret. I could not tell you then, Edmund. Now it is different; come nearer and listen. It is a long story."

His grey eyes gleamed like steel under his bent brows.

Bitter words rose to his lips; he checked their utterance. This was not a time to reproach her for the wrong he had pardoned!

"Enough!" he muttered; "I do not ask your confidence. You refused it once; I no longer need it."

"I must tell you!" she exclaimed in low, passionate tones. "I was bound over to secrecy then, and I had to bear your cruel blame! I cannot endure it any longer, Edmund. You must hear everything, even if you make yourself my enemy—even if you betray to death a life that I would give my own to save!"

Her voice dropped for a few moments, and her breathing came hard and quick. Her gaze never wandered from his face, and presently she said very quietly:

"Edmund, do you remember I used to speak to you sometimes of my brother? I believed him dead. News had reached me that he had met his death out in Australia."

"Well?" with a smile that seemed to freeze his lips.

She lifted her wasted hand, and drew him down on to the seat near him. Instead of letting his hand go from her clasp again, she drew it against her cheek, and half raising herself, leaned her head against him.

"What a cruel pain has come into your eyes?" she murmured, shivering. "Yet you did love me!"

"God knows I did! But it was a false worship—it left my heart empty of faith."

"Only because you misjudged me."

"Misjudged you! Had I not evidence enough against you?"

"You should have trusted me. I told you that you wronged me—I had never deceived you; but you disbelieved and thrust me from you, and afterwards would not give me a hearing. Edmund, it is true I met somebody in the woods, and it was to escape detection I urged you to do all in your power to keep everybody away from the spot where I knew my brother was concealed. It was for my brother's sake. The report of his death was false. Quite suddenly he returned to England, and traced me to Deepwood. He told me he had a terrible secret, and that I was never to say he lived, for to the world he was already dead."

"Go on," Sir Edmund whispered, hoarsely, when she paused, almost overcome.

"I have not told the worst yet," she said, wearily. "I could not rest till he had confided his secret to me, and, in trusting you with it now, I place at your mercy his life-long liberty. Shall I go on?"

"If it will ease your mind to do so."

"Bend closer. The wind and the waves might carry our secret to other ears, and it is only to you I would dare trust it. Frank fell into great trouble. He was convicted on a charge of which he was as innocent as you or I, and he broke loose and escaped."

Sir Edmund watched her steadfastly, his face undergoing many changes.

"Is this truth?" he asked, after a deep silence.

"As that there is a God in heaven!" she answered, fervently.

"Where is your brother?"

"In pursuit of his enemy. He has sworn to use his freedom but to one purpose—to find, and deliver up to justice, the man whose crime he was forced to bear. If he had met you he would have told you what I have told you. He could not endure that I should suffer through him. He did not foresee the danger this secret would expose me to. Afterwards he tried to find you, hoping to explain everything, but you were gone!"

"And the photographs—what did they mean?" he asked, still only half convinced.

Gladys sighed, and her face wore a more troubled look.

"I do not know. Someone must have seen us together, and have managed to secure a likeness while I was wishing Frank good-bye. I knew nothing of them till—till they were held up as proof against me."

"It is a desperate story!" Sir Edmund said, in a strained voice. "A strange truth if it be true."

Gladys flushed, and a hot gleam came into her eyes, making them unnaturally brilliant.

"Do you repay my confidence with doubt—with unbelief?" she exclaimed, drawing slightly away from him. "I have suffered so much through this secret, because I was afraid to speak; now that I have unburdened my heart, is the same suspicion to stand between us?"

Sir Edmund covered his eyes with his hand.

"Gladys, is it true that I have wronged you?"

"How deeply I can never tell you. Long, long ago, I told you I had a secret that must part us—that I dared not be your wife, lest in after days you should reproach me for having bound my life with yours. You understand now why I shrank from the love that was so sweet to me. My brother, though innocent, was an exile—branded!"

"Poor child!"

She felt his hand tremble as he laid it on her head, and his eyes had softened strangely under his bent brows.

"You believe me at last?" Gladys asked, eagerly. "And you will not betray Frank? Some day his innocence will be proved. You will wait and trust him, will you not?"

"If what you say be true—"

"Still if!" she exclaimed, turning away from him, and clasping her hands with a bitter moan. "It must

be so! I know no word that will convince you! I
forgive you your fault, Sir Edmund—forgive mine."

The words were a heart-broken cry, and she did not
try again to soften his mood by look or touch.

She seemed to droop into a bent heap, rocking herself
to and fro in her anguish.

When at length she lifted her face, the sweet eyes
were full of scornful, resolute pride.

"Leave me—leave me!" she exclaimed, putting out
her hand as though to motion him from her sight. "I
have stooped my woman's pride in this weak pleading!
I have become unworthy in my own eyes, as I seem in
yours.   Since you insult me with disbelief, your opinion
deserves only my contempt! Why did you let me tell
you—why did you let me endanger my brother's
safety—for this?"

Hot tears were in her eyes, and her voice quivered
with passion.

He had wronged her with cruel doubts, had turned
the world against her.

And now, when she had tried to prove her innocence,
when she had forgiven him, he still disbelieved!

She thought how Frank would have resented this
deep insult had he been near.

"Sir Edmund should go down on his knees and ask
her pardon," he had said, and she felt she had humbled
herself to this man who was treating her with such
cruel and unrelenting injustice.

"I forgave you your blind suspicion while I kept
the truth from you," she said, after a dull pause;
"but now the injury strikes harder on me. I cannot bear your presence, knowing what is in your
heart against me. I wish I had never met you—
I hope when this voyage is ended we shall never
meet again!"

Sir Edmund left her side and paced the deck in fierce
silence.

His heart ached with a strange bitter tenderness for
her.

Every reproach she had uttered had quivered through
him with a sharp pang, and he felt a longing to raise

her in his arms, to tell her he knew her soul was pure and bright as the stars in heaven.

Yet had he not too blindly put faith in her before? Might not this be the continuation of a dark deceit? Was he weak enough to let the old spell wind round him because her fair childlike eyes were looking his soul away?

He did not trust himself to glance at her while this struggle was going on.

When at length he turned towards the spot where he had left her she was no longer there.

"Poor little Gladys!" he thought, as he hurried to the saloon. "What a brute I have been! And to doubt her after she had explained everything. She must hate the sight of me!"

He was full of remorse now.

He knew it was only because he had loved her that he had tried to shut his heart against the truth she spoke.

"Love is blind." He had kept these words well in mind, and had been over discreet.

He was disappointed not to find Gladys in the saloon.

He was anxious to be at peace with her—to bring back the sweet, trustful smile to her face.

The deep burning sorrow that had been in her eyes when she last looked at him haunted him.

He sent a message to her by the stewardess, and in reply received from Gladys a short note.

"You repent too late," the lines ran. "I can neither forget nor forgive your last insult. Besides, to what purpose would it be? To-day you believe, to-morrow you will accuse. As your mood changes so you buoy up my hopes, or cast me down to despair. You love me, but that love would be torture if barren of faith. I think we had best live apart—as strangers. I repeat, I never wish to see you again."

This did not satisfy Sir Edmund.

He scrawled a few words on the back of her letter, full of tender pleading, and passionate self-reproach.

He must see her, or he should go mad.

Gladys, without reading, tore the paper into fragments, and sent it back to him.

Sir Edmund went up on deck like a man who had been stunned.

He realised now all that he had lost—all he had thrown away.

He had wronged his pure little love—his child-wife, and when she forgave he doubted.

Now what power had he to heal the sting his suspicion had left on her soul?

If only he could see her!

He understood her well enough to know that to thrust himself into her presence now would only be to harden her pride against him.

Yet, must he abide by her word—the word she had taken up from his own lips—separation?

He felt the depth of the suffering she was inflicting upon herself, and his heart ached for her as he pictured her alone in her grief—shut away from the comfort he so longed to give.

Hour after hour he paced the deck in bitter reflection—solitary, undisturbed.

The night lowered, and a dense heaviness gathered round the vessel—a suffocating dullness that was presently lit up with a fierce flash of lightning.

A crashing peal of thunder shook the night, and for a few seconds Sir Edmund was deafened by the awful echo, blinded by the sharp, piercing light that again broke the gloomy sky.

The sea rose high, and the ship heaved from side to side, labouring against the strong rush of the tide.

A louder and more fearful boom summoned all passengers on deck—the men with white set faces, the women shivering with terror.

"HAD MAN EVER SO SWEET A FAIRY IN HIS HOME?" HE EXCLAIMED.

Sir Edmund scanned the pale group eagerly.

Gladys had not followed. She remained below alone.

"My poor little one!" Sir Edmund thought, as he went down to look for her. "She will be frightened to death. I will not have her left by herself."

The door of her cabin was locked, and finding she did not answer when he called, he gave the bolt a fierce blow that burst it open.

She was kneeling on the ground, with her face hidden against a chair, her hands folded as if in prayer.

She had not heard him enter.

The storm was raging so furiously now as to drown every other sound, and she did not know how near he was till she felt herself lifted in his arms, and carried upon deck.

Everyone had gathered round the captain, as though his presence was a safeguard against the night's peril.

Sir Edmund carried his pale little wife to a deserted part of the deck, and placing her gently on her feet, he stood by her side with both his arms clasped round her.

"Are you frightened, Gladys?" he asked, turning her face against his breast, as the blue, darting light whirled across her eyes.

Gladys drew his hand away from her head, and steadily faced the storm.

"When you left me an hour ago I prayed for death," she said, a strange terror in her voice. "Do you think my wretched prayer has been heard, and this is my punishment—to see all these other poor lives perish with mine?"

"God grant no life on board will be lost to-night," Sir Edmund replied, gravely. "We are in His hands, dear. Do you imagine one little weak voice could raise a storm like this?"

"I prayed for death," she whispered, gazing with wide frightened eyes at the lightning flashing down from the sky. "If anything should happen, if we should never see the daybreak, will the doom of this ship be on my soul?"

"My darling! You have no right to torture yourself with such miserable thoughts. We are in great peril, but you have not made the danger. Kiss me, dear, for we are face to face with death, and I do not know how long we may be together."

Gladys drew coldly away from him.

"No; we are strangers," she said, even at this moment remembering the bitterness which kept them apart; "as such we must live—or die."

"Cannot you forgive me, Gladys? A little later and it may be too late."

"Forgive you—yes, but I can never forget. Why did you bring me up here? It would have been kinder to have left me to myself."

"To meet danger—perhaps death, alone. Gladys, through all these months of cruel suspicion and separation, I have loved you; now I know you innocent, how much dearer must you be to me?—my wife, who has borne such deep wrong at my hands! Gladys, let the past die out of our lives, and you shall never have cause to reproach me for one unjust word. This cannot go on any longer, darling; you are my wife, the one love I have ever had; I can never let you go from my side again."

Once more he had drawn her to his heart, and as the storm raged more furiously, she clung to him in terror.

Two of the masts had already fallen under a stroke of leaping light, and those on board the tossing vessel wondered if she would ever reach her anchorage.

A wider flash of lightning showed every face white with a terrible unspoken dread, and for a moment the disabled ship seemed to be rushing headlong into a sea of flame.

Then amid the terrific roar of the thunder there was a sudden shock.

The vessel rebounded, shuddering like a living thing in agony, a great gap yawning in her side, the remaining mast shattered into splinters.

She had struck on a rock.

When next the lightning flashed over the sea it revealed a scene of horrible despair, and the wild cries of those on the sinking ship were drowned as one voice in the storm.

"The boats—quick! We can clear the wreck before she goes down!"

The words came from Sir Edmund's lips.

He was already at work with the captain, cutting the ropes, and almost flinging the passengers into the boats.

"There is room for all—all can be saved!" he exclaimed, as the desperate cries broke out afresh. "Take courage, and keep a steady hand. Now, men, row for your lives!"

CHAPTER XX.

N the darkness and the confusion, it was impossible to distinguish who were the first to leave the vessel.

Sir Edmund had lifted Gladys into one of the boats before he gave a thought to anyone else, and he and the captain were the last left on board.

With a silent hand-clasp, the two who had borne up with such calm courage in this deadly peril, climbed down into the light craft that was to bear them on to life or death.

"With God's help we shall reach a safe harbour before daybreak!" the captain exclaimed presently. "Steady, men! Keep in the wake of the other boats!"

Sir Edmund grasped an oar from one of the sailors, and pulled with all his might.

Gladys was not with them, and he wanted her to know everyone was safe.

He heard the hull of the doomed ship strike a reef, as the waves washed over her deck, and involuntarily he turned to take a last look at the shattered masts and torn flowing sails.

Was it only a shadow, or did he see a form standing erect and motionless on the flooded deck—a white, horror-stricken face, lit up for a moment by the fierce lightning blaze?

Sir Edmund hastily thrust his oar into other hands.

"Look!" he said, hoarsely, pointing to the wreck; "we have forgotten one. Pull back again, for the love of Heaven!"

"Too late!" one of the men muttered, shading his eyes with his hand, as he gazed in the direction of the dark broken mass. "If we go back we are lost. We should be swamped or sunk under the wreck; besides, there would be a man too many."

The captain half rose, his brave face composed and resolute.

"I have his place," he said, firmly. "Do you understand? Put back!"

The men rowed on in sullen silence, still keeping in their first course.

Was it likely they would obey the order their captain had given them—leave him to sink with the wreck, while they took up another struggling life?

The captain stood up, his hands clenched hard.

"Put back!" he commanded, almost fiercely.

"It's too late!" was again the muttered answer. "She is sinking fast; we could never reach her—unless we go down under water. No, no, captain; each man for himself now!"

Sir Edmund turned on them with a look of scorn.

"Cowards!" he exclaimed. "Will you see a fellow-creature—a fellow-sufferer—perish without offering the help you have power to give? Dare you expect to receive mercy to-night, while you yourselves condemn another to the death from which you are praying deliverance? You are unworthy the strength God has given you, since you only use it in your own service. 'Each man for himself!' you say. Aye, then you are not men!"

While he spoke he tore off his coat and shoes, and before they could stop him he plunged into the sea, and struck out towards the wreck.

He was a bold swimmer, and the expanse of tumbling waves sweeping between his out-stretched hands and those dark, swaying beams seemed nothing.

The refuge he had just left might glide beyond his reach for ever.

He would not leave this desolate being to perish while aid was so near.

The storm raged wildly over his head, and the waves rolled darkly round him.

With unwavering strength he forced his passage through the dull sea, slowly but surely nearing the black object that with a sullen crash had hurled itself over on the reef.

Sir Edmund thrust his way through the great waves with almost superhuman power.

The vivid lightning showed him it was a woman to whose rescue he was hurrying—a girl with flowing hair, and forlorn arms held pitifully towards him.

Hurried as had been this last desperate act, he had the thought to thrust a life-belt round him, and warned by the ominous creaking sound that filled the breathless pauses in the storm, he uncoiled the rope and flung the belt to her.

"Throw it round you, and leap as far out as you can!" he exclaimed, his voice sounding strangely above the furious sounds deafening the night; "don't lose a second, for Heaven's sake!—get clear of the wreck, and for the rest trust to me!"

With a piercing cry she threw herself towards him, and he snatched her from the black, shadowy mass just as it sunk silently under the sea.

"Thank Heaven I was in time!" he said, huskily, as he struck out for the boat. "Cling to me with all your strength; I will save you!"

Either the captain had enforced obedience, or the men had repented their unwillingness to again risk their lives.

The little craft was coming steadily to meet Sir Edmund, and as he placed the girlish form in the strong hands held towards him, a feeble cheer mingled with the storm's tumult.

"She is a light weight, and will not make much difference," he said, as he was drawn up over the side of the boat; "anyhow, it is worth the risk."

Two or three of the sailors hung their heads in shame.

They felt reproached, and in the silence which followed Sir Edmund turned his attention to the girl he had saved from certain death.

She was half lying in the bottom of the boat, close to where he was sitting.

As he bent over her she tried to raise herself, and clasping her hands on his knee, let her head fall forward on her arms.

Sir Edmund gave a slight start as he looked at the dark outline of her form.

The touch of those tender hands sent a sudden thrill through him.

Scarcely daring to analyse the thought prompting the action he gently stroked back the long, wet hair, and gazed earnestly at the drooping face.

"Gladys!" he whispered, a strange tremor vibrating in his voice.

He felt her trembling against him.

Without a word she drew his hand down to her lips, and that soft, shy caress brought a tender gleam in his eyes.

"My darling!" he murmured, clasping her passionately to his heart, "how was it you were left behind? I placed you in the first boat we launched, and I believed you safe. I should have been mad with horror had I known it was you standing alone on the wreck!"

"I crept back again to your side, Edmund. I thought there might not be room for all, and I wanted to be last. I meant to leave the ship when you did; but in the confusion someone rushed against me, and I fell. When I struggled to my feet, and looked towards the spot where I had seen you standing, I was alone!"

Sir Edmund pressed a long kiss on the sweet lips—a kiss that was full of reverence and silent thanksgiving.

"My poor little love," murmured Edmund tenderly. "Why did you not call to me?"

"I did," nestling closer to him, like a shivering child; "but how could my voice be heard above so fearful a storm? You saved my life bravely and unselfishly, and from to-night it is yours, Edmund, to use as part of your own!"

"I shall keep you to your words," he said, glad that at last this peace had come between them; "my little wife shall never repent having given herself to me."

Once more he kissed her, as though to seal this new promise, and pressing her pale face against his cheek, Gladys sank into a dreamy happy silence.

"You must not sleep with all this wet about you," he said, full of care for her. "You are shivering, darling. Let me put some of these dry coats round you."

He wrapped her up warmly, and tried to persuade her to lie at the bottom of the boat, where she would be more sheltered from the storm.

Wet as she was, she preferred remaining by his side. Her tired head could find no dearer resting-place than over the passionate heart that thrilled with every beat of her own pulse.

"Let me stay as I am now," she said, softly, as she half knelt at his side; "I am so tired, and I do not want to go away from you."

"You shall not, dearest," he answered, a light flitting over his handsome face. "I could hold you like this for ever, Gladys. I am thankful that at last there is a true understanding between us."

Gladys was silent.

She slipped one arm softly round his neck, and rested quietly against him.

Her tired limbs had found repose at last, and in the safe warm shelter of his arms she fell asleep.

Sir Edmund looked tenderly down at her white face, his heart thrilling with a strange pain, as he thought how close those sweet eyes had been to everlasting darkness.

Only by what seemed a miracle had she been saved to-night, and as he clasped the slender form, nestling like a folded flower against him, he felt that the purest light of life would have faded if she had drifted from the world.

Once or twice he bent over her in almost breathless dread, when some changing light showed the marble-like stillness of the young face.

How fearfully like death this pale slumber seemed! Yet she was breathing gently as a child, her lips parted with a dreamy hushed happiness.

The storm passed away, and the breaking dawn flushed wave and sky with a faint rose hue."

There was no trace of the wreck.

The sea, with the new-born day smiling on it, was as calm as a lake, and but for the fair head pillowed on his breast, Sir Edmund might have imagined the night's peril part of a strange dream.

Help came to them from Naples as soon as the boats were visible through the pearly mists.

The danger was passed, and those who had pulled so bravely through the dark storm put the little crafts safely ashore, inwardly thanking the Providence that had spared them to greet this bright new day.

Towards noon, the great white sails of a beautiful vessel gleamed in the sunlight not far from where the sailors had anchored the boats.

She was bound for England, and most of the ship-wrecked passengers went on board, eager to reach the dear homeland, which a few hours ago they had despaired of ever seeing again.

Gladys, with her hand resting softly on Sir Edmund's arm, waved them a bright *bon voyage*, and as the ship glided over the crested waves, she turned away with a little sigh.

" Would you rather I had let you go with them ? " Sir Edmund asked gently.

" No—but I was thinking."

" Sad thoughts ! Of whom ? "

" Of Frank. I wonder if he is safe ? If he wants me ever so much he will not know where to send."

Sir Edmund looked gloomy.

He could not bear her mind to wander away from him, even to her brother.

" Couldn't we telegraph ? " he asked, conquering the jealousy which for a moment had made him selfish.

She shook her head :
" The message would never reach him. He did not tell me more than that he was going to England."

" To find his enemy, didn't you say ? "

" To find Richard Garth."

Sir Edmund gave a slight start.

"What had he to do with it?"

"Not much, perhaps—perhaps everything. I cannot tell you more than that I know Richard Garth to be the greatest traitor in the world. He knew my secret from the very day the picnic was put off. He saw me with my brother and recognised him."

"He kept the secret well, Gladys," Sir Edmund observed coldly. "I hardly comprehend your reason for blaming him."

"Do you think he would have kept it without a motive?" she asked, bitterly. "I have no faith in his friendship for my brother. I believe, as he could have explained away the suspicion put on me, so he could lift from Frank's life that shadow which hangs over him like a curse. The invalid you met in Cairo, with all her beautiful hair turned white with grief, is Mr. Garth's wife. His cruelty drove her mad."

"I understood he had lost both wife and child before he went to Deepwood," Sir Edmund said, incredulously.

"So he though, perhaps; but only the baby is dead. I wanted Florence to tell me more, but I was afraid to ask anything. Her past was so recent; the strange horror of it darkened her mind whenever she tried to recall what had been."

"My dear little girl, do you mean to say you set any importance on the word of a madwoman?"

"She has been very ill—her mind seems to be wrapped in a kind of torpor, but when she spoke to me about these things, Edmund, she was not mad."

Her words failed to convince Sir Edmund.

"It has been a case of desertion then, according to this poor creature's account? Is she quite reconciled to her fate?"

Gladys looked up into his smiling face reproachfully.

"If you mean, does she ever want to see her husband again—no! She recoils from the very thought of him. I think she would rather he were dead than he should cross her path again."

"Very unnatural," Sir Edmund interposed grimly. "Did she ever try to instil the same thought in your heart towards me? I richly deserved it from you,

Gladys. Come, answer me truly, sweet; would you have been glad if I had died and left you free?"

"No."

"You do not hate me because I have been cruel to you—because I made you suffer half of what I suffered myself?"

"No."

"One more question, Gladys. Does my wife love me?"

"With her whole heart and soul!"

"My darling, will you be happy with me, after all the bitter pain I brought upon you?"

"I made that misery for myself, Ned, and it is you who have lifted me from it. I do not think I shall ever be unhappy again."

Fair words; was there yet another shadow to fall between these two, who, though linked in one destiny, were always so strangely parted?

No matter how dull and wearisome the despair she had endured, the sudden brightness that had broken over her life made up for everything.

The soft sunny grandeur of the scenes she found herself in, thrilled her with intense delight, and, as she travelled along the wild mountainous paths, or lay back in a gondola, with the dreamy splash of the water making music for her, her soul seemed sometimes to stand still, awed by the too-perfect joy it held.

"Shall we live like this always?" she asked, when they had seen nearly all the beauties of Italy. "I shall be sorry when the time comes for me to die. This world is very beautiful; I can think of no sweeter rest for the soul than this deep, calm happiness. Will life be always so full of golden smiles?"

They were drifting gently down one of the fairest of Italy's rivers, Gladys looking very sweet in a soft dress of the most delicate pale pink tint, with a bunch of white blossoms in her waistband, and a heap of them scattered in her lap.

Sir Edmund watched her tenderly, taking in every shade of the loveliness that, nurtured these few days in the warmth of his love, had bloomed to such rare perfection.

"If human power can make it so, Gladys," he answered her, "life to you shall never be anything else but sunshine."

" I don't think it could be such bright sunshine anywhere but in Italy," she said, looking dreamily at the blue water that mirrored back the soft light of her own eyes. "I almost wish we might stay here always."

Sir Edmund leaned towards her, and laid his hand on the two little fair ones caressing the flowers.

"I thought you could be happy anywhere with me, Gladys!" he exclaimed in low, half-earnest tones.

"So I could," meeting his gaze rather wistfully. "Only here you and I seem to live for each other—to think of nothing but the present. There is no one to mar the harmony between us. Can you understand me, Ned ?"

"Perfectly, wild flower. But I don't think, in any part of the world, there is one living who could spoil our peace now. Own that on second thoughts your opinion is the same as mine, Gladys. I shall not allow you to have any ideas on the subject different to what I have."

A smile chased away the sadness from the pretty pouting lips.

It was so easy for Gladys to be happy when that deep tender voice was murmuring words of hope to her, and of undying love.

Visions of Beatrice and of Richard Garth crossed her mind like shadows.

But looking into her husband's face, she forgot them, and her bright spirit rose gladly, lit up by the impassioned fondness shining in the eyes she loved.

CHAPTER XXI.

HE next few months were like an enchanted period in her life.

They wandered through Switzerland, and after leaving that land of white beauty, Sir Edmund took his wife to Paris. Here they were not so much alone.

Sir Edmund met many of his earlier friends, whom of late had sometimes wondered what had become of him.

There had been rumours of an "unfortunate marriage" connected with his name, and there was quite an excitement amongst those who had shared this vague understanding when Sir Edmund introduced "Lady Etheridge—my wife."

"By Jove, a very lovely one, too!" was the thought that flashed through many of the masculine minds. "I envy him his fair choice."

Everyone admired Gladys. Wherever she went she was the chief attraction, and Sir Edmund often caught a gaze watching, with more than common interest, the varying expressions on her bright young face.

He was conscious of a thrill of pride when he saw how much a single smile from her was to some of these men.

Yet too much attention was paid her for him to be satisfied with this new admiration she created, and he grudged almost every glance she bestowed on her little train of worshippers.

"I don't think it would be good for my peace of mind if I kept you in Paris," he said to her, half laughingly, when they were at some brilliant assembly, surrounded with everything costly and beautiful.

"Why not?" she asked, smilingly.

She knew why he had spoken thus, and felt a shy glad pleasure in tormenting him.

"I should lose my head with jealousy," he replied, clasping her hand for a second, under pretence of buttoning her glove. "There, I have broken one of those pretty pearl fastenings. You had better let me undo them all and take the glove off altogether."

"No thank you!" then, glancing up into his jealous eyes: "I really do believe, Edmund, you are mean enough to—to have done that purposely."

"My darling, Gladys——"

"I am sure you did Edmund—just so that my wedding-ring should be uncovered! You are growing most horribly exacting."

"And you, my little one, are growing most tormentingly beautiful. I can hardly blame those poor wretches for adoring you."

"I should imagine not, considering they are only following your example. It is your example—isn't it, Edmund?" with the slightest shade of wistfulness in her clear eyes.

"If you say so, of course it must be."

"You say so. I want to hear it from you."

"You strange child! Must I tell you again what you know so well? I love you, dear."

"Thank you," she said, softly, and she linked her small bare hand on his arm. "I would give up all the world to please you, Edmund."

He looked at her remorsefully.

"What a selfish brute I must seem to you, Gladys—to draw you away from every little pleasure that does not come through me! You were full of happiness just now, yet I could not bear to see your lips smiling for others; I could not rest till I had got you away from those who were watching you with such ardent admiration, devouring every word and every look I thought I alone had a right to. I was unjustly jealous, darling. You must not let me become your tyrant."

"I am not afraid," she answered trustfully. "Will you take me home now? I feel tired."

"It is early to leave. Are you sure you wish to go?"

"Quite. After Italy and Switzerland, Paris makes my head ache."

"I thought you liked Paris. Yesterday you were enchanted with the glories it showed you."

"At the Opera? Oh, yes, that was beautiful!" the young face flushing with enthusiasm; "but—"

"Well?"

"I like better the poetry and the music that fill Italy."

"Will it make you much happier if I promise to take you there again before the winter is over."

"Will you?"

"Decidedly—unless anything serious should happen to prevent."

"What could happen? Do you think anything will happen, Ned?"

"No, darling. I hardly know what made me say that. My words meant nothing."

He wrapped her up very tenderly in her white fur-bordered cloak, for the night-air was keen, and, after the desert-heat of Cairo, and the sunny warmth of the south, a chill wind might be dangerous to her, as to a fragile hot-house plant.

It was very pleasant driving through Paris under the clear moonlit sky.

Sir Edmund was so gentle with her, humouring her changeful moods, and eagerly seconding every new thought she expressed.

It would have been strange if she had not been happy —if she had doubted the sincerity of the love he lavished upon her.

December had set in before they returned to Deepwood.

A telegram had been dispatched to the Towers the day after the shipwreck, and everything was in splendid order when Sir Edmund welcomed Gladys to the home he had thought never to share with her.

Everyone knew there had been a reconciliation.

The vicar, Joshua Heath, who, without asking proof of her innocence, had befriended Gladys when all others forsook her, greeted her with honest pleasure.

He did not know her secret, but he knew she had never been guilty of what she had been accused, and his kind face glowed as he shook hands with husband and wife—the two between whom he had pronounced the deathless bond which, at the beginning, had been so rudely rent.

"Heaven bless you both!" he murmured, fervently. "God has joined your souls, and only when it is His will shall they be put apart."

There was not much time to think over the past.

They intended staying in England for only a short time, and before they set out on fresh travels there was a great deal to be done.

There was a letter waiting for Gladys, which had been forwarded from Cairo.

It was from Frank.

He had not yet found Garth. He enclosed a London address where she was to write him news of herself, and she was not to be anxious on his account, for healthy freedom had changed his haggard looks, and there was no chance now of his being recognised as the outcast.

Gladys wrote a long reply, telling him everything that had happened since he had left her.

She begged him to seize the earliest opportunity to pay her a visit, and to accept the friendship her husband was all eagerness to give.

There was also a letter for Sir Edmund from Beatrice.

She seemed to be tiring of her wild life, and she spoke of returning to England.

"Osman adores me as madly as ever," she wrote, "but it is in a savage kind of way. Sometimes I am frightened of his hot fierce nature; I think if I displeased him he would kill me."

She did not hint anything about Gladys, for was not her name a forbidden word between them?

Sir Edmund bit his lip as he remembered how he had disowned his wife in the presence of his half-sister, and he felt he could not say enough in Gladys' praise to recompense the wrong he had done her.

How did he know Beatrice might be Gladys' worst enemy? That her restless unsatisfied soul still craved after the wealth he held so lightly—the wealth which was to pass to her, and to her children, if Sir Edmund should have no nearer heir.

He wanted Gladys to send Beatrice a message, pressing her to join them in some fair winter city.

But in this he found his little wife very stubborn. Her pride rebelled against giving pardon unasked to the girl who had insulted her with such cold cruel distrust, and she sent no word to Beatrice.

Frank went to the Towers a few days after hearing from Gladys.

He was in the best of spirits when he arrived, and seemed determined to make everybody else as cheery as possible.

"My sister has told you what I am?" he asked Sir Edmund, when Gladys had introduced them.

"She has told me everything, poor child."

"And you have sufficient faith in her and in me to believe when I tell you I am not guilty of that for which I was condemned."

"I never yet doubted the word of a man of honour—such I believe you."

"Thanks!" Frank exclaimed, and then, for the first time, he grasped Sir Edmund's extended hand, too proud to press acquaintance on one who had once doubted, till he knew no shadow of the old suspicion remained.

They persuaded him to remain their guest till their appointed time for leaving Deepwood, greatly to his danger and their own.

If he were discovered there, what proof had they to shield him from the iron grip of the law?

Frank would not encourage any misgiving of this kind.

He had completely escaped detection. He felt his liberty now was quite his own, and with his fortune, which Gladys managed to place entirely at his disposal, he was enabled to live like other independent men—no longer a fugitive.

Gladys hinted once or twice that it might be better to let things rest in their present state, and not try to penetrate the strange mystery of crime surrounding him.

Frank indignantly rejected the idea.

"What! live all my life under a cloud without daring once to face the world openly? Not I. I do not fear my enemy enough for that. It is he who shall fear me—he who shall cringe before me, as a slave before his judge. His own guilt shall accuse him, and he will not escape his punishment."

"By Jove! I admire your pluck," Sir Edmund exclaimed, looking approvingly at the flushed boyish face —so like, and yet so unlike Gladys'. "It's a dangerous game, but I think it is worth the run, and as far as it is in my power to aid you, you know you can place full reliance on my assistance."

Sir Edmund got on capitally with Frank. The straightforward enthusiasm with which he expressed his feelings, at once won confidence, and Sir Edmund only had one regret concerning him—that he had not met his wife's brother sooner.

They were leading a very quiet life at the Towers, yet it was by no means a dull one.

The old homestead was to be vastly improved upon in their absence, and there were long consultations over the choice of a new set of panels, or on the advisability of replacing old Dutch-tiled stoves with new ones.

"You may say what you like on the subject," Gladys said, looking lovingly at some dingy hangings in a chamber which had not been occupied since Mary Queen of Scots had once rested there; "but I don't think the modern antique is anything compared with the real *bona fide* Early English. I wouldn't have this dear old tapestry touched for the world."

"Then you won't have the new stove in the west drawing-room, after all?" Sir Edmund observed, amused to see what a little animated her, when that little was in the interest of their home.

"It would certainly be a great improvement," she answered, thoughtfully, "and the design we selected was very lovely. What do you think, Frank?"

"If that's the west drawing-room we just came through, I think it is in a thoroughly dilapidated condition, and, unless it is to be shut up altogether, its antiquity would lose nothing by being revised; and there would be a good deal more comfort to be got out of it."

"This wing has not been occupied for more than a century," Sir Edmund put in. "It is quite Gladys' idea to have it thrown open. I had intended having a new wing added, but she wouldn't hear of leaving this old tower to crumble into ruins; I believe she was right."

"Of course she was!" Gladys declared with an air of pride. "You ought to adorn every stone of this wall, for hasn't it been your forefather's stronghold since the Conqueror defeated poor Harold on the field of battle?"

"It's awfully cold, though," Frank said, unsentimentally, "and intensely gloomy on a day like this. I wonder you are not afraid of a ghost stealing behind you in your shadow Gla."

She laughed, and then shivered slightly as the long-closed-in dampness struck round her.

"I wish you had not spoken like that, Frank," she murmured, all the careless gaiety leaving her face; "I shall dread coming here by myself. The place really does look fearfully weird."

She had grown quite white, and when Sir Edmund touched her, her hands were icy cold.

"Why has this wing been unused for so many years?" she asked, looking straight into his eyes.

He drew her close to his side.

"I hoped the foolish story would never be told to you, darling. It was once believed this tower was haunted, but of course it was all nonsense, and since Sir Egbert's time, nobody has thought much about it. Now that you know why this corridor has so long been deserted, would you like it shut up again?"

"Yes; you and I can go through the room sometimes when we are together. I don't think we should like any alterations made in this tower. There may be a ghost standing behind every one of these panels—it would be terrible to disturb them!"

"You are trembling, Gladys. I ought not to have allowed you to come. Who thought that you were a little ghost-believer? I imagined you would treat such a fancy with scorn. Frank is right; this gloom is awfully depressing. We had better get back to our own quarters."

Gladys did not regain her spirits till she was in the dining-room, where there was a great fire blazing on the hearth, and the warm glow of shaded lamps making everything look cheery.

Dinner was not yet served, but after having been startled about ghosts, she preferred waiting till Frank and Sir Edmund joined her.

They followed almost directly, and were both grateful for the pretty home picture she made, kneeling on a magnificent tiger-skin in front of the fire, her black velvet dress, with its deep ruffles of fine old lace, looking quaintly picturesque.

A King Charles spaniel was in her lap, its head nestled against her hand; and as Sir Edmund took in the exquisite grace of the half-recumbent figure, he felt proud to see her there and to know she was his.

"Had man ever so sweet a fairy in his home as this one who makes my hearth beautiful?" he exclaimed, as he sank in a chair beside her.

Gladys sprang lightly to her feet, the little King Charles hugged up in one arm, her eyes radiant as they met her husband's gaze.

"Yet you would have let me live in those weird rooms without even telling me the ghost legend," she murmured, with a reproachful smile; "a dreadfully mean thing to do!"

Sir Edmund gave a short contented laugh.

"Be just, Gladys. Whose wish was it to have the old wing used?"

"Yours."

"Gladys!"

"It was to please me."

"Ah, that's better. Come, lady hostess, when are you going to take your place?"

Gladys' bright glance flashed over the great solemn-looking table, then she took her seat close by his side, Frank opposite.

"I cannot imagine why we do not have the house full of guests," she said, suddenly, looking rather disconsolately at the blank stretch of table-cloth. "Since I know the place is haunted, I think we ought to fill the rooms with as much life as possible. It would never do to let the ghosts have it all their own way."

"I do not remember ever hearing of more than one ghost in connection with the old tower," Sir Edmund observed, placing a dainty helping of roast fowl before her. "And that a very harmless one—the ghost of a little child."

"Have you seen it?" with breathless interest.

"I don't think anyone has. It is only supposed to haunt the place with its cries. It is thought that the child was murdered, but his fate is not known to this day—he disappeared."

"How terrible!" Gladys said, with a shudder. "I shall not mind the ghost now I know it is only a poor little child. It is strange I never heard the story before."

"It was thought best to let the superstition die out of date. I almost wish I had kept it from you. You must promise me not to think any more about it. That's a jolly little dog, Gladie; where did you pick him up?"

"Frank got him for me."

"You ought to have your picture done with him, Gladys. I must look up a good artist."

"There's one very near you. Frank paints splendidly, but I shall not sit for my portrait yet. It isn't necessary, is it, Ned, unless you think I am going to die. Do you?"

"My darling, I had not such a thought! What put such an idea into your head? I think I shall have to follow the suggestion you made just now, and ask a few friends down till we leave Deepwood."

The blood leapt up into Frank's face.

Was it not for his sake the doors were closed to visitors, lest any should question his presence and detect the shadow hanging over his head?

He rose impulsively, and stood with his hand on the back of his chair.

"I have much to thank you for," he said, quietly, addressing Sir Edmund. "I know my presence has prevented you having any friends. To-morrow I will leave. It is not right that I should throw a cloud on your home."

Sir Edmund understood the fierce deep pain which had wrung these words from the outcast.

He, too, rose, and laying his hand on Frank's shoulder, pressed him down into his seat.

"Not another word like that, Frank, or I shall think you have not understood me. One thing is clear—if filling the house means driving you out of it, we three must be content with each other's society."

"I had almost forgotten that," Gladys murmured, angry with herself for her thoughtlessness. " How selfish I must seem to you, Frank! Now I reconsider the matter, I will sit for the picture. I should so like you to paint it, Frank. What shall we do this evening—go to the piano, or to the billiard-room?"

"Billiard-room," Sir Edmund replied, promptly, and when they were all three bending over the long green table, watching every turn of the game, their faces were as eager and as intent as if life itself depended on their skill.

Frank had the first game, and after a hot close fight, he gave a triumphant "Hurrah!" as Sir Edmund's last ball shot into the silken net.

Mentally, he had staked the chief aim of his life.

If he lost, he was to take it as a sign that he would lose in the great struggle he was bracing himself for— that struggle with an unknown enemy ; if he won, it was to be the signal of his future success.

The interest of the game had run high—how high was known alone to Frank—and he had won !

CHAPTER XXII.

THE next morning the lake having been well grounded by three days' hard frost, they all went skating.

Frank had not been on the ice since he was a lad, nevertheless he managed to leave a few strange figures in his track—extraordinary devices that Gladys looked at with wonder.

With her hand firmly clasped in Sir Edmund's, she skimmed along by his side as lightly and as swiftly as a bird, her face aglow with the free fresh exercise.

The morning was beautifully clear.

No snow had fallen, and the lake looked like a huge sheet of glass, brightened by occasional gleams of sunlight that shot out through the white clouds.

"How would it be to have a race by torchlight to-night?" she exclaimed.

"I think you will find this morning's run nearly enough. I wouldn't advise you to do too much all at once. We have one more week at Deepwood, and, if the weather does not change, you can have as much torch-skating as you like; but to-day——"

"To-day you will not let me! Why?"

"I am not sure the lake is sound enough to bear."

"Hicks tried it, and said it was as solid as if it had been freezing for a month."

"Hicks would say anything to please you, Gladys; I suppose he trusted to my looking after you. It is as firm as a rock where we are now; but I wouldn't answer for what might happen to anyone who outstepped Hicks's boundary."

"I believe you are not half enjoying this fun. Are you really anxious? Stay here while I test our safety."

Before he could prevent, her hand broke from his clasp, and she glided swiftly away from his side.

SIR EDMUND'S HANDS CLENCHED AND HIS EYES GLITTERED STRANGELY AS HE MET HIS SISTER'S GAZE.

He called to her, his voice weighed down with anxiety. She only looked back over her shoulder and laughed—fearless, because she felt sure of her safety—because she believed Sir Edmund's misgivings to be the consequence of his over-care for her.

She did not know her danger; she had been on riskier footing many times, and no harm had come to her.

She reached the outer line Hicks had marked—the line of danger—and, governed by some daring impulse, she rushed heedlessly on—on to the far end of the lake, where the ice looked dark under the bent trees.

Again Sir Edmund's voice, stern in its great dread, made her glance back.

He was close upon her, his face white with angry pain.

"Gladys, take care—stop!" he exclaimed. "Gladys—do you hear me?—stop!"

Frank, suddenly roused to her peril, took up the cry, and tore after her.

Then came a moment when the two men paused in horror.

There was a sharp brittle sound. Sir Edmund, with his lips set like stone, flung himself forward and seized Gladys' dress, snatching her from a dark brink as the ice broke under her.

He reeled slightly; the glassy ground heaved beneath him. Another instant, and they would both have been struggling in the deep caved water.

There was only one way to save her.

He felt the ice give way under his feet, and holding her firmly, he swayed backwards, and bore down on his shoulder.

His arm struck with a dull sharp thud, and he released Gladys.

"Don't lose a moment—drag yourself backwards!" he exclaimed. "The ice is breaking! Frank, take care of her for Heaven's sake!"

Frank drew her out of danger, and sprang to Sir Edmund's assistance.

"A narrow escape, old fellow!" he said, as he clutched Sir Edmund's coat. "Gladie deserves to be bullied for this."

Sir Edmund's face had grown deathly white; he shook off Frank's hold, and seemed to wrench himself to his feet. For an instant he stood erect. Then there was a crashing grinding sound, and he disappeared—down—down—one hand alone groping above the closing waters.

With a terrible cry, Gladys rushed to the jagged edge of the ice, and would have flung herself into the lake to clasp that wandering hand, had not Frank thrust her back.

"Keep away, Gladie, and I will save him," he muttered huskily. "Fetch help!"

Gladys could not move.

She stood looking on, powerless with fear and horror.

She saw the dear face rise above the floating ice, then sink down into darkness; once more it rose, and the despairing hand clutched Frank's outstretched arm.

Gladys could look no longer.

She shrank down shuddering. A struggle was going on—a struggle against death, and she had no strength to save her husband from the dread power that had seized him.

Someone rushed past her.

Frank's words rang dimly in her ears—"Fetch help!"

With a wild effort she conquered the faintness weighing upon her, and rushed after the flying form.

Her cry had been heard by one of the gamekeepers, and Sir Edmund was saved.

"Thank God!" she whispered, as she knelt beside him, and lifted his head in her lap. "My dear, dear love!"

He smiled up into her white face, then consciousness left him, and he lay on the chill ice like one dead.

"I am afraid his arm is broken!" Frank said in a low voice. "He threw all his weight on it at first. We had better carry him into the house, Morrison."

The gamekeeper helped to raise him, and Gladys held one of the cold numbed hands in a passionate clasp as they bore him home.

They laid him on a couch in an ante-room, where a bright fire was blazing, and a surgeon was immediately sent for.

Gladys waited in an agony of suspense until medical help arrived.

"It is all my fault," she moaned despairingly. "I have nearly cost him his life! How selfish—how utterly unworthy his care I am!"

She flung herself down by the couch and called his name pitifully.

He was deaf—immovable—and when the doctor came, she looked at him with wild eyes, and asked if her husband would die.

"I trust not," was the reply she received. "He is in a critical condition, but I have no doubt in an hour or two he will be conscious that he lives. I think it will be best for you to leave him for a little while, Lady Etheridge. You shall know directly there is a change for the better."

Gladys left the room reluctantly, and waited miserably for the word that was to summon her to her husband's side.

No day had ever seemed so long as this one weary hour of suspense.

When Frank went to her, and told her Ned had asked for her, hot tears blinded her eyes, and she could find no voice in which to express her overwrought feelings.

Sir Edmund had been removed to his own room, and he was lying in bed, his face white with suffering.

His eyes brightened as Gladys entered, and he put out one hand to her—only one—for the other was bound helplessly to his side.

His arm was broken, and where his head had struck against the ice there was a deep gash, covered with a linen bandage.

"Can you ever forgive me for this?" Gladys murmured, kissing his hot forehead. "I shall never skate again, Ned. It is a terrible lesson."

"I do not care, darling, so that you are safe."

"But you—you are suffering horribly. I wish I had fallen through the ice before you had time to know what had become of me! It was what I deserved. I am not worth the pain you gave yourself in saving me."

He closed his eyes and drew her hand against his lips.

"This does not hurt much," he said, resting his aching head against her arm. "But if harm had come to you, I should have gone out of my mind. I am thankful the suffering fell to me instead."

Orders had been given for him to be kept quiet, as a guard against brain-fever, and Gladys was afraid to encourage him to talk, precious as his tender forgiving words were to her.

She and Frank watched by him all through the day, and late in the evening the surgeon looked in again.

"Will he get well soon?" Gladys asked wistfully. "Is he better than when you left him?"

The doctor shook his head.

"I don't wish to frighten you," he replied gravely, "but it is best to tell you at once. Sir Edmund will have much to go through before he can get about in his old way. There will be a painful operation on his arm when his nerves are more settled. In the meanwhile, the only thing we can do for him is to keep his mind entirely at rest."

Gladys was wretchedly disappointed.

She went back to her post with a heavy heart, and kneeling down by the sick man's couch, she laid her head on his pillow and gave way to a few silent tears.

Sir Edmund lay so still she imagined he was sleeping.

A soft touch on her head roused her, and she saw his tired eyes gazing compassionately upon her.

"Don't grieve, darling," he said, stroking her bright hair; "I can bear anything except seeing you unhappy. So long as you stay near I shall not complain about being ill."

"But when I know I am the cause of all your suffering!"

"Nonsense, sweet. I am only disappointed about one thing—we shall have to finish the winter here instead of going abroad. When Frank goes you will find it dreadfully dull, Gladys."

A look of measureless love shone in her large clear eyes.

"With you?" she asked, a tremulous smile giving the purest touch of beauty to her face. "I could not be dull anywhere with you, Ned."

"You do not know yet, little love."

"Yes I do," hiding her face so that he could not see the soft tears in her eyes. "I can never forget what my life was away from you—it nearly killed me, Edmund."

"What misery can come of one mistake!" he exclaimed dreamily. "This is a strange world, Gladie."

"A sweet world when we find love in it," she whispered, with shy happiness. "I am almost glad we are not going to Italy. Here we shall have to be everything to each other—you and I. I shall not let anyone except myself nurse you, or do anything for you while you are ill. You must make me your second life."

He smiled fondly into the child-like face, so full of gentle faith and love.

"'The life of my life' is what you should say," he replied, tightening his clasp on her warm clinging hands. "Sweet little wife, God keep you always by my side!"

He closed his eyes, and sank into a fitful sleep, his breathing heavy and irregular; he had no power to control the fever oppressing him.

Frank looked anxiously at the pale face, with its heavy eyes and parched lips.

To him Sir Edmund seemed to be sinking into a worse state, and he hardly knew what this restless sleep boded.

After midnight he persuaded Gladys to go to her room, and leave him to watch the patient.

"There's a couch at the foot of the bed, where I can lie down," he said, gently compelling her to go towards the door. "I shall hear if he makes the slightest movement, and I am really a capital nurse, Gladie."

"I shall not rest away from him," she murmured, turning wistfully from her brother. "I would rather stay, Frank; I cannot bear leaving him. He may miss me when he wakes."

"He would be sorry to see you sitting up, wearing yourself out," Frank argued. "Besides, it would be a wasted watch, Gladie. While he sleeps, what pleasure can there be for him in your presence? To-morrow, when he would be glad to have you near him, you will be tired out and fit for nothing. Take my advice, dear, and save your strength for greater need; you don't know what may be required of you yet."

Gladys went to her room reluctantly, having exacted a promise that if Ned should ask for her, Frank was to knock softly at her door.

A fire was burning brightly in her room, and her maid waiting to know if her service would be required any more that night.

Gladys had made up her mind to sit the night out in a cosy chair wheeled near the hearth.

The presence of her maid dispelled this idea, and she thought it best to act on Frank's advice.

"Get me my white quilted dressing-gown, Mary," she said, putting her hand wearily to her head; "I shall keep it on all night, so as to be ready if Sir Edmund should wish to see me."

"Yes, my lady," Mary responded in a subdued voice. "Shall I sleep in the ante-room to-night? You may require me if you are disturbed."

"You may as well, Mary. Put a shade over the candles, and then you can go to bed at once. I will call you if I want you."

Mary shaded the light, and drew the rose-coloured curtains round the bed.

Then, finding there was nothing more for her to do, she left the room.

Gladys could not make up her mind to lie down.

Sitting with the fire-glow warm about her, she rested her head back on her clasped hands, and kept her gaze fixed anxiously on the door.

She was listening for a sound—for a breath, and she could not put her heart at rest.

She knew she could trust Frank to take her place to-night.

Yet she could not get her thoughts away from the sick-room.

Perhaps while she sat there brooding, Ned was awake, and looking round for her; perhaps he was in horrible pain, his head tossing restlessly on his hot pillows?

With these thoughts throbbing through her brain, it was torture to shut herself away from him, to gaze into the fire, while the clock ticked time to the long weary night.

It seemed an endless time, yet only half an hour had passed since she had said good-night to Frank—since she had watched Sir Edmund's feverish sleep.

If he were awake and in pain, how lonely—how long the night would seem to him!

The suspense prayed on her soul. She started up, and went quietly to her husband's door.

Only silence. Some instinct must have warned Frank she was there, or else he heard the sweep of her dress against the panels.

He opened the door, and motioned her not to speak.

"He is still asleep," Frank whispered, standing aside, so that she could see Sir Edmund's colourless face, deathlike in the shadowed light, made uncertain by the flickering fire-flames.

"Will he be better when he wakes? Is this sleep a good sign?" Gladys asked in a low tone.

"In his case it is the safest medicine—the best healer," Frank replied, cheerily. "Go to bed, Gladie, and leave him to me. If you worry yourself like this, you will be invalid to-morrow instead of nurse."

Gladys' gaze lingered wistfully on her husband's face as she moved away.

She turned once, and sighed heavily. She was disappointed. There was nothing for her to do. Her presence only made Frank anxious, and the sound of her step might perhaps disturb Ned's rest.

She must wait till to-morrow.

She went back to her room, and, sinking on her knees, sent a brief prayer up to Heaven.

A hot tear fell on her folded hands as she murmured Sir Edmund's name. Then she rose, and cast herself wearily on the bed.

She had no thought of sleeping, but gradually she lost herself in a dream, and when she awoke the candle had long burnt out, and the grey winter morning sent a dull light into the room.

She sat up and pulled the bell-rope—lightly, lest the sound should reach Sir Edmund.

Mary answered the summons almost immediately. She had been up since daybreak, knowing that directly Lady Etheridge awoke she would want attendance.

"Will you enquire at once if Sir Edmund is better?" Gladys asked, hurriedly.

"I have done so already, my lady. They say there has been no change. He is the same as he was yesterday."

"Let me have my bath, Mary. I promised to relieve Mr. Frank directly the night had passed."

Gladys was not long completing her toilette. A refreshing plunge in clear bright water; the tangle of gold-bronze hair gathered in a rippling knot; then, hurrying on a pretty morning robe, she went straight to Sir Edmund's room.

The door was shut against her. The doctors were before her.

She paced anxiously up and down the corridor, and when she was at last admitted, Sir Edmund was prostrate on his pillows, his lips drawn with suffering.

"The worst is over," the surgeon said in answer to her looks of wild questioning. "He has only to keep quiet and get as strong as he can. Everything now depends on the care he receives. I think we shall have to send a trained nurse——"

Gladys glanced appealingly at Sir Edmund. He understood, and at once rejected the offer.

"I have an old housekeeper who thoroughly understands the order of a sick-room," he interposed. "For the present, at least, the stranger would only be in the way. If I am not able to help myself in a day or two, I will consider the matter again, and give you a different answer."

A reproachful look from Gladys brought a smile to his lips.

"Do you think you will not tire of the task before half the week is out?" he murmured, when the doctors had taken their leave. "It would not be fair to let you wear yourself out in a sick-room. I have acted very selfishly in refusing the nurse."

"Is it selfish to please me, Ned?"

"I pleased myself more, I am afraid."

"That is impossible. I should hate anyone who took my place."

In spite of his sufferings, Sir Edmund could not repress a smile.

How much sweeter to have this flower-like face bent over him in wistful despair, than to endure the practised care of a stranger!

"I cannot allow you to give up all your time to me, darling; you must go out with Frank——"

"When you are well enough to go with us, I will."

"Come, wild rose, that's a very unpractical way of speaking. Because I am locked up for a time, is your health to be sacrificed? You are not over strong, my little one, and I cannot afford to have you ill again."

"Only one thing could make me ill," Gladys persisted, "and that would be if anything prevented my being near you when you most need me. I shall make this our drawing-room till you are quite well. We will have a big yule-log on Christmas Day, and shut out the snow and wind; and I will sing you all the sweetest carols I can remember. I only wish I could be the sufferer instead of you."

"I wouldn't change places for the world, Gladys."

He spoke in such a careless contented tone, forcing a smile to his lips, she could scarcely understand the agony he had endured within the last hour while his injured arm was being operated upon.

Her presence had a soothing influence. The touch of her hand dispelled pain, and when she was near he forgot his suffering, or felt it only as the penalty paid for the deeper love she was giving him.

"As we are going to have it all to ourselves, I hope Frank will give up his idea of leaving us, at least till some change takes place," Sir Edmund said later in the day. "We shall miss you awfully, old fellow."

Frank looked pleased.

"I shall not go till something very urgent drives me away," he answered, the fire sending a ruddy glow over him, as he stirred the red embers into a blaze. "I would be your guest always, if I dared."

"What is to prevent it," Gladys asked, forgetting the danger of the secret which had branded his life.

Before anyone could answer, a servant entered with a letter.

Gladys took it from the tray, and gave it to Sir Edmund.

"From Beatrice," he muttered, glancing at the inscription.

The utterance of her name seemed to invoke an ominous silence—a silence broken at length by Sir Edmund.

"She will be in London in a few weeks, and will visit us at the earliest opportunity."

"I must leave before she arrives," Frank remarked gloomily. "There need be no secret about my being

Gladie's brother—but I don't think it would be wise to let her see me—not if the mistake could be explained without my presence."

So the home-harmony was to be broken.

"You must stay until after Christmas," Sir Edmund persuaded, his voice betraying little pleasure at the news of his half-sister's home-coming. "We shall not give you up, old man, before it is absolutely necessary. Beatrice is so changeable: we may have a letter to-morrow contradicting this."

His prophecy was not correct; no other message came from Beatrice.

CHAPTER XXIII.

HEY spent a very quiet but a very happy Christmas.

Sir Edmund was able to leave his bed, and to lie on a couch in the dining-room, where they had spent so many homely evenings together.

The dark walls glowed with holly, the tasteful arrangement of which had been Frank's work, and he amused them with such a store of lively anecdotes that they had no cause to regret having no other company.

He wished them both good-bye on New Year's Day, promising to write from time to time, and to send them word where their letters would reach him.

There was no more skating for Gladys that winter.

All her time was taken up with Sir Edmund, and often when she gazed at his pale patient face, a pang went through her heart. He seemed to get well so slowly. Sometimes she feared that he would never have the free painless use of his limbs again.

The bitter January snows faded from the earth, and Beatrice had not arrived at Deepwood.

She came one windy March evening, looking bright and beautiful as in the old days before she had become Osman Omar's wife.

She had not sent them word when to expect her, and when she arrived at the Towers, Gladys was at the piano singing a sweet half-forgotten duet with Sir Edmund.

The lamps had not been brought in yet, and as the firelight revealed the two figures to Beatrice, she gave a start of surprise, and hurried forward.

" Edmund ! "

The song ceased.

He turned at the sound of his name, and greeted his sister.

"Well, Triss, I thought you had quite forgotten us!" he exclaimed, all the aching pain gone that had been in his voice when he bade good-bye to her at Cairo. "Are you alone? Where is Osman?"

She gave a short petulant laugh.

"Oh, you may depend he is somewhere in my track," she answered, carelessly. I told him to remain in London till I sent for him. I hardly think there is any hope of his carrying out my wish," then turning suddenly to Gladys:

"Do I know this lady? It is not——"

"It is Gladys," he said, putting his arm round his wife and drawing her gently forward. "Kiss her, Beatrice; there has been a dark mistake; we did her a great wrong."

"When?" Beatrice asked, coldly.

"On the morning of our marriage. You remember those photographs? The gentleman was her brother."

"Did she tell you this?" with quiet scorn.

"Yes. Come, Triss, no sneers. Gladys has much to forgive. She must be a saint to look over the past. Our harshness came very near to killing her, poor little girl! At least tell her you are sorry for what she has suffered."

Beatrice drew back proudly, a contemptuous smile on her lips.

"You should have prepared me for this, Edmund. I cannot so easily change my ideas concerning the girl you married. You are ill—mad, I fear—or you would not for a second time have given way to her influence."

Sir Edmund's hands clenched, and his grey eyes glittered strangely as they met his sister's gaze.

It was hard to stand by while Gladys received this insult.

Had the sting came from any but Beatrice's lips he would have fiercely resented it.

Yet, remembering the bitter blame he had once cast on Gladys, how could he expect a different bearing from one who did not know that which he had since learned?

"There must be an understanding between us at once, Beatrice," he said, firmly. "You must take my word and Gladys' for the truth of what I tell you. She has been truer to me than I deserve, and we all did her a great injustice when we believed otherwise."

"A pity she did not explain this sooner," Beatrice interrupted sarcastically.

"Her silence proved greater courage than many, tried as she was, would have possessed," Sir Edmund replied hotly; "with one word she could have righted herself, but she would not speak, because she would have been compelled to tell another's history as well as her own. It is not necessary for me to say more. If you choose to blind yourself to the truth, I shall not try to persuade you further—only my wife shall not receive anyone as a guest who will insult her with sneers and unbelief."

Beatrice gave a low, derisive laugh.

She was fiercely disappointed. After Gladys' name had so long been a forbidden word—when she had built all her hopes on the thought that her brother had lived down the memory of his short wild love-dream, she found him reconciled to the wife he had sworn he would never acknowledge.

"I must commend you on the easy way in which you have allowed yourself to be deceived," she said, mockingly; "your faith in woman does you credit. I am grateful for one thing, that you and I no longer bear the same name."

"I don't think you have gained much by the change," he replied dryly.

The proud face flushed angrily.

"We need not quarrel, Edmund. I am only sorry for you, because I know to what this blind trust will lead. I should not have come had you warned me of the state of affairs. I think I will return at once to my husband."

She held out her hand to Sir Edmund.

He took it and retained it for a moment.

"Be reasonable, Beatrice. I only ask you to believe what is true and just. There is no need for you to rush off in this rash headstrong way. If you go, you will regret parting like this, some day. Gladys, see what you can do convince her."

Gladys slipped her hands on his arm and shrank closer to him, preferring that he should fight her battle.

"I can do nothing," she answered, gravely; "if she cannot trust your word, how will she mine? Besides, so much is against me, and I can explain so little. You know my heart—you have full faith in me; I can bear distrust from everyone else—for poor Frank's sake."

The last words were added in a very low tone—so low that they did not distinctly reach Beatrice's ears.

Sir Edmund gave the little hands resting on his arm an affectionate pressure—a warm firm touch that re-assured Gladys, and brought a cloud of contempt to Beatrice's brow.

"We must give her time, my darling," he murmured, glad to find she had strength to endure the old hateful accusation without burdening her soul with misery; "Triss will understand by-and-bye."

"I understand too well already," Beatrice responded, bitterly. "You were mad, Edmund, once having rid yourself of the girl, to let her steal again into your life! She came to us a stranger, and with a lie on her lips. Did she not say her brother was dead—that she had no relative living? Even if her last story was true, and her supposed dead brother had conveniently taken up an existence, what reason had she for not identifying him with the man she met in the woods? It was time, I think, when her name became the byword for a revolting scandal. I pity you, Edmund!"

"Does a man, who feels himself one of the most blessed on earth, need pity?" he asked, with a proud smile.

Beatrice turned away impatiently.

"You are blind!" she muttered.

"Not I. It is you who will not see the truth."

"If you could explain this mystery, which seems such a mass of contradiction, I should be glad to believe the best. Where there is no sin, there should be no secret."

"There is a secret, though—a very heavy one, too."

"I suppose you share it?" with soft sarcasm.

"Yes; thank Heaven, Gladys told me everything. The only fault I have against her is that she did not confide in me sooner. I was blind when I doubted her, Beatrice; now all her past actions come back to me with a different meaning. If these should be my last words, I solemnly declare that Gladys met nobody but her own brother in the woods."

Beatrice felt this belief was firmly rooted in his mind, and knew she would do no good by holding out in opposition.

It would be best, she thought, to appear unconcerned, and to let events take their course.

A more penetrating look into Gladys' face had made her fate seem less certain. Sir Edmund's wife had changed since she had seen her last; though her face was flushed and her eyes full of dreamy love, there was a *spirituelle* delicacy about her, a flower-like purity of form and colouring that belong to those destined to die young.

This idea struck Beatrice forcibly, and she felt a shadow was hanging over her brother—a shadow he little dreamt of : his fair wife would fade from his side, and leave him desolate.

Beatrice was comforted by this thought. If all progressed as she imagined, there would still be a chance of her dead father's fortune reverting to her.

Already she had felt the need of civilised wealth.

Arabian life, when once the novelty had dulled, became irksome. She had never cared much for the young chief.

His passionate adoration for her had been the one charm he possessed in her sight. Now even that had lost its fascination, and she saw in him only a handsome savage who, at the slightest provocation, would become her tyrant.

It was a relief to be out of reach of his dark, fiery glance.

After a few moments' consideration, she made up her mind it would be better to remain at the Towers, and keep a vigilant watch over Gladys.

She could lose nothing by acting thus, and there was much at stake that might be won.

Sir Edmund was glad she had come to more peaceful terms, and Gladys was of too sweet a nature to bear malice.

Instinctively she knew Beatrice disliked her, but, while she was sure of Ned's love, she could pass over every unkind word levelled against her, and, if she could prevent it, no domestic discord should make their home miserable.

Beatrice rebelled against the quiet life they were leading.

"I could not endure this existence!" she exclaimed, when she had spent two days at the Towers. "It was gloomy enough in the old days, but it is unbearable now! I hope you are not going to turn invalid for the rest of your life, Ned. I never knew anyone else make such a fuss over a broken arm."

"It was not only his arm," Gladys said, reproachfully. "His accident was a very serious one."

"So I imagine, seeing the dull state it has brought him to. The best thing would be to invite a few nice people down. I don't believe in shutting oneself up when one is ill."

Sir Edmund laughed good-naturedly.

He had expected this from Beatrice; he knew too well her passion for pleasure to dream that she could live with them as Frank had done, and he was ready to fall in at once with her wishes.

"Give me the names of all the friends you would like to meet, and Gladie and I will send the invitations," he replied, willingly. "I have shut myself out of society so long that I hardly know where to begin."

"Would it not be best to let Gladys choose her own guests?" Beatrice asked, kneeling down on the hearth-rug, and gently stirring the fire so that the flame lighted up the face she was scanning.

"I do not know any whom I should care to ask, except those I met in Paris."

"Were you in Paris with Edmund? You did not tell me this."

Gladys met the piercing glance with proud wonder.

"We travelled there from Naples. We were ship-wrecked on our passage from Cairo. Ned did noble work that night. His cheering voice and steady hand gave courage to everyone on board. I shall never forget him as I saw him then!"

"Then you both stood the chance of drowning?" Beatrice said, lightly. "Did you make any friends or acquaintances while you were in Cairo, Gladys?"

"One—an invalid lady."

"Do you mean to say you did not have any admirers? I should have thought, being alone in a strange country, everybody would have been interested in you. You ought to have no end of romantic stories to tell us, or are you afraid of rousing Ned's jealousy?"

Beatrice noticed the quick flush of pain which passed over Gladys' cheek, and her suspicion against her deepened; she was surprised when Sir Edmund answered for Gladys:

"I could give a very sad account of a man's head-strong love, but I think my little girl would rather not have it mentioned."

"Did it concern her?"

"Greatly."

"What was the man's name?"

"Ernest Dudley."

"Did you meet him?"

"I never heard of him till he was dead. He fell desperately in love with my poor little wife, almost before he had exchanged a dozen words with her, and when he discovered she was already married he stabbed himself."

"What a tragedy!" Beatrice exclaimed with a curious laugh.

She was jealous; she herself would have preferred being the heroine of such a mad romance.

It was waste, she thought, for a man to throw away his life because Gladys had crossed his path.

This trustful understanding between husband and wife annoyed her, too.

She had imagined her persistent questioning would plunge Gladys into a state of confusion. She was surprised by the easy manner in which Sir Edmund answered her, and she felt that whatever had been in the past, Gladys had no secret from her husband.

"So you do not care about asking anyone down?" Beatrice said, after a pause. "I assure you, you will not persuade me to remain long in this seclusion; I have had to bear enough of it with Osman."

"But, my dear girl, have I not told you that you only have to say whom you want to meet, and we will act at once on your suggestion."

"Well, begin with old friends—Sir Montague and Lady Diedrich, Captain Morris, Chris Randall, Richard Garth——"

Gladys started up with a low exclamation of terror.

"Not Richard Garth," she whispered, with white lips.

"Why not?" Beatrice asked, her quick suspicions aroused.

"We do not even know where he is," Gladys said, brokenly.

"But I do; and what is more, I have asked him to call as soon as he can. I don't think he knows there has been a reconciliation between you and Ned. It will be almost as great a surprise to him as it was to me."

Gladys looked at Sir Edmund with horror in her eyes.

"He must not come," she muttered, feverishly. "He must not be our guest, Ned. Remember what I told you——"

"My darling, do not alarm yourself. He shall never cross this threshold till he has answered the question with which I shall confront him."

Then turning to his sister, Sir Edmund said, firmly:

"Richard Garth must be left out of the party. I dislike and mistrust him; until I know more of him I cannot allow him to become my guest. I should be glad if you could tell me where he is. I have business with him."

A bewildering silence followed his words; before Beatrice could frame a reply the door opened, and somebody was ushered into the room.

"Mr. Garth!"

He stood before them, the firelight shining full on his dark evil face, the old mocking smile in his eyes and on his lips.

His gaze flashed on Gladys like lightning, and taking all in at a single glance, he stepped hastily forward, and held out his hand to her.

"I am happy to meet you thus," he answered, bending his handsome head, "by your husband's side."

Gladys drew back, and slipped both her hands in Sir Edmund's strong clasp.

"I am sorry you have come," she said, coldly; "I did not want to see you."

CHAPTER XXIV.

GARTH'S face clouded ominously.

He shook hands silently with Beatrice, then turned again to Sir Edmund.

"I do not know what I have done to merit such a strange reception," he said resentfully; "I have always tried to serve Lady Etheridge, as far as it was in my power; but it seems I am unfortunate enough to have invoked her displeasure, and yours. I should like to know how I have offended."

Sir Edmund looked sternly into Garth's face.

"Follow me into the library and I will tell you," he answered shortly; "we can speak more freely alone."

Garth hesitated.

"What is there to conceal from these ladies?"

"Much. Come."

Gladys watched them anxiously as they left the room, longing to follow them, yet not daring to leave Beatrice, who might want to share the confidence between them.

"Really," Beatrice exclaimed, fiercely pulling the bell, "this is most singular behaviour. Edmund must certainly be out of his mind; he must have injured his head greatly in that accident. I think Mr. Garth hardly understands him. It is to be hoped nothing serious will come of their interview! I am quite uneasy about them."

She turned to the maid who had entered the room in answer to her summons, and ordered lamps to be brought in directly.

"I beg your pardon, Beatrice," Gladys said, lighting the pretty painted candles on the mantel-shelf with her own trembling hands; "I am ashamed to have been so forgetful. You must be tired after your journey. I will order dinner to be served at once, and while they are getting it ready, I will take you up to your room.

It is just the same as when you had it in the old days. Before Ned's illness, we thought of having the Dark Tower redecorated, but I persuaded him not to have it touched when I discovered it was haunted."

"Haunted? What nonsense? Whoever told you so?"

"Ned did."

"Another proof of his madness! I wonder you are not afraid to live with him, Gladys."

Gladys smiled, and her large trustful eyes softened.

"Afraid?" she echoed, gazing at Beatrice, as though she feared the Arab's beautiful wife were the one who had lost her reason. "Oh, you do not understand Ned —or me."

"You certainly are a very strange pair," Beatrice replied coolly, flinging down her hat and cloak, and going to the looking-glass. "It is not an easy thing to make either of you out. I should like to know what this new prejudice is against Mr. Garth. Is it one of poor Edmund's manias to see in him a possible rival?"

"He knows I dislike Richard Garth more than I do anybody else in the world."

Beatrice raised her delicate eyebrows contemptuously.

"What nonsense! I wonder Ned takes notice of your absurd fancies. I am sure if Richard Garth was good enough to be dear mamma's guest, you need not have your doors closed against him, especially when he comes as my friend! I shall not think of snubbing him."

"Please yourself, of course," Gladys answered, wearying of the subject; "but I think if you knew as much of him as I do you would not care to shield him. Are you ready to go down now?"

"Quite. I hope that mysterious interview is ended— and, Gladys, for goodness sake do not send Mr. Garth off. If you and Ned are company enough for each other, you must remember that I want a little cheerful society. I like Richard; I often wish I had been his wife, instead of Osman's."

Gladys gave a look of cold horror.

"You may thank Heaven for having spared you such a fate," she said, gravely. "I advise you not to place too much trust in him till you know more of his past. I do not speak without a reason."

Beatrice turned away from the glass with a careless laugh—proud, defiant, dauntless.

"Such vague hints cannot frighten me, prophetess," she replied as they went downstairs. "I am determined not to take up this prejudice. I shall keep true to Richard."

"He is unworthy the trust," Gladys answered, sighing as the remembrance of Florence's fair pathetic face rose before her. "Ned will find better friends for you. Mr. Garth is a traitor!"

Gladys uttered the last words with suppressed passion, and for the first time Beatrice noticed how white she was, and that her eyes were full of a watchful dread.

Evidently Gladys was pressing some great strain on her feelings.

She had been talking lightly, as if all her mind had been with Beatrice.

But one glance at her, as she passed under the big hall-lamp, on her way to the dining-room, showed that she was suffering from nervous excitement.

Beatrice noticed the swift uncertain step, the feverish clasp of the small hand on the balustrade, and the look of subdued terror and suspense directed towards the library.

She saw all this, and wondered more and more what this mystery meant—what this secret was which was being kept from her.

HER ARMS CLUNG ROUND HIS NECK, AS THOUGH SHE DREADED SOME UNSEEN FORCE WOULD TEAR HER FROM HIM.

Beatrice followed Gladys into the dining-room, and waited.

Once or twice they heard Sir Edmund's voice raised in anger; but they could not understand what was said, and they each drew their own conclusions.

"I think we have left them long enough," Beatrice exclaimed impatiently. "Ned is so dreadfully hot-headed. One hardly knows what insult Mr. Garth may have to bear."

Gladys' pale lips trembled a little, yet she controlled herself, and drew Beatrice into a cosy chair placed near the fire.

"We had better wait till they come to us," she said, stooping to stroke the silky ears of the King Charles who had been faithfully following her since Beatrice's arrival. "I wonder if they will leave the library friends or foes."

One glance at the two angry men would have set any uncertainty on this point at rest.

Sir Edmund was standing on the hearthrug, the leaping fire-flames seeming to set his grey eyes ablaze, his broad brow fiercely knit, his hands clenched, as though his sinews ached to grapple at the enemy who smiled on his rage.

"I kept her secret," Garth was saying. "What else was I to do, knowing her sensitive nature? It would have been a sure way of killing her to have exposed her brother."

"You, at least, could have given me a clue to the truth. What I cannot forgive is that you, knowing her innocent, stood by like a coward while she was grossly insulted; you even left her to the mercy of strangers, who knew nothing of the noble self-sacrifice those meetings meant. Besides, what reason had you—you who could do no good for the sake of good—what reason had you for screening her brother? What do you know of him?"

"Only that he was charged with fraud, and condemned. You know best what his life has been since his escape."

"Do you believe him guilty?"

Garth threw himself back in his chair, as though the keen penetration of Sir Edmund's eyes annoyed him.

"Should I have helped him if I had thought the punishment he escaped just?"

"I don't know. I think you would do anything to serve your own purposes."

Garth started, so slightly that his surprise could scarcely have been noticed by any but the closest observer.

"What motive could there be in sheltering a poor devil driven as Frank Clifton was?" he asked carelessly. "Out in Australia I was always his best friend, and the shock was as great to me as to him when they arrested him. I never believed him guilty. He was such a confiding, such an open-hearted lad. It seemed impossible to me that he could have evil in him. There is not much chance of his innocence being proved, but as long as he can keep the law-hounds out of his track he need never be the worse for the miserable accusation. I'm glad to say I succeeded in getting him a safe berth in Cairo."

"Rather a dangerous place to send him to," Sir Edmund put in dryly.

"For him?"

"No; for you!"

Garth's lips tightened fiercely, and his hands clenched on the side of the chair.

"Of course, of course!" he muttered hoarsely. "It is risky work helping an escaped convict to conceal himself."

Sir Edmund was watching him with eyes that seemed to dart into Garth's soul.

He moved uneasily in his seat, and a look of smothered hatred came over his dark face.

"You mistake my meaning," Sir Edmund said with chill decision. "I refer to danger to you that might arise through the discovery of your own secret—your wife."

"She is dead. Why do you call back the past pain? She is dead—poor Florence!—let her name rest."

Garth had risen to his feet, his face ghastly white, his strong frame trembling.

"Your wife!"

Those words seemed to have stunned him. His breath came short and thick through his clenched teeth.

Was his sin finding him out already? Had the Arab betrayed him? What did Sir Edmund know of Florence?

"Don't call up the past," he repeated huskily; "she is dead!"

"Dead!—so you thought when you left her. Afraid to look on your crime, you left the work but half done. Florence Garth lives!"

"Whoever told you so is mad," Garth said in a low distinct voice. "I tell you again that she is dead."

"Then who is the girl who calls herself Florence Garth—Richard Garth's wife?"

"A lunatic most likely. I know nothing of her."

But she knows much of you. She told Gladys everything—more than enough to place you in a murderer's dock. She believes you caused her child's death, and tried to poison her. If what she says be true, you—"

Sir Edmund stopped, silenced by a fierce grip on his shoulder.

Garth had confronted him, his face pale and clammy, his eyes dull, like lead.

"What are you saying?" he whispered with livid lips. "The woman is mad—mad, I tell you! Why do you repeat her ravings to me—me, on whose misfortune she has set her frenzy? If even the story were true—if Florence lived—do you think she would not follow me—the more surely to bring her wild charge against me—supposing such a crime as you speak of to have been committed? Do you think her loss was no grief to me? The sight of her dead face froze my soul; she was like a lily, so pure and so beautiful. To hear her name linked with this horrible story sets my heart on fire—my poor sweet Florence!"

Sir Edmund had never seen a man moved as Garth was now. His voice, husky with desperate passion, broke down, and his breast heaved tumultuously.

He acted his part well. It was hard to disbelieve him —hard to doubt the cause of his emotion.

Sir Edmund disliked him; yet he could not help feeling pity for him as he saw the fierce spirit torn by this tempest of pain.

Perhaps, after all, he had misjudged him. Florence's story seemed vague and improbable; and what Garth had said was true—she was mad.

Sir Edmund's fierce suspicions were overcome at sight of Garth's grief. The man could feel. He was not the hardened callous brute Sir Edmund had thought him; and the girl, with her white wavy hair and her weary eyes—the girl who shrank from Richard Garth's name with such wild horror—was mad!

"Bear up, Garth," he said in a kinder tone; "you know best whether what I have said be true or not. To me it seems impossible that any man could take pleasure in life with such a vile blot on his conscience. I don't think you are so bad as that, Garth. The story was strange, and the girl's manner impressed Gladys."

"Lady Etheridge is only a child," Garth muttered, pulling himself together. "I can forgive her her belief against me, though I thought my loyalty to her brother should have secured me a better opinion. She chose to suffer rather than betray his secret; I took my cue from her and kept silent; besides, how could I prove the man's figure in the photograph to be that of her brother? The face was hidden. At the time I was as mystified as anyone else present. The truth did not flash into my mind till long after."

There was a covered meaning in the last words that sent the blood flying to Sir Edmund's brow.

"What do you mean?" he exclaimed angrily. "Are you trying to throw poison on the faith I have in my wife?"

Garth smiled, and put his hand to his forehead, as though the discussion wearied him.

"Certainly not," he answered gently; the fact I want to point out to you is, that where every proof is missing, either of innocence or guilt, suspicion becomes dangerous. We are too ready to believe ill of our fellow-creatures."

"Well—well, let it all end here. You have given me your word that there is no truth in the story told by the poor girl in Cairo——"

"As God is my witness—no!"

Sir Edmund shivered as he looked at Garth, standing with the red glow of the fire on his upturned face, his right hand lifted above his head, as though invoking the heavens to bind him to his oath.

What curse had he called upon himself—this man who had no faith in the power to which he appealed?

He smiled, as he saw Sir Edmund turn away, for in his heart he knew he had lied—lied deeply and successfully.

CHAPTER XXV.

HE smile was still on Garth's face when he followed Sir Edmund into the dining-room.

Gladys drew back a little when she saw him, and glanced enquiringly at her husband.

"How white you are, Edmund!" she whispered, as she took her seat by his side. "Are you not so well to-night?"

"Better than I have been for a long time, pet," he answered, not wishing to impress her with the gloom that had suddenly come over him. "How the wind howls! It is like the roar of a hundred lions."

"A bitter night to turn a starving dog out," Richard Garth put in, in his rich persuasive voice. "Have you the heart to do it, Lady Etheridge?"

Gladys' brow darkened with fear as she met his gaze, and she looked at Sir Edmund for an explanation.

"We have misjudged him," was all he said to her, for he felt that Beatrice was watching them, and he wanted her to have no clue as to the cause of their disagreement.

Garth smiled, and sank into the chair next to Beatrice, unasked. Impelled by an uncontrollable impulse, Gladys rose, and moved away from the table.

"The bread would choke me that was shared with him!" she explained, her lips quivering with scorn. The air he breathes seems to stifle me. I cannot stay in the same room with him."

"I never saw so much home-tragedy in my life," Beatrice murmured, amused at the scene. "I shall imagine soon that I have fallen into a house full of lunatics. This kind of thing has been going on ever since I arrived. Pray do not take any notice, Mr.

Garth; I assure you, as there is so little courtesy shown, the only thing is to look upon the place as a Liberty Hall. I have had a tremendous journey. I wish you would get me some soup before it is too cold to be touched."

Gladys' little hand closed feverishly on a string of pearls clasped round her throat, and her sweet face grew pale with the outrage put upon her pride.

Knowing what she did of Richard Garth, was she to be forced to endure his presence—to have him at her table—he, a deserter—a murderer?

She recoiled with horror from the thought, and all the firm strength of her pure nature rose up against him.

She glanced at his white, cruel-looking hands, that had poured death into a child's innocent sleep, and her thoughts flew to Florence, the pale wraith-like woman, whose story to her rang with saddest truth.

Sir Edmund had all the straightforward truthfulness, all the honest unsuspicion of a grand old Saxon race.

He was always ready to believe the best of everyone, and Gladys felt that Garth had been successful in deceiving him.

Beatrice, too, was taking part against her. Gladys wished she had never come. Had they been alone, they could easily have sent Garth away; but Beatrice seemed to have made up her mind to entertain him as her own guest, and Gladys felt her will would be set at defiance by them both.

Sir Edmund knew Gladys was making for herself a bitter enemy, and he wished she would bear with this dark man's presence, for her own sake.

My darling, don't let us keep Triss waiting any longer," he said, taking her hand, and trying to draw her again into her chair. "No Etheridge has yet been accused of inhospitality; besides, dear, Garth has quite cleared himself of the strange suspicion we had against him."

She shuddered, and drew back like one shrinking from some great terror, for the first time bringing her will before his.

"No, no!" she exclaimed passionately; "he has deceived you! He is cruel and base as a man can be! I will not count him amongst my friends—I will not degrade myself by receiving as my guest one I so utterly despise! If you wish him to remain, I can do nothing to prevent it; but I will not stay in the room where he is!"

Her spirit was roused; she felt every word she uttered, and her eyes gleamed with an intense scorn as her gaze swept down on Richard Garth.

If innocent, would he brook this insult? If he had any righteous pride, would he stay after that speech?

Gladys watched him with feverish intensity, her gaze searching deep into his soul; and for a second time her fair beauty called an image of Florence to his mind.

He could have struck the sweet accusing eyes, that had in them the deep soft light which had shown in the guileless face of his wife.

She understood the look he gave her—the look of hatred which shot out a mute challenge. She saw the power, the triumph, and turning from him to Beatrice, she knew that with these two might rest the destruction of her life's happiness.

She lifted her hand and pointed to his evil face, a strange smile on her hot lips, her heart throbbing fast under the necklace of costly pearls.

"Look!" she said, her voice vibrating with scorn. "Would he bear this, if I had wronged him as you say I have? Who, with man's pride in him, would sit there, while I stand, offering no apology, though he knows I am leaving the room to avoid him! Believe him, or believe me, I tell you he is a traitor!"

An expression of distressed pain crossed Sir Edmund's brow; but Gladys did not wait for an answer.

She flung Garth a look of bitter reproach, and then turned her back upon him.

Swift as her movement was, before she reached the door, his had was on the handle.

"Allow me," he said softly. "I am sorry to have incurred your anger; I hope before I leave Deepwood to win back your favour."

"It was never yours," she answered coldly; and as she passed through the doorway, she caught the fierce whisper meant only for her ears:

"Take care! If you betray me, your brother's freedom—perhaps his life, shall pay the forfeit! Remember the power I hold over him! Offend me, and I will set men on his track who will drag him back to the living death from which there will be no second escape! He shall stand again in the felon's dock, again in the convict's cell, and your name shall share the dark brand that is on his!"

The door closed between them with a sharp click, and Gladys stood out in the great oaken hall, stunned, trembling in every limb, those cruel words burning into her brain.

She pressed both her hands to her brow, and leaned faintly against the carved panelling.

To what had her pride led? She in the power of this man she hated—hated because of his evil doings!

What did he expect her to do? To endure his presence in her house always? Perhaps, as she was to bear his secret, he would in time force her to become his accomplice—force her to help him in his wicked scheming against poor Florence.

He seemed suddenly to have become a living terror to her.

She knew he would not spare his power over her—knew that he would make her suffer for the scorn she had given him to-night.

To her, those brief sentences hissed in her ear were the confession of his guilt.

He feared her as much as she feared him. If by word or look she accused him, he would denounce Frank.

They were quits; silence was bought with silence; she dared not defy him.

She could hear his voice, soft, musical, alluring, and she knew he was trying to put Sir Edmund's mind at rest concerning herself.

"And Edmund believes him—Edmund will trust him!" she thought, sickening at the sound of the low mocking laughter that seemed intended for her ear. "Oh, how much more must I bear for Frank's sake? If only there had never been that first terrible secret!"

A servant, passing through the hall to the dining-room, found her standing there, staring blankly before her, like one stunned by some heavy shock.

"Are you ill, my lady?" the girl asked in a frightened voice.

Gladys started, and tried to overcome the wild beating of her heart.

"It is only a slight faintness," she murmured, passing swiftly up the staircase. "If Sir Edmund asks for me, say I have gone up to my room to rest. Do not bring anything up to me; I have no appetite to-night, and I want to be left quiet."

"Very well, my lady."

It was no use giving way to dreary reflections. If troubles would come, the best thing was to bear them as lightly as possible; and, determined that Garth should not be their sole guest, she dashed off invitations to everybody she knew, including those whose names Beatrice had mentioned.

Sir Edmund was surprised to find her busy with her pen when he went to see how she was getting on an hour afterwards.

"How desperately determined you look!" he said, smiling as he stooped to kiss her. "What a pile of letters! I had no idea you had such a heavy correspondence."

"I am asking a party down," she answered, laying her pen aside, and slipping her hand in his. "The more people we have, the more time we shall have to ourselves; they will look to each other for amusement instead of to us. It is difficult, when there are only two guests, to leave them. What is Beatrice doing?"

"Playing billiards with Garth. They seem to get on wonderfully well together, those two."

"Yes; I don't think either of them will miss us much. I wish Beatrice had never formed that friendship for him. Has she asked him to stay?"

"Her invitation was a command, and the fellow seemed willing enough to obey. I don't see what excuse we can find for sending him off. We have been hard on him, Gladie. I wonder he took it so quietly. He said the woman who imagines herself to be Florence Garth is mad. He was right; you told me the poor girl had lost her reason."

"When she spoke to me about herself she was sane," Gladys replied, looking at him with intense earnestness. "I wish we had never left her as we did! We might have brought her over, and have let her meet Richard Garth, only the sight of him would be death to her. She shrank from the thought of him as if he were some great hideous serpent. I shall never forget the horror that was on her face when she heard his name."

"My darling, it was simply the exaggerated terror of a frenzied brain. Garth would not have dared take the oath he did if there had been truth in the story. You must try and conquer this fancy, dear."

Gladys shook her head with a sharp little sigh.

"It is no use, Ned; you will never change my opinion of Richard Garth."

"Am I to tell him to go?"

She started, and her eyes had a frightened look in them, as she answered him:

"If he wants to stay, let him—for Frank's sake."

"But if his presence annoys you, Gladys, he shall not remain under this roof a day. I couldn't have my little wife made miserable for anybody."

"We must think of Frank. I am frightened for him, when I remember that Richard Garth has the keeping of his secret."

"He has guarded it well enough all this time; I hardly think he is likely to turn traitor now. Did they bring you up any dinner?"

"I told Mary I did not want anything."

"Well, you will have to eat something now to keep me company. Your absence quite took away my appetite."

Sir Edmund rang the bell, and gave a brief order to Mary, and in a few moments a dainty repast was placed on the table, drawn cosily up near the fire.

"I am afraid you spoil me terribly," Gladys said, the great love she bore her husband rushing high in her heart, as she saw with what thoughtful care he tended her. "Somehow, you make me feel like a penitent child, Ned; as if I do not deserve the dear kindness you lavish upon me."

She caught the hand that was ministering so gently to her, and pressed her cheek against it, then her lips.

"My king! If you only knew how much I love you!" she murmured passionately. "Kiss me, Ned, and look into my eyes. This sweet love seems to lift my soul away from me; it is like a touch of heaven—a living dream! Oh, Ned, if anything should part us now, all the world would not hold such anguish as would be in my heart! I think I should kill myself in the mad torture."

Every pulse in the slight frame was thrilling with the tumult of feeling that shook her.

Her arms clung round his neck, as though she dreaded some unseen force would tear her away from him.

Sir Edmund's eyes softened as he looked at her—as he drew her bright head in firm warm rest against his breast.

"My own! Why do yo pain yourself with such cruel thoughts?" he said, his voice full of fond reproach. "We are together—man and wife—nothing but death shall put us asunder. Poor little Gladys—poor little heart! I wonder when all this restless fear will be forgotten? Let me see you smile, darling, or I shall imagine I do not know how to make you happy."

"I am too happy," she whispered, with a deep restful sigh; and then she looked at him with such a glorious light on her face that for a moment Sir Edmund felt the dull dread of her words.

If they should be again parted—if he should lose her —what would his life be worth?

He crushed her to his heart with unconscious passion, then, afraid lest she should read the sudden fear which crossed his soul, he kissed her softly, and released her.

"How soon will you be ready to come dawn, Madame Truant?" he asked, when he had coaxed her to eat a little. "We shall have Beatrice in search of us presently."

"It is so sweet to be by ourselves," Gladys said dreamily; "I wish we could live in some beautiful Paradise right away from the world, where we could love on for ever and ever. I feel sometimes that I do not want to hear any sound but your dear voice, or to see anything but the smile which comes to your face when I am near you. I want to live only for you."

Sir Edmund gave a short happy laugh.

Those tender words were very precious to him; they were treasures that gladdened his soul.

He felt the worth of this pure love, wrapped so slosely round his life, and inwardly he prayed that Gladys might never be taken from him.

CHAPTER XXVI.

EATRICE and Garth did not long remain the only guests.

Gladys' prettily-worded invitations met with a prompt response, and the house was soon full.

She had asked Beatrice to persuade Osman Omar to come down.

But the Arab's wife scarcely seemed to wish for his presence, and Gladys learned afterwards that there had been a quarrel, and Beatrice, in one of her proud bitter moods, had left him.

There had not been so much gaiety at Deepwood for a long time as there was now.

There was plenty of good fishing for the gentlemen in the fresh breezy mornings; and Sir Edmund kept a fine stud.

Garth made himself famous by writing a play full of sparkling incident, and he and Beatrice took the leading characters, delighting everyone with their splendid acting.

"It is a pity her husband is not with her," one lady said, her thoughts diverted from the play by something in Garth's voice and look, as he repeated his passionate love-sentences, Beatrice, her brilliant loveliness brightened by a dress of glittering embroidery, clasped to his breast. "She is very young, and very, very beautiful. Richard Garth—not *Leslie*—is the lover, and it is Beatrice he holds to his heart. That is not acting."

"Not acting? It's the most superb acting I have ever seen!" another answered, not understanding, and the one who had spoken first was silent.

Nobody else saw what was being enacted before them —nobody else suspected that the fiery words they applauded in *Leslie* were uttered with all the fervour of heart-felt passion.

Long after the play was ended, Richard Garth and Beatrice still kept up the characters they seemed to have lost themselves so completely in. Garth was always *Leslie*, and Beatrice never ceased to be *Cynthia* —his love.

No arrangements were made for a return to Italy.

At the end of six weeks all the guests excepting Beatrice, had left the Towers, and she, dreading the return of the old monotony, urged Gladys and Sir Edmund to go up to town for an early season.

There they were again thrown in contact with Richard Garth.

Riding in the Row; in a crowded ballroom; at the opera; even at the slowest reception, he was always one of the first to greet them.

They seemed never free of his presence.

The Arab paid a visit to his wife directly he knew she was in London, but Beatrice did not hide the dislike she felt for him, and he left her with words full of hot fierce pain.

He was compelled to go to the East to aid in the recovery of some rare jewels that had been stolen from him; treasures that would, perhaps, buy him a kind word from Beatrice when he could place them in her hands.

He had asked her to go with him, and she had refused.

"I cannot," she had answered, with scorn on her bright lips. "The jewels are not worth having if I have to fetch them myself; but if I know you have risked your life for them, why then, of course, they will be very precious."

"More precious yet, if for them my life is lost!" he retorted, his eyes flashing like covered fire as he looked at her. "Hark you! If it should be so," he added, seizing her hands in a fierce grip; "if the price of them should be my life—if ever you forget me—if you shut me out of your life, a cold blighting curse shall come to you from the grave! Woe be to you and to the one who usurps my place! In my absence I trust you, because you are my wife; but—if you deceive me, Beatrice, I will kill you!"

He uttered the words in a hoarse whisper, his hands clenched hard on her delicate wrists, his eyes glaring into hers.

Then, with a passion of wild love, he seized her in his arms, and covered her face with burning kisses.

"Good-bye!" he muttered. "Good-bye! One day you shall love me, Beatrice, or one day I will kill you!"

A sudden fear shadowed Beatrice's eyes, and she shuddered in his embrace.

He did not heed that she shrank from him almost with loathing.

He kissed her lips again and again, then with a passionate lingering look, left her.

"I wish we might never meet again," she murmured, when the sound of his step had died away. "It was a mad fate that threw him in my way! I believe in the end he will kill me."

Before he left England, Osman called on Richard Garth, and begged him to take care of Beatrice, if, in his absence, she should need a friend.

Garth promised, and the Arab started on his journey, eager to fulfil the long task before him, that he might the sooner return to Beatrice.

Gladys had seen much in Beatrice that made her sorry for Osman, and the *bon voyage* she had wished him at parting was full of unconscious sadness.

Beatrice disliked him, and to Gladys, in whose gentle little heart love was the sweetest hope, his lot seemed cruel and undeserved,

She knew what it cost him to take this journey alone, and she felt that Beatrice's place was by his side.

Beatrice scarcely seemed to notice his absence.

She was already the rage of the season. Her marriage with the Arab, the wandering, extravagant life she had led with him in the East, wove a charm of romance about her, and she was courted, admired, and flattered, more than she had ever been before.

To her the time seemed to burn itself away like wild-fire, and as the season drew to a close, and Sir Edmund talked of returning to Deepwood, the old restless discontent came back to her.

"Why can't we go to Paris for a month?" Beatrice asked petulantly; "I hate the thought of Deepwood—I know what it means!"

Sir Edmund bore her remarks good-naturedly.

"We will go wherever you like in a few weeks, Beatrice; but I have business down in the country which must be seen to first, unless you and Gladys would care to go by yourselves, and leave me to follow?"

"We could do that very well," Beatrice answered eagerly. "I really do not see what occasion there is for us all to go down."

"I do, though," Gladys said quickly, slipping her arm through Sir Edmund's, and nestling her head against his shoulder. "As if I could leave you! I would rather stay with you at the Towers than go to Paris."

"Well, what is it to be, Beatrice?"

"Oh, let Gladys decide!" she exclaimed scornfully. "I have told you once what I wish."

Gladys looked distressed; she could not bear to thwart Beatrice—to cross her will so often; and yet, how could she make up her mind to leave Ned?

"It would be much better to put off the journey, and all go together," she said wistfully. "I think a week in the country would be very enjoyable just now. London is so dreadfully warm."

"But who wants to stay in London?" Beatrice asked impatiently. "Everybody is going to Paris; why should we not follow? We can get up a party for Deepwood afterwards. As for the business you have there, Edmund, I dare say you could get through it easily in a day. I suppose it is only to look at some improvements you have had made."

After a long discussion, it ended in Beatrice having her way.

Sir Edmund postponed his appointment, and arranged to go to Deepwood early in September.

He did not like to disappoint Beatrice, and he thought it would be as well to spend a month in Paris, and return in time for a good shooting season.

As to Gladys, it mattered little to her where she was while he was with her; and she was relieved that Beatrice's pleasure was not to be sacrificed to hers.

There, as in London, Garth followed them like an evil shadow, Beatrice always encouraging him; Sir Edmund trusting him; Gladys hating and fearing him; not daring to betray the loathing with which she shrank from the touch of his hand, when in the presence of others he forced her to endure the familiar greeting that was such a bitter ordeal.

She had to be guarded in her manner towards him.

If she gave anyone a clue to her dislike for him, she knew how he would resent it.

The world must not see him as she saw him—not yet. When Frank's innocence was proved; when Frank was beyond the power of his threat—time enough then to search out Garth's secret.

Often and often Gladys wished Osman would come back and take his wife away.

She felt that while Beatrice was with them they would never be rid of Garth, and there were times when his presence was a constant terror to her.

A sharp despair gripped her heart when, just before they left Paris, she heard Sir Edmund ask him to join them at Deepwood.

She was not prepared for Garth's answer.

"Thanks, my dear fellow; but I do not think there is any chance of my returning to England till after Christmas. I am obliged to go to Germany to look after an estate that will one day be mine. It doesn't do to neglect those things too much."

Gladys gave a sigh of relief; for a time at least this evil shadow was to move away from her life!

Directly Garth had gone out of the room, she hid her face on Sir Edmund's arm, and burst into a fit of passionate tears.

"Oh, Ned, I am so glad he is not going back with us," she exclaimed; "I could hardly believe when I heard him say he could not go—it seemed too good!"

Sir Edmund turned her face gently up against his breast, and looked long and searchingly into her beautiful eyes.

"What a strange little girl you are!" he said, and there was almost pain in his voice. "I had no idea his presence could affect you so much. I will not ask him again."

"It does not much matter. He will come whenever he wants to," she replied wearily. "Still, it is a relief to know we shall not see him for a few months."

It was a relief indeed to Gladys. She went back to the Towers as light-hearted and happy as a child.

Sir Edmund smiled sometimes as he watched her. It was as if some bond had been lifted from her bright spirit, and she reminded him of a bird released from its cage.

"What makes you so happy to-day?" he often asked her, when he had listened to a snatch of some sweet song that rippled from her lips as she walked under the great rose-boughs, gathering flowers for her vases.

"Because Mr. Garth is not here," she would answer, with a brighter light in her eyes. "It is lovely to wander about without the fear of meeting him."

Even Beatrice did not much regret Garth's absence when some of Sir Edmund's college friends came down for the shooting, and they scarcely ever started out on their morning excursions without her.

They tried to persuade Gladys to follow and watch the sport.

The shrank from the proposal, her gaze resting on Sir Edmund, full of grave reproach.

"The sight would be one of pain, not pleasure," she said pitifully. "Do you think I could see a bird fall with its poor wings broken, and leave it for the dogs to tear? It is most cruel amusement! You do not seem to understand how horrible it is to make targets of living things."

Her words did not impress her hearers very much.

Sir Edmund laughed and kissed her, amused at the reproachful glance she gave him as he took up his gun.

He was glad she preferred remaining at home.

Trudging over the moist fallen leaves, with the wood-mists clinging about her, would do her no good, and he knew she could choose this time for writing to Frank.

It never occurred to him that she might fret those hours away in watching and listening for his return.

One morning he was struck by a wistfulness in her eyes, as she watched him strapping on his bag.

"I don't think I shall shoot to-day," he said, throwing his gun aside. "How would you like me to drive you down to the White Pass, Gladys? We might get those doves you took such a fancy to."

"Don't be too rash, Ned," Beatrice put in quietly. "We arranged that we should take our last shots to-day. There are so few of us left; I hardly see how we can spare you. If Gladys would rather not be left at home, why doesn't she come with us? She would find it much more amusing than the drive."

"I am afraid not. What do you think, Gladys?"

"If this is to be the last time, I would rather wait till you come back for the drive. You will not stay out later than two, and I can finish my screen; it will be my only chance, and I want to paint all the lilies myself."

Sir Edmund looked at her doubtfully.

Her eyes did not meet his quite steadily, and the sweet voice had a tired ring in it.

Was she disappointed because he was going shooting again, knowing he could not take her with him, or did she really wish to finish her lilies?

Beatrice's voice broke in upon his thoughts:

"We are wasting time, Ned. Is it to be yes or no? Are we to start without you?"

"You had better go," Gladys urged, feeling it would be a sacrifice for him to give up this last day's sport. "It is only parting for a little while," she added, smiling tenderly into his bronzed face. "We are making nearly as much fuss as if you were going on some long strange journey! Here is your gun, Ned; everybody is waiting for you."

He took his gun from her fair little hands, and pressing a warm kiss on her cheek, he made at once for the woods.

He turned often to wave his hat to her, as she stood watching him from the window, a gleam of autumn sunshine resting on her head, her soft lips parted with a smile that made his heart lighter, his step quicker and more buoyant.

How handsome he looked, as he turned for the last time, and stood with the brown leaves falling on his bare head, the steadfast love in his eyes reflecting a silent message to her.

"Good-bye—good sport!" she murmured, pressing her lips to her hands, and stretching them out towards him. "Pride of my life, my love—for a little while, good-bye!"

He could not hear the words, but he almost knew what she was saying; and as he stepped into the thicket he kept his face turned towards her, waving his hat again and again, till the trees hid him from her sight.

Good-bye for a little while!

Alas! they knew nothing of the fate that was waiting to rush between them.

A last smile, a last fond signal—and they were parted.

Long after he had disappeared, Gladys stood there gazing at the spot where she had seen him force a passage through the tangled branches, her eyes full of trustful love.

She fancied she could still see him, still hear his quick firm tread, and she smiled dreamily as the soft breeze played on her brow, the breeze that swept up from the woods where he was walking.

Was there nothing to warn her—nothing in the sigh of the wind, in the dull falling of the withered leaves?

He had gone with careless words on his lips—lips that would have clung to hers in mute agony, if he had known what this parting meant!

Gone—for how long? When would that brave face turn to her again?

 *   *   *   *   *

Dream on, Gladys! Smile before the knowledge of what is in store deadens the light in your eyes!

When the sun sets there will be a dark awakening, a bitter heart-broken cry for the one who is gone!

CHAPTER XXVII.

IT was the last time Ned would leave her for his gun—that cruel toy she could never touch without a shudder.

Gladys consoled herself with this thought, and tried to feel contented as she opened her paint-box, and put a few finishing touches to her screen.

She was in too restless a mood to sit long over the lilies. She threw down her brushes, and skimmed a few chapters of a novel Beatrice had left on the table. The story did not interest her, and laying the book aside, she went to the piano.

Music had no charm for her this morning. She got up impatiently and looked at the clock.

They had scarcely been gone an hour. How long the days were! After all, it was a pity she did not make up her mind to go with them. Perhaps they would come home earlier than usual.

She walked through the conservatories and cut a basketful of flowers; then selecting a lovely rose, she laid a spray of maidenhair against the pale-pink petals, and stuck it in her waistband, ready to give to Ned when he came back.

When he came back! Alas!

She could hear them firing, and she shrank from the sound as though with each shot the life sacrificed were that of a man, instead of a bird. It seemed cruel sport to her, and she wondered how Beatrice could delight in it.

She went in, and looked again at the clock. The hands had scarcely moved. How the minutes dragged!

Gladys walked to the window, then went back to the hearth—undecided, restless, impatient.

GLADYS KNELT ON THE GROUND AND DREW BACK SOME OF THE TANGLED VINES.

No. 11.

" I will go and meet them," she thought; " I am not in the humour for painting this morning. Those lilies look so meaningless and staring; I am tired of them."

She ran up to her room and put on her hat and cloak, then hurriedly leaving the house, she followed in the track of the shooting party.

When once she plunged into the brushwood, it was not an easy task to find what paths they had taken.

She only disturbed the game, and ran the risk of getting shot.

She called, but nobody seemed to hear her, and determined not to be baffled, she went on fearlessly, thinking if she took a circular path she could not fail to come upon someone belonging to Sir Edmund's party.

She had gone deeper into the woods than she imagined, and she was rewarded at length by seeing between the brown leaves a flash of crimson she knew belonged to Beatrice's dress. Gladys tried to overtake her.

" Beatrice, wait for me!" she called, pushing her way through the thick brambles. " I have had such a wild chase after you! Where is Ned?"

Beatrice must have heard her, yet she did not pause or look back. She seemed to dart away as though that bright clear voice had startled her—stealthily, like one seeking to conceal herself.

" I did not know Beatrice was so nervous," Gladys thought, stopping the pursuit, as the glow of crimson vanished swiftly in the distance. " I have given her quite a fright. She ought to have known my voice, though. I hope she does not take me for a poacher! She had her gun with her. Under the circumstances it is lucky for me she did not fire in this direction. I wish I knew how to let Ned know I am here. I suppose I shall come across somebody else soon. Beatrice would not be by herself."

It seemed to Gladys that the shooting was going on far away at the back of her, but Beatrice having just fled past her, she felt certain she was in the right track.

She called again, and listened eagerly for an answer.

One of Sir Edmund's dogs bounded between the trees, sniffing the ground as he ran backwards and forwards.

"Good dog—good Cæsar!" Gladys said, trying to keep him at her side. "Where is your master? Find him!"

Cæsar hung down his head, and ran forward. Gladys followed, wondering vaguely if the dog were in pursuit of his master, or of game.

He was searching for someone or something, tearing back from time to time, and throwing up his head with a dismal howl.

Gladys followed him into the very heart of the woods, and when once or twice she lost sight of him, a strange fear took possession of her.

Alone in this wild deserted spot, what would she do if her guide forsook her? how find her way out of this dark labyrinth?

A long miserable howl from Cæsar sent a chill through her veins. Her heart gave a dull throb, and she felt every drop of blood recede from her lips as she hurried to the spot from whence the sound came.

Cæsar was tearing up the dead leaves with his paws, and scattering a mass of brambles that trailed on the ground.

"What is it, Cæsar? What do you want?" Gladys murmured, shivering as the dog's piteous howls echoed around. "Fetch your master; you will not find him here."

The dog did not seem to know her voice, it was so low, and had such a frightened ring in it. What did she fear?

Impelled by sheer force of instinct, Gladys knelt on the ground, and drew back some of the tangled vines.

Beneath, and deep down, was the dark gleam of shadowed water—a well, black and fathomless, with handmarks and footmarks on the rugged edge that told a cruel heartbreaking truth.

Gladys pushed off her hat, and with both hands pressed to her temples, looked wildly round.

Her eyes caught the glitter of something lying near, and her gaze fastened on it with mad horror.

It was Sir Edmund's gun, fallen like a dead thing on the wet moss at the edge of the well.

Oh, sad token of a pitiful fate!

No more need to wonder, no need to search farther. She had looked her last on the face she loved—all ended here.

The horrible truth flashed like lightning into her brain, and she crouched there in a pale frozen heap, the dog's deep howls sounding like a dirge in her ears.

Ned was dead—dead while the day was still fair and bright. Close by, where shots sounded, they were all laughing and making merry. Nobody had missed him yet. He had gone down to his death alone, and his dog had brought her to the spot that was his grave.

His grave! She had lost him for ever! Had heard his voice for the last time—for the last time had felt the clasp of his strong caressing hand.

He was dead—drowned! And she had parted with him with light words, had watched him go with a smile on her lips.

Her agony seemed to crush her. An hour ago her life had been sheltered against sorrow by the strength of his love; she had never thought that she might lose him, that her spell of happiness could be so suddenly shattered.

He had sunk down under the dark still waters. Oh, if she could only see his face once more! But to know that he who had been so full of strength and careless ease one brief hour ago, was lying there maimed, broken, lifeless, beyond human reach, swept from the face of the earth for ever!

"Ned—Ned! Edmund!"

She called his name in wildest anguish, but the cry, so full of racked pain, did not seem to come from her poor white lips.

A dull cold heaviness made her limbs like stone. It was as if all feeling were being drawn from her by some slow power, a power that deadened the body, and left the mind tortured with vivid thought.

Her brain was hot with the frantic desire to fling herself down the well, to join in death the one she had loved with all her life.

She looked at the black stirless waters with wide hungry eyes, and had not power to hurl herself forward.

The dog whined dismally, and licked her hand.

The touch roused her; she gave a piercing cry, and seizing the gun that lay against her dress, she hugged it to her bosom, and pressed her lips to the chill steel.

Was it true she had looked her last on him? Were these the only traces she would find of her dear lost one —the gun he had carried so lightly on his shoulder, and the dog that had followed at his heels?

She rocked herself to and fro in an agony of tearless grief. Suddenly, before she was conscious of the danger, the lace on her sleeve became entangled round the trigger, and there was a sharp report as the charge in the gun exploded. Fortunately Gladys, though greatly startled, was unharmed. The sound of Sir Edmund's gun brought those who were by this time searching for him to the spot, and they crowded round Gladys with white faces and scared voices.

"What has happened? Why are you here?" Beatrice exclaimed, seizing Gladys arm, and shaking her from the faintness stealing over her. "Where is Ned?"

Gladys started to her feet, and, throwing herself wildly in the midst of Sir Edmund's friends, she urged them to the brink of the fatal well.

"He is there! He has slipped through the false ground of leaves!" she said in a hollow voice. "Look, there are the marks of his feet where the branches are broken. Save him for pity's sake! You will not leave him there? You will not go back without him?"

There was a horrified silence. Those whom she dragged to the well looked from the broken brink to the water below, then shuddered, and covered their eyes with their hands. If this horrible thing were true—if Sir Edmund had slipped down into that fathomless depth—what hope was there? His fate was sealed.

Beatrice, with her brow resting against the barrel of her gun, her face hidden, was weeping hysterically, and two or three of the younger men gathered round her, not daring to express the sympathy they felt so bitterly.

"It cannot be—it is too awful!" they murmured, recoiling from the thought. "Was Lady Etheridge with him? Did anyone see him fall?"

"I came too late—too late to save him!" Gladys moaned, wringing her pale hands in agony. "It was all as you see it now—silent and terrible! His dog ran howling to the spot, and I followed. He came here to find Ned."

"It is some dreadful mistake—it cannot be," they said, trying to draw Gladys away; "we will search the woods, and not give up till we have found him. I am sure, wherever he is, he is safe, and will treat this as a fine joke. Come, dogs, find your master! Find him, good dogs!"

Cæsar whined dismally, where he crouched by the downward-sloping footmarks, and nothing would induce him to leave the spot.

"I believe the poor brute is hurt," somebody observed, bending to examine a patch of blood staining the shaggy paws. "By Jove!—yes. He has been shot."

"I should like to know who has done that," another exclaimed indignantly.

"It was I," Gladys said, looking at the dog in a dazed kind of way. "The gun went off when I took it up. I did not know I had hurt him. Poor Cæsar!"

The dog turned his faithful eyes on her, and tried to move towards her. Then swaying, he rolled over on his side—dead.

Gladys gave a strange little laugh—a laugh that sounded sadder than a cry of pain.

It had not been for the sake of his lost master that the dog had crouched there so wretchedly. He had been wounded unto death, and bodily injury was the cause of his howling.

Gladys laughed again, as she tried to frame this thought in her hot brain. Yet there was an aching misery in her eyes pitiful to see, and her face was white as the face of one dead.

"Ned—Ned!" she called, her voice piercing the silence of the woods. "Where are you, Ned? My darling—my love—answer!"

Only the echo of her own words came back to her.

Others took up the cry, and the deep glades resounded with Sir Edmund's name.

All that day they scoured the woods, but they could not track Sir Edmund's steps from the well.

The hounds led them always to the same spot where his gun and his dog lay side by side.

"Not there—not there!" Gladys would cry each time, drawing the wanderers back with her ice-cold hands. "It is the dog they scent. We are on the wrong track still!"

The day faded, and the moon rose behind the clouds.

Yet nobody had found Sir Edmund.

Throughout the night they traversed the woods, their path lighted by lanterns and torches, Gladys always first, plunging through the dense leaves like a white spirit, the torch she held high above her head throwing a weird light on her flowing hair and soft clinging dress.

"Do not stop!" she said, speaking as a queen giving a command, when, after fruitless toil, they paused like lost pilgrims, and looked blankly into each other's faces. "Ned has missed his way, and has perhaps thrown himself down under a tree to sleep till daybreak. If we go on we must find him soon."

They went on—on until their lanterns glared at the faint dawn—on till the sun rose up and mocked them.

Then each separate party gave up hope and returned.

Those who were with Gladys led the way back without a word.

A dead silence had fallen over them.

Nobody spoke.

It was as if they were marching in a funeral train, bowed down, and pale with speechless grief.

Gladys went straight up to her room, dry-eyed, and stonily calm, with the look of one who had received her death-blow.

She sank into a chair by the window, where she had watched him walk away, with yesterday's sun shining on his face.

She was weary—oh, so weary! but she would wait for him.

He would come soon; soon his brave true eyes, full of sunlight, would smile up at her.

Who said she had lost him—that he was dead?

She had been dreaming as she sat there, with the autumn breeze blowing in upon her; all those wild hours of misery had been suffered in a short troubled sleep!

Ned had only been gone a little while—yet why had the shooting ceased? Why did this dreary silence pall on her senses? Who was crying—Beatrice? What cause had she to weep?

When darkness came again, and the serving-women went to see how it was with Gladys, she was still sitting at the open window, with wide unseeing eyes turned towards the lowering night.

They spoke; she did not hear.

With gentle pitying hands they touched her; still she did not move.

They held the light closer to her face and saw that she had fainted.

They took off her moss-stained dress, and removed the torn shoes from her little bruised feet; then they laid her on her bed and brushed the damp leaves out of her beautiful hair.

"It's the best thing that could have happened to her," one old servant said, brushing the tears from her worn cheek. "Let her rest so a while, poor heart; once she wakes, it will be many a long day before she again forgets her misery. God help her—if Sir Edmund never comes back!"

Still they hoped—still they watched for his return.

How could they know that Beatrice, for the sake of his fortune, had urged him on to where the well was hidden—had given him a sudden sharp push as he stood on the brink, and hurled him into the awful depth yawning at his feet.

Beatrice—who since his disappearance had refused to be consoled; who had aided, day and night, in that fruitless search—alone could have told his fate.

Her hand had sent him to his death. Nobody saw—nobody heard. Her secret was safe.

What stood now between her and the wealth which had been her brother's? What?

CHAPTER XXVIII.

HEN Gladys recovered from that death-like swoon, she never spoke of Sir Edmund—never even uttered his name.

Her great dark eyes opened heavily, and gazed up at the faces bending over her.

Then her whole frame quivered, the fringed lids drooped, and once more she lay motionless as one dead.

That one agonized look was enough. He had not come back.

"How long is it?" was all she asked.

Those who heard started at sound of the changed voice—so hollow, and broken, and joyless.

"This is the fourth day," they answered sadly, and it seemed to them that Gladys did not hear the low-toned reply.

Day after day she lay with her pure face upturned on the pillows, pale and cold as a frozen lily.

Doctors gathered round her bedside, but what cure had they for this dumb heartbreaking anguish?

They could only hope, and wait for a change.

"Is she dying?" Beatrice asked, unable to curb her anxiety.

"I am afraid so," the doctor replied gravely. "I had best be plain with you. Her life his hanging on a thread. I think it hardly possible she can recover."

"Can you do nothing?"

"Nothing; her life rests in God's hands."

After this, Beatrice seemed more reconciled.

Every day she watched for an hour by Gladys—watched her fading slowly, like a flower, her life sinking lower with every breath.

The guests had all departed, shocked—scarcely able to realise that Sir Edmund was dead.

They had seen Beatrice in her heavy black dress, and knew his sweet young wife was dying, and they went away with a stunned sense weighing upon them—went with heavy steps to bear the sorrowful news abroad.

One stormy November night, a little child came to Gladys, bringing new light to her life—a fair babe, with grey-blue eyes, and downy curls that made a halo of pale gold round his head.

Gladys turned wearily when they laid him on her breast.

How could this new little life recompense her for the dear one she had lost?

"You only link me closer to the dead," she murmured to the child; "and yet for you I must live. I almost wish you had never been born, baby. Oh, if I could take you to your father now—you and I together!"

Together—no. If Gladys went, she must bid farewell to her child. He would live to bear his dead father's name proudly, while she—her life was still despaired of.

She seemed to get no better—no worse.

She had lost all interest in the world she lived in. Even the child failed to rouse her from the strange apathy she had sunk in.

His cry wearied and distressed her; she wanted always to be left alone.

As for Beatrice, she scarcely looked at the little one. She hated children, she said, when her coldness was commented upon; so the baby was left entirely to the mercy and the love of his nurses, who watched over him with unceasing care.

The nurses could forgive Gladys' indifference to her boy, because they knew how she was tried, and that the sight of him only filled her with bitter yearning.

But Beatrice's harsh manner they could not understand, and they grew to dislike and mistrust her.

"She seems to grudge him his little life," one of the women said indignantly, as she rocked the child proudly on her heart; "I believe she would be glad if he were to die."

Beatrice must have been rather unguarded in her manner for them to have guessed the truth.

This child was a cruel disappointment to her. She had not counted on the baby-life which would come between her and the Deepwood property.

"It cannot live, it looks half dead now," she had thought, when for the first time she looked at the little heir, and she went back to her room, unconcerned, expecting every hour to hear that he was dead.

A jealous hatred gnawed at her heart when, as the days flew by, the child strengthened and grew—a fair princely boy that Sir Edmund would have been proud of.

Nothing could save Gladys. She might linger on for a few slow weeks, the light of life growing fainter and fainter; but she would never rise up from her bed again.

The minister and his wife were the only visitors she ever received, and they would not be denied.

"You must try and think more about your boy," Mrs. Heath said gently, when she was sitting with her one snowy day; "he is such a pretty little fellow; let me lay him on your pillow."

Gladys took him in her weak arms almost for the first time, and pressed her lips softly to the baby face.

"You came to me at the wrong time," she murmured, looking sadly into the sweet blue eyes. "My heart is dead. I have no love to give you."

The child, attracted by her voice, put his warm clinging hands against her face, and smiled.

The touch sent a thrill through her. She seemed to understand the new love that was given her to cherish. She pressed the tiny form closer to her heart, and kissed him again and again.

Then, for the first time since Sir Edmund's disappearance, the passionate tears welled up to her eyes, and fell hot and swift on the little head nestled on her breast.

Mrs. Heath let her weep on. She was glad to see this burst of feeling. These tears might save her life, she thought.

"You have not told us yet what you will call him," she said when Gladys had become calm; "time is getting on, and we are waiting for you to decide."

Gladys shivered as though she shrank from the subject.

"I should like to give him Ned's name," she whispered, her eyes filling with pain, "but it would break my heart to call him by it. What other family names are there?"

"I do not think there has ever been more than one son born to the house, and each successive heir has been called Edmund. This little one does honour to his race —he is a true Saxon."

"Let that be his name, then," Gladys said wearily— "Sir Saxon."

Beatrice heard the decision with contempt.

"It does not much matter," she muttered with gloomy prophecy; "I have an idea the child will not live to enjoy his title long. One never knows what may happen, and though the boy may be well to-day, you cannot answer even for his life to-morrow."

"There is not much to fear where he is concerned," Mrs. Heath replied, instinctively drawing the child farther away from Beatrice; "all our sorrow now is for poor Gladys."

Beatrice knit her beautiful brows as she glanced at the baby, the unconscious source of all her bitterness, and the dark thought preyed on her mind that something would happen to destroy this frail blossom-like life, and leave her free to grasp the fruit of the evil deed she had committed.

The long winter days passed slowly and drearily, but she did not speak of leaving the Towers.

She wanted to wait for the end; she felt if she left Deepwood now she might never return as its mistress, and she watched anxiously for some change to come.

When the Christmas-bells rang out, things were going on in just the same way, and Beatrice was beginning to despair.

Gladys was weaker, if possible, and on Christmas night the doctors were hastily summoned to her bedside —she would never hear the new year's chimes. Poor Gladys—poor stricken flower! perhaps when the morning came she would have faded from the earth.

The greatest confusion reigned; weeping women were wandering helplessly from one room to another, wringing their hands and asking what was to be done.

Gladys was once more consciousless, her pale face resting like sculptured marble on the soft pillows,. her hands, grown thin almost to transparency, clasped nervously on the silk coverlet.

Beatrice never knew how it happened, but she found herself alone in the nursery.

The child was asleep.

A breathless half-terrified longing came over her as she watched him.

If she could only hide him—if she could only put him somewhere out of the world !

Nobody would miss him now; and afterwards, when Gladys had closed her eyes on this life for ever, what would it matter?

Her heart was on fire; she dared not pause—dared not think.

One hasty look round, then she tore the child from his cot, and fled noiselessly along the deserted corridor with him in her arms.

She scarcely knew where she was taking him.

Her thoughts flew to the deep snow without. Then, as suddenly, she remembered the footprints that would betray her.

She rushed on—on towards the old lampless wing they said was haunted.

A mad, horrible thought was in her mind.

Long ago she had seen in one of the tapestried rooms a great ebony chest. She had never thought of it since.

Now it seemed to open itself to her as a refuge.

She remembered exactly where it stood, and she groped her way swiftly to it.

A faint streak of moonlight fell through an opening in the window-curtains, and rested on the golden head drooping over her arm.

She would not look down at it; she could not witness her own crime; she felt surer of her aim—safer when darkness concealed her.

Shrinking into the black shadow, she bent down and pressed her hand on the spring.

The lid flew up silently, and without a moment's pause she thrust the sleeping child into the chest.

For a second time she touched the spring; the lid slid down. Her night's dark work was finished.

She put her hands to her ears and turned swiftly away—turned to see the curtain drawn back from the window by a ghastly hand that seemed familiar to her.

Her heart stood still with terror. A shadowy form was standing in the moonlight, and gazing down at her were the horrified eyes of the brother she had murdered.

The dead man's face was before her; the dead man's hand was raised in awful accusation against her.

The curtain dropped from his hold, and in the darkness he moved towards her, a streak of livid light following him.

Beatrice recoiled as he approached. Powerless with fear, she dared not fly away from this terrible form. That hollow unearthly gaze seemed to magnetise her. She moved back before him—back till she crouched beside the chest that concealed her crime.

Even then the mute command governed her. Her shuddering hand felt its way to the spring, and as the lid rolled back she fell on the floor in a dull heap.

Another moment, and a clamorous alarm rang through the house.

Nobody knew what had happened. Even those who had gathered in the chamber of death left their post to obey the wild summons that had startled them. They followed the sound of the madly-ringing bells till they had reached the haunted room.

"A light—for God's sake, a light!" a hollow voice called; and above the din a baby's pitiful cry rang out.

White with fear, they rushed into the room, holding the flaring candle in front of them.

They could not understand what this strange scene meant—the senseless form of Beatrice; the open chest;

the child they left asleep in the nursery lying at Sir Edmund's feet.

Yes, Sir Edmund—changed almost past recognition, like one who has been near to death—but Sir Edmund beyond a doubt.

"Sir Edmund! Oh, thank Heaven—thank Heaven!"

The cry burst involuntarily from the lips of all, and they crowded round him, looking at him through tears of gladness.

He whom they had searched so vainly for, whom they had mourned as dead, was before them, his eyes full of haggard life and human pain.

Oh, the joy of beholding him once more—even to those faithful servants! To Gladys might it not mean new life?

"You are surprised to find me here," he said with a grim smile. "I am afraid I gave you all a scare. My sister evidently took me for a ghost, and I see you are all in mourning for me. I don't know that I like the idea." Then pointing to the baby he had laid on the floor in safety : "Whose child is this?"

"Your own son, Sir Edmund."

"Thank God I was in time!" he muttered, his lips tightening as he glanced at Beatrice.

Then he lifted the little one gently in his arms, and his face softened as he kissed his boy's brow.

"Attend to her," he said, motioning them to go to Beatrice. "Who has charge of the child?"

The nurse came forward and took him from Sir Edmund.

"Look more to your duty in future," he commanded in a low firm voice, and the woman wondered what meaning there was in the words.

"All our attention was given to her ladyship," the nurse murmured. "Oh, sir!"

A hand of ice seemed to grip his heart.

"What is wrong?" he exclaimed, seizing the woman's arm, and glaring into her startled face. "Where is Lady Etheridge?"

"In her room, Sir Edmund. She has never left her bed since she received the shock of your disappearance."

He swept the woman out of his path, and sprang towards the door, his face drawn with anguish.

Half-a-dozen hands were stretched out to hold him back.

"Let us go first, Sir Edmund! It must be broken to her gently. The sight of you may be too much for her."

"Is she in danger?" he whispered hoarsely.

"Dying, they say."

He reeled back as though he had been shot.

"Dying!" he repeated in a voice of agony, and, breaking from the beseeching hands, he rushed past them like a madman.

"If I have lost her," he muttered with ashen lips, "woe be to the one who parted us. Gladys, Gladys, you shall not die!"

On his way to her room he came against one of the doctors.

Sir Edmund clutched his arm.

"You know who I am," he said hurriedly; "save her, and I will do all for you that one man can do for another. But I will not be kept from her side now."

"There is no need," the doctor replied, looking pityingly into the husband's wild eyes; "you can do no harm by watching. She is unconscious."

CHAPTER XXIX.

IR EDMUND'S heart seemed to freeze within him as he entered the room where Gladys lay, sick unto death.

One glance at the small, pace face, at the wasted arms flung over the coverlet, revealed to him all the terrible change in her.

She was so white and still; for a moment he thought he gazed on one dead.

His strong frame shook, and he walked blindly to the bedside.

"Gladys — Gladys!" he murmured, laying his trembling hand on the golden hair. "Gladys—my darling! I am come back to you—come back from the verge of death! Open your dear eyes, and let me see that you are glad!"

No response.

Chill and white as a snow-flower she lay before him, and as the breathless seconds flew a great anguish wrung his soul.

He knew the worst. She was sinking fast.

With a bitter groan he bent over her, and covered the sweet face with passionate kisses—kisses that kept the faint life warm on her lips, and put new breath in her heart.

Half mad with despair, he hardly knew what he was doing.

He lifted her head from the pillows, and raised her up against his breast, holding her close in his arms that the strong beat of his heart might stir her pulses afresh.

How long he waited for some sign of life in her he never knew.

All the house had grown very still when the child-like head moved, and she sighed and opened her eyes, as one awakened from a deep sleep.

No start of surprise at sight of him.

She looked straight up into his haggard face, her lips parted with a smile of infinite love.

"Ned!"

She breathed his name in a dreamy whisper, one weak arm stole across his breast, and nestling closer, she shut her eyes again—exhausted, and caring only to rest in his sheltering clasp.

A sudden thrill ran through Sir Edmund, a wave of colour rushed to his brow, and his lips quivered as they pressed hers in a long, clinging kiss.

"I thought I had lost you, my darling!" he murmured, huskily. "Thank Heaven, you are safe!"

To Gladys his voice sounded indistinct, like a dream-voice; the words fell sweetly on her ears, but they conveyed no meaning to her.

She had forgotten everything—even the existence of her little child.

That broad breast was such a natural resting-place for her head.

In this new awakening all the dark pain vanished, and she did not remember she had mourned Sir Edmund as dead.

The doctor stepped to the bedside, and looked on anxiously, scarcely daring to build a hope on that frail, fitful life.

"Give her this," he said, placing a cordial in Sir Edmund's hand. "We need not disturb her then."

Gladys drank the draught gratefully, and once more her great eyes opened to Sir Edmund's gaze, a slow, bewildered fear gathering in them.

"Ned," she whispered, trying to lift herself in his arms, "tell me what I have been dreaming? I forget—"

"Forget what, love?"

She clung convulsively to him, her eyes growing very wide, strained by intense thought.

Presently she broke into a faint laugh—a laugh that rang out wildly, while the great tears gathered on her thick lashes.

"I have had such an absurd dream," she said, her lips quivering pitifully.

Then a sharp sob broke her voice, the delirious smile left her face, and she clasped both her hands on her head.

How much of her dream had been real?

"I remember now!" she murmured, slowly. "You went away from me, and I thought you were dead—because you told me that only death would part us. What was it, Ned?"

"An accident," in short, husky tones.

"Tell me all of it, Ned. I cannot understand—"

"By-and-by, sweet Gladys, you shall know everything. You must rest now. I want you to get well very soon."

She nestled down in his arms, and drew his hand softly against her cheek.

"You are my strength," she said, with a shadowy smile. "The sight of you has brought new life to me—I could not die now."

A dreamy silence followed her words, and Gladys lay quite still, her eyes gently closed as though in sleep.

A slight check in the faint, irregular breathing, a stifled sigh, made Sir Edmund look more intently at her.

"Gladys!"

Her name fell tenderly from his lips.

With a shiver she opened her eyes, and he saw they were full of tears.

"Are you in pain, darling? My poor little Gladys!"

His own eyes softened with something more than love, and he let his lips rest against her brow that she might not read the agony on his face.

She clung to him feverishly.

The same thought which had chilled her heart had racked his soul with fresh torture.

Everything had come too late.

She was dying.

"Don't let me go, Ned!" she moaned, a wild pathetic pain in her eyes. "Our lives seem to be crossing. Ned—Ned—shall I die? It will be so hard —now!"

No answer; only a passionate kiss on the quivering lips, only a quick upheaving of the man's strong heart.

"You will not give anyone else—this love, that I love more than my life—when I am gone? Ned, don't take anyone else to fill my place. Whatever happens, do not forget, that we shall meet again—and I shall be your wife—there—as here. It will not be parting for ever and ever."

The effort to speak exhausted her; her head drooped wearily, and when she spoke again her voice was fainter.

She had been thinking of Dudley, wondering, in a vague painless way, if in severing his life from hers, the same heart-sick suffering had come to him as would come to her when her dying gaze should linger for the last time on the face she loved.

"I wish my life could be measured with yours," she said, wistfully. "I don't want to die, Ned—to be away from you! I seem to be drifting farther and farther from you; and we might be so happy—you and I, and our little child. I have never seen him with you; I should like once to put him in your arms, Ned."

A smile flickered over her face as the little one was held gently to her, and, with a broken sigh, she lifted him towards Sir Edmund.

"Whenever you look at him you must think of me," she murmured, one hand linked in Sir Edmund's, the other clasping the child. "You must give him my share of love; I have not cared very much for him, because I thought his life was only sent in exchange for yours. I made a mistake, dear—he is sent to you."

"Hush, Gladys! I cannot bear this, my darling, my little love! I will not lose you! I have been as near death, but I have come back to you. You are so young, so full of sweetness, and it is not time yet for you to die. Gladys, surely I have not been spared for this!"

There was a dull agony in his voice, and his passionate eyes peered down into hers with a haggard dread.

Gladys shook her head sadly.

"It is no use," she said, kissing her baby with yearning lips, as someone took him from Sir Edmund.. "I know I must leave you soon, Ned. Do not look at me with such pain! I am not suffering now. Hold me up —higher. Dear, dear Ned!"

The words sank to a dreamy whisper; her violet eyes darkened as they gazed into his face.

With a faint, tremulous sigh she sank gently down in his arms, her long lashes shutting in the light of her eyes, an unconscious smile resting on her parted lips.

Sir Edmund's glance seemed riveted to the pale face upturned on his arm.

Scarcely breathing, he bent over her and listened.

Was this stillness sleep or death? Was it only the firelight dancing? or did any more life-like glow come on to her silent lips?

The doctor had gone to the bedside unobserved. He touched Sir Edmund softly on the shoulder.

"She is asleep," he whispered. "There is a change for the better. I have no doubt with good care we shall pull her through. Let her find you here when she wakes."

Sir Edmund did not stir from his post. He looked tired and ill; but he could not think of himself while Gladys lay there in the sleep that was to give her a new hold on life.

Her breathing, so faint at first, became more regular, and once or twice she moved restlessly, as though in a dream.

He caught the murmur of his own name linked with broken words of love, and a gleam of the old brightness came back to his face.

That sleep worked wonders.

When she awoke she was on a sure road to recovery; and though it would be long before she could get back the strength she had lost, there was little fear of a relapse.

Sir Edmund would not allow her to talk.

"Wait till you are better, darling," he said, when she tried to speak. "All we want you to do is to get well as quickly as ever you can; and, for the present, your best remedy is rest."

When the morning broke, and she was again sleeping, he went to his own room to get through a hurried toilet.

Amid the confusion of the past night he had not been forgotten.

A fire burned cheerily in the grate, and everything was in readiness for him, as though he had not been absent a single day.

Afterwards he learned that during his disappearance his room had never been closed.

At any moment he might have returned and found everything prepared for him; Gladys would not have it left desolate.

Sir Edmund threw off his coat, pulled his dressing-gown on, and, stretching himself in a big armchair, he settled down in a thoughtful mood.

What a powerful fate governed his life!

Straight up from a bed of fever, he had come on the scene in time to save the child he had never seen, and the wife he loved so dearly.

He could hardly trust himself to think of Beatrice.

His brow grew dark, as he remembered how he had found her on his return, and something between a groan and a curse broke from his lips.

He must have an interview with her as soon as possible.

He could not sit there with the thought of her in his brain.

He started up restlessly, and hurried on with his toilet.

Then, refreshed, he rang for his valet, and for the first time asked after Beatrice.

She was better.

Sir Edmund went at once to her door, and dismissing the maid, he stood with folded arms half-way across the threshold.

Beatrice was lying on the outside of the bed, in a warm white wrapper, her long dark hair trailing over the pillows, her face partly hidden by the arm that was flung up over her head.

" Beatrice, will you try to look at me ? I want all your attention."

She shuddered, and turned away from him.

" Not glad to see me, Beatrice ? " he said, his voice full of stern reproach. " For your own sake I should have thought you would be thankful I am living."

" Have you come from the dead to torture me ? " she muttered. " I wish I had never seen your face again ! The sight of you is hateful to me."

" And the child — was he in your way, too ? Beatrice ! Beatrice ! where did you find your sin ? "

She cowered down, and pressed her lips till all the colour faded from them.

There was a scornful bitterness in his tone that stung her more deeply than if he had confronted her with a more vengeful accusation.

Shame overwhelmed her ; she dared not look in his face.

He knew how guilty she was, and she felt herself at his mercy.

" What do you intend doing ? " he asked, presently. " After what has happened it is not possible for you to stay under my roof. For my own sake as well as for yours, you may depend no one will ever know the cause of my disappearance, or for what reason you took the child out of his nursery last night ! You must go, Beatrice, and try to live down the evil in you. Thank Heaven, no harm has come of your mad impulse ! The only atonement you can make is to go, and take the remembrance of your sin away."

Beatrice raised herself on her elbow, and for the first time turned her face towards him, her eyes full of wonder.

" You rebuke me kindly," she muttered, shuddering as she thought of the punishment she deserved at his hands. " I can scarcely believe anyone could forgive such as a wrong as I have done you."

" What good should I do by harbouring resentment ? " he asked, coldly. " I would rather let you go and repent as you have sinned—in secret. I never want to speak of this, or to see you again, nor need I say your home is no longer with me. If you like I will telegraph to Osman, so that you can meet him at once."

"I do not know where to send him word," she replied, gloomily. "It is nearly a month since I last heard from him, and he was travelling then."

"I can make no plans for you. Choose your own course—you cannot remain here."

He could say nothing more. He looked at her for a moment in silence, then left her.

Beatrice knew he meant this to be their last interview.

If she went in peace, his vengeance would not follow her. It was all he had commanded her—to go!

To go—where?

She rose up from the bed and paced the room restlessly, her eyes glittering with fierce thought.

She had never imagined this bitter hour would come to her. Her crime had been an impulse of jealous envy.

It was a dull ending to all her wild ambitions. She had forfeited every claim on Sir Edmund, and she hardly knew where to look for a friend.

In this reckless, passionate mood she thought of Richard Garth, and she sent her message to him.

WHITE WITH FEAR THEY RUSHED INTO THE ROOM.

No. 12.

CHAPTER XXX.

ORE than a week elapsed before Beatrice left the Towers, and she saw nothing of her brother or his wife.

To silence the remarks of the servants she was compelled to go about the house in her usual way, but as she had seldom visited the sick-room or the nursery, it did not seem strange that she should hold aloof now.

No one regretted much when, early in the new year, she attired herself in a dark rich travelling-dress, and went away in a strange carriage which had been sent down for her.

The snow was falling thickly, and the rushing wind swept it along in huge drifts, making the road dangerous for the horses.

A bitter night! and Beatrice had to face the storm alone, her heart full of desperate anger against the one who had sent her forth.

There was no shamed droop of the proud, young head.

Her wayward spirit rose hotly above the humiliation of this cold departure, and she went out into the whirling snow with a light step and curling lips.

The world was never dark to Beatrice. Her callous nature was closed against pain, and she left her brother's roof without remorse.

Nobody at the Towers knew where she was going—nobody cared.

Half-way to the station the horses stopped, and someone sprang into the carriage and took the opposite seat.

It was Richard Garth.

He clasped Beatrice's hand for an instant, then in a firm, quick tone told the men to drive on with all the speed they could.

"So you want me to befriend you, Beatrice?" he whispered, drawing her hands once more within his clasp. "Have you quarrelled with Sir Edmund?"

"He has quarrelled with me," she replied, with a strange little laugh; "I would rather not speak of him."

"How suddenly he came to life after that mysterious disappearance!" Garth said, with almost startling abruptness. "I came across more than one paragraph announcing his supposed death, and before I could make anything out of the story I discover the whole rumour had been a mistake. Do you know how it happened, Beatrice?"

She looked away from him impatiently.

"No; he never thought it worth while to give an explanation. He seems to have no thought for anything apart from his wife and child. I found it dreadfully dull lately, and I am quite glad to be able to escape. I hardly know where I am to go. What do you advise me?"

He bent towards her, a passionate smile quivering on his lips.

"Come with me," he murmured, his cruel eyes softening to tenderness. "I love you, Beatrice, you know how deeply—how fatally—as I have never loved before in my life. You seem to have lifted an iron bar from my heart, and every word, every look of yours, burns into my soul. You called it folly once, and laughed at me, so I went where I could not meet you. You have summoned me again to your side—for what, Beatrice?"

"I have no other friend—that is all," she answered, without looking at him; "the depression I have endured was beginning to tell on me, and my thoughts flew to you as being the least susceptible to gloom. I hate to feel miserable, and I dreaded a long journey alone."

"You want me to travel with you to the East?"

"Yes."

"To join Omar?"

"Of course; though I have not the faintest idea where he is. I put off answering his letters, and lately he has not written. Out there it will not be so difficult to trace him."

"How lightly you speak!" Garth exclaimed, his chest heaving with a fierce breath. "Beatrice, what if we never find Omar? Will you wander with me always? I know you love me!—why should you put yourself away from me? You and I, now we have met again, cannot live apart."

Garth's bold words roused no anger in Beatrice's heart.

His rich soft voice thrilled to her soul, and a passionate light came into her eyes.

"Are you forgetting Osman?" she asked, leaning her head back against the dark cushions of the carriage.

The veins rose on Garth's brow.

"If I thought he were the only obstacle between us, I would——"

"Kill him?"

"Yes."

"It is not easy to kill," she said, with a touch of bitterness, remembering how the two lives she had tried to drive from the world had struggled from her power. "I advise you never to make such a rash attempt, Richard; you would sure to be the sufferer. Besides, am I worth it?"

"Your love is worth everything to me, Beatrice; I would shrink from nothing to gain you! As for Omar, had it not been for me, he would never have seen you —never have won from you that mad promise to become his wife. Why should he be favoured more than I? It does not seem like robbery to take what one has given; and in a way, Osman owed all his happiness to me."

"Why did you not think of this at first?" Beatrice asked quietly. "It was you I loved, not Osman! I was alone, and his love was better than none. I had no choice."

"It is not too late to choose between us now, Beatrice!" he muttered passionately. "We can escape so easily together. I am sick of the world and all its masked mockery! Would it not be better to dash through those few miserable ties that make such a feeble barrier between us? Already you seem to belong to me. In you I have found the partner of my soul! Without you, my life would be only half complete. And you, Beatrice—you love me!"

The words were uttered with hot intensity, and Garth bent forward and kissed her lips—lips he had caressed once in feigned acting, when she had rested in his arms as the *Cynthia* of his play—lips that breathed no reproach against him for the love he had set beating in her heart.

This man, with his handsome face and his soft passionate voice, fascinated her.

Her soul seemed to be swept under a wild spell, and in some vague way she felt he had gained power over her.

In this man she loved she had found her master.

"If Osman should know he would kill us both!" she murmured, shuddering.

"Do you fear him—while I live?" Garth whispered, the old cruel gleam flashing over his face. "Who is stronger, do you think—he or I? If my chance of winning you depended on strength of muscle, I should not long have a rival! Which one would you rather see dead, me or your dark husband?"

Beatrice shrank away from him, her eyes looking almost painfully brilliant in the uncertain light of the lanterns.

"Why do you ask such horrid things, Richard?"

He gave a short laugh.

"Well, I will put it in other words. If the struggle should ever come, who would you have victorious?"

"I cannot say; I do not want to think! I hope you and Osman will never meet!"

"And you Beatrice?"

"He must forget me."

Garth took both her hands, and held them close against his heart, gazing fervently into her beautiful face.

"You will risk all?" he murmured.

"All. Take my answer now, if you care for me; presently it may not be the same."

The snow was still falling heavily, and they seemed to progress more slowly every moment.

Garth shouted to the men to push on faster.

"We shall be blocked in if you don't hurry," he said irritably. "You need not spare the horses."

The carriage lurched and rolled heavily onward, the blinded horses running knee-deep through the snow.

The driver kept them hard at it, though they had missed the line of the road, and seemed to be tearing over a frozen wilderness.

Suddenly there was a sharp shock, the vehicle was lifted and thrown over on its side, and the horses dragged down. They had stumbled over a bank, and two of the wheels had sunk into a marsh.

The windows and the lamp-glasses were shivered to atoms, and they were thrown into utter darkness.

"Get the horses up!" Garth exclaimed, bursting open one of the doors and leaping out; then, turning his attention to Beatrice: "Are you safe, my darling? You must come out while they get this confounded thing up. If you climb nearer, I can lift you."

Beatrice seemed unable to follow his directions.

Terror had taken all the courage out of her, and she crouched down where she had been flung, with her head against the framework of the broken window.

Garth shouted to the footman for a light.

"I am afraid the lady is hurt," he said with a dull fear in his voice. "Put a match to one of the wicks, never mind about the glass!"

The footman groped in vain for the lamps.

Both had been dashed from their sockets, and he did not know where to put his hand on them.

Garth raved out again for a light, and somebody struck a match, which was instantly extinguished by the wind.

"Fools! What use is that?" Garth hissed. "Get a light, or by Heaven——"

He did not finish. A sudden fiery glare leaped from the black heap before him, and the scene was lit up by a great scorching flame. The carriage was on fire!

It seemed that Fate had a hand in this, for as the smoke curled up the snow ceased to fall, and the blaze burst forth with blinding heat.

The driver's first thought was for his horses, and his own safety. With a firm hand he cut the harness, and pulled the frightened beasts up; then flinging himself across the back of one, he gripped the bridle of the other, and dashed off towards the village.

Garth stood looking round him like a madman.

He understood it all.

The lamps were dashed to pieces, and the oil had upset over the burning wicks. The fierce flames, lashed by the keen wind, darted up on every side, and broke over the cushions in a whirling blaze.

He sprang into the hot glow, and clutched the flames in frenzied despair for a hold on Beatrice.

Through the mass of fire he could see her white panic-stricken face, the breathless agony in her eyes.

Already the pitiless flames had caught her beautiful hair, and the great fiery tongues lapped round her like devouring fiends. Garth sickened at the sight.

In a few moments she would be burnt to death!

Putting his arm up to screen his eyes from the heat, he made a frantic dash forward, and tried to drag her from her danger. He was beaten back by the bursting flames, his face blackened, and smarting with cruel pain. He shrank back from the scorching glare.

He could not for a second time plunge into the stifling fire; and he shrank back with a shudder as a piercing shriek from Beatrice rang on his ears, a shriek that broke from her parched lips again and again, with horrible despair.

Garth shut his heart against feeling. He could do no more for her. She was not worth the risk of his life.

He turned away and left her to her doom—left her burning there without succour, with no one near to hear her shrill cries for help. She must perish; he could make no further effort to save her.

In this hour of trial, the selfishness and cruelty in him were greater than his love.

His own life was more precious to him than her safety —he could only leave her to her fate.

A nervous hand caught his arm in an icy hold. He swung round, and met the scared gaze of the footman.

"Oh, sir, do something, for pity's sake! Don't leave her there!"

"It is too late!" Garth muttered. "I dare say she is already dead!"

"Sir, can't you hear how she is shrieking for help?"

Garth heard, but her cry did not move him, and he turned his white face calmly to the glaring light as the man shot past him, and leaping into the burning carriage, hurled Beatrice out on to the snow.

With a shout to Garth, he darted under the flames, and crawled out through an opening on the other side, scarcely receiving a scar.

Long before the man could get round to where Beatrice lay, Garth was at her side, his coat flung off, and wrapped tightly over her smouldering garments.

He shut his eyes with a sickening shudder as he looked at her—a few moments ago so beautiful, so brilliant, and now, only a darkened unsightly form, with blistered hands, and hair singed closely to her head.

"Poor Beatrice! Poor Beatrice!" he muttered hoarsely, as he saw her writhe in torture. "Shall I lift you? We must get farther away from the fire."

He tried to raise her, but in his fear of hurting her, he staggered, and bore down on his knees.

An instant later, there was a loud crash just over his head, and with a stream of blinding smoke, the red beams heaved and fell together—fell with dull suffocating force on the startled face of Richard Garth.

Had his arms been free, he might have saved himself. Beatrice lay a dead weight across him, and he had no power to avoid the danger he knew was coming.

The tottering mass crashed down on his head, and one beam, striking sharply against his bare throat, threw him back on the pile with a stifled groan.

*   *   *   *   *

When help came, they were dragged from the *débris*, and carried to the nearest inn.

"How did it happen?" was asked in half-a-dozen horrified voices. "Are they dead?—both dead? Burnt to death while the snow was freezing round them. How terrible!"

"Aye, but look!" others exclaimed when a candle was held over the ghastly faces. "There's a gash across the gentleman's throat, and his head hangs strangely! Hold the light nearer. Don't any of you know his face? It's Mr. Garth! And the lady, don't you recognise her? Ride to the Towers, some of you, and rouse an alarm!"

CHAPTER XXXI.

T three o'clock in the morning the inmates of the Towers were alarmed by the loud harsh clanging of a bell, and Sir Edmund, leaping from his bed, hurried on some clothes, and hastened down into the hall.

"What has happened?" he asked, looking from the butler's scared face to the man who had brought the news from the inn. "Is anything wrong?"

"There's been an accident, Sir Edmund."

"Speak out, man? What is it—who is hurt?"

"Mr. Garth's one of them—I think he's killed—and the other is—oh, Sir Edmund, I don't like to tell you —for I believe she is dead, too!"

"Where?" Sir Edmund asked huskily, a cold pallor coming over his face.

"They're at the inn—at the Sportman's Rest. I've brought the dog-cart, if you wouldn't mind. There's no time to be lost."

A group of shivering servants had gathered at the foot of the staircase.

Sir Edmund turned to them before he followed the man out into the bitter snow.

"Do not disturb Lady Etheridge," he said hurriedly; "I will see her on my return."

As he spoke he glanced up instinctively, and on the landing above he saw Gladys standing in her night-dress—a pale, wraith-like form, with soft flowing hair, and frightened eyes shining down on the little group below.

Since her illness it was the first time she had left her room, and a startled exclamation broke from those who caught sight of her.

Sir Edmund looked at her almost angrily.

"Gladys, what madness is this?" he muttered, distracted by this doubled anxiety. "Go back to your room at once—unless you wish to kill yourself!"

"But where are you going? What is the matter, Ned?" she asked, putting her hand to her head in a bewildered way.

"There has been an accident, darling, and I am called away. Do not add to my anxiety by letting me go with the impression that you are exposing yourself to all kinds of danger. I will get back as soon as possible and tell you the news. Don't stand in the cold; let me know you are safe in your room before I start. Go, dear; you cannot understand how you are worrying me."

His look more than his tone made her obey, and with a miserable feeling that something terrible had happened—something she dared not question—she went back to her bed.

Sir Edmund did not lose a second. It had been a hard task to control himself—to hide from her the dread which weighed in his mind.

The word "Beatrice" had not been breathed; but the truth had flashed into his brain with sharp conviction. He knew the one they had shrank from naming was his sister.

The door was flung open as he approached, and striding past those near him, he sprang up into the dogcart, and, tearing the reins from the driver, dashed furiously through the darkness.

"I suppose there is a doctor there?" he asked once.

"Some of the lads had gone for help before I started," the man answered gruffly.

It was a long, silent, hard drive. Nobody but Sir Edmund could have driven over the frozen snow at that whirling pace.

When he alighted and entered the inn his face was almost rigid, and he let the woman lead him in silence to a dimly-lighted chamber where Beatrice lay.

Sir Edmund was prepared to see her, but not thus. He recoiled as his glance rested on the poor scorched face and disfigured hands. How horribly she had changed! Had he sent her from his roof for this?

She stirred slightly on her pillows, and a sharp cry of pain broke from her lips.

Even now a fire seemed to be consuming her—torturing her with endless agony; and look where she would she could see nothing but the red flames leaping round her.

"Do you know I am near you, Beatrice?" Sir Edmund asked, his voice more gentle than it had been to her for weeks past.

Her breath came harder through her parched lips.

"Is it Ned?" she moaned, turning her lustreless eyes towards him. "I cannot see anyone. I think I am blind."

"Why, you are looking at me, Beatrice!" trying to speak lightly. "I must be standing in the shadow."

"It is all shadow," she answered pitifully. "I am blind!"

"You have had a bad accident," Sir Edmund said, trying to soothe her. "Your sight will be clear enough in a little while. You must not expect to get well in one night, dear."

She shuddered. Remembering her sin against him, his kindness smote upon her, and she wondered that he could have found it in his heart to forgive her.

"I don't think I have done much good by living," she whispered after a long pause, the words coming slowly and painfully. "I wonder what I was born for? My life has been like a blight. I have been so selfish always. I wish my nature had been the same as yours, Ned."

"Hush, Triss! I am not better than anybody else. Don't fret about those things," he muttered, knowing to what her mind had wandered. "Perhaps I judged you too harshly."

"Not harshly enough, Ned. You do not know all. To the very last I have been false. If this had not happened, there would have been even another sin told against me. I despise myself for that wickedness now, Ned. While a better feeling is on me, will you forgive me everything?"

"Everything, Beatrice—everything dear!" he said huskily. "Try and forget all that, and let all the best thoughts come first. Can you see me now?"

"It is darker—darker—and darker! I am in such horrible pain. If I could only sleep and forget! I heard somebody say I shall never be better. It seems strange to be dying so soon."

After this she lapsed into silence, exhausted and full of pain.

The doctor came noiselessly into the room, and looked from her to Sir Edmund.

It was a glance full of meaning, and Sir Edmund felt something tighten at his heart, as he let his gaze rest dully on the face from which all the beauty had gone.

He laid his hand softly on her pillow.

"Beatrice!"

She looked up at him with a convulsive smile—a smile that wrung a moan of agony from her.

"I can see you now," she murmured, her breath growing more and more laboured. "And mamma, standing at the foot of the bed. Why doesn't she come nearer? Oh, Ned—Ned! Don't leave me—don't leave me!"

With a shuddering cry she raised herself upright in the bed; a great shiver that seemed to clutch away her breath, trembled through her, and lifting her arms, she sighed, and fell back—dead!

The severe shock and exposure to the cold had done the worst towards hastening the end, and as Sir Edmund gazed down at the blind passionless face, he could scarcely realise that death had closed round her heart.

It was so sudden.

Only a short time ago he had seen her full of reckless life; only a short time ago he had prayed he might never look on her again!

He knew her youth, and her weakness—knew how sadly she wanted guiding, and he had left her to her own wayward impulse.

There was a heavy gnawing at his heart as he stood in the fitful candle-light, with that dead face before him.

Even now she might have been sheltered in his home —held away from temptation.

He had left her too much to herself; and she was dead.

Dead! The word seemed to fall like a stone on his heart. He turned away with an icy shiver.

"What of the other—of Mr. Garth?" Sir Edmund asked, in a hollow voice, as he passed from the room where Beatrice lay so still and mute.

"Progressing favourably, I am thankful to say," the doctor replied, gently. "He has one or two severe injuries, and strong inflammation exists, but he is out of danger, and if kept quiet will get on nicely. Would you like to see him?"

"No," Sir Edmund muttered hoarsely, and without another word he left the inn, and once more dashed off in the dog-cart.

The faint grey dawn was before him when he reached the post-office.

Almost before the door could be opened, he thrust his way to the desk and filled in half-a-dozen telegraph-forms.

"It is a message of death," he said, as he handed them in. "Let no time be lost."

They were all to different directions, but bore the same name, "Osman Omar."

In this time of need, he did not know where to find the one who should have been there first—who knew nothing of the blank desolate grief waiting for him.

Sir Edmund sent wherever he thought the message might reach him; and then, racing back to the inn, he went again to the room where Beatrice lay.

Even now he could hardly force himself to believe what had happened.

Beatrice dead! Beatrice, who had gone from his home in perfect buoyant health?

The suddenness of the calamity seemed to have dulled his power of understanding; he could not grasp the bare horrible thought thrust upon him!

Yet again the awful silence of that darkened room palled on him; again the cold unchanging face was before his gaze, and he knew the dark beautiful eyes would never open—the curved lips be always mute.

He heard how it had all happened—heard with aching ears and smarting heart; then, with the morning breaking round, he walked back to the Towers.

In the hall, he almost mechanically threw off his snow-flecked coat, then passed straight up to Gladys' room.

She met him at the door, looking very delicate and sweet in a pale-pink morning-robe, trimmed with soft lace and swansdown.

Her face was nearly as white as the snow he had left outside, and there were dark shadows under her eyes as though she had been crying.

"Don't scold me for being up," she said, putting both her arms round his neck, and leaning her head against him. "I know everything. Dear Ned!"

His lips trembled as he kissed her cheek.

"It was a horrible accident!" he exclaimed, shivering. "Poor Beatrice!"

Gladys clung closer to him, and her tears fell on his breast where she hid her face.

"Shall I go to them?" she asked, after a pause.

"You, my darling! What could you do?"

"Sit by Beatrice. And Mr. Garth—is he dying, do you think?"

"No; he will recover."

"I hope he will try to make his life a kinder one," Gladys said, softly. "But poor Beatrice, she had done nothing; it was hard she should have had such a cruel fate. I shall never leave off regretting that I did not see her before she went away. I cannot understand what made her act so strangely. Was I ever unkind to her, Ned? I never meant to be!"

"I am sure you were not," he replied, huskily. "Don't grieve, dear; we have much to be thankful for—even now."

Beatrice's secret was safe with him. Not to Gladys would he reveal the mystery of those two dark acts that sullied the memory of the dead.

Nobody ever knew how near death the baby-heir had been on that wild Christmas night when Sir Edmund had returned—returned, as it seemed, from the grave, and the part Beatrice had played in his own disappearance was never told.

He was anxious about Osman, and as the day wore on, he wired off message after message, hoping that one at least would bear him the awful news.

None ever reached the Arab.

Fate was playing a cross-game with these lives, and without a word of warning Osman arrived at the Towers that night.

He had regained his treasures—treasures Beatrice had bade him risk his life for, and he was flushed and eager with triumph.

The silent gloom of the house struck a chill to him as he entered.

He halted, and gave a quick glance into the butler's white face, like one suspicious of an enemy.

Those who saw the sudden change from glad greeting to perplexed fear, knew he was unconscious of the shock in store, and each one drew back, shrinking from dealing the blow that would rend this passionate nature with direst anguish.

It was heart-breaking to see the pleading dread with which he looked from one face to another.

"What has happened?" he said, knitting his brow in a dazed kind of way. "Why do none of you speak? Are you not my friends? And Beatrice—where is she?"

Sir Edmund laid his hand on Osman's shoulder, and led him into the library.

"My telegram did not reach you?" he muttered vaguely. Then meeting the Arab's bewildered eyes fully: "I have sad news for you, my poor fellow. Beatrice is gone."

"Gone! Where?" Osman echoed, not grasping the meaning of those few dull words. "She said she would wait till I came back. Perhaps I am too soon; she may return."

"No, it is not possible, Osman. Prepare yourself for the worst. There has been an accident, and—and nothing could save her."

Osman gave a sudden start as though a knife had gone through him, and a look of blank horror came over his face.

"Is she—dead?" he gasped, seizing Sir Edmund's arm convulsively. "What are you telling me? What have you done with Beatrice? Give her to me—let me go to her—or I will kill you!"

His breath came in sharp heavy gasps, and a savage pain burned in his eyes.

What had they done with Beatrice? They to whose care he had left her. Dead! Then he would bitterly avenge her. She was his, and he loved her, and they had destroyed her!

The truth rushed upon him with maddening force, and he drew his breath fiercely through his clenched lips.

"Tell me where I can find her!" he muttered incoherently. "You are playing with me dangerously. You forget—she is my wife."

There was an anguish in the last words that sent a thrill through Sir Edmund. He had prepared himself for this passionate outbreak, but he knew the wilder the storm the sooner a calm would come, and he stood by, full of silent sorrow for the man in whose soul he was pouring such deep agony.

Gladys entered the room unobserved, and slipped her hand softly in Osman's dusky palm.

The touch roused him. He wrung her hand with unconscious strength, paining her.

"Where is Beatrice?" he asked in a hoarse whisper. "You—you will tell me?"

Gladys looked from the despairing eyes burning down on her to the haggard face of her husband.

Sir Edmund folded his arms on his breast and bowed his head. There was nothing more for him to say; the answer might bear less pain coming from Gladys.

She felt the hand grasping hers tighten, like a vice, and as she glanced up the one word trembled upon her lips:

"Dead!"

He gazed at her for a moment, his eyes freezing, his features drawn into ghastly lines. Then, with a terrible cry, he flung up his arms and fell forward.

CHAPTER XXXII.

AYS after, when Beatrice had been laid to rest like a dead queen, with jewels clasped round her, Osman found his way to the room where Richard Garth was sleeping. A shrill wind was beating against the windows, and the hail pelted down in frozen showers.

All sounds inside the house were drowned by the noise without. While the fierce blasts whistled through every crevice, and shook each hinge, nobody downstairs could hear what was going on in the sick-room.

The Arab was staying at the inn, a morbid fancy making him occupy the dreary-looking chamber where Beatrice's last breath had been spent.

Since that deathly shock this was the first time he had seen Garth.

Osman paused stealthily by the bed, and, like a panther ready to spring, gazed down at the disfigured face.

"You killed your own wife," he hissed, "but what right had you to let harm come to mine? You have lost her to me. You saw her suffer while you saved yourself! Weak-hearted traitor! do you think to escape the death that was her doom?"

Garth gave a slight smile.

"My dear fellow, your grief vents itself in wild words! Don't spare me; I forgive the bitterest thing you can say to me, for I know the sharp misery that prompts you. I loved Beatrice, even as you did, and the loss to me was as great!"

"You took her from me!" Osman whispered, the words thick and disjointed. "But for you she would not have died—you were the cause—you who were alone with her, the only one to whom she could cry for help. Oh, if I had been near to save her—to thrust you in her place, there would not be this bitter reckoning, this ordeal of vengeance!"

Garth raised himself with difficulty; there was a fierce vindictive glare in the Arab's eyes he did not like.

He felt himself at his mercy, and instinctively he raised his hand to the bell-rope.

With a quick noiseless movement Osman drew a knife from his breast and cut the rope.

"I would rather deal with you alone," he said, replacing the knife, and keeping his hand in his breast, grasping on the cold steel. "What do you fear?"

"Not you," Garth replied, with another of those nervous painful smiles. "I thought I would get up. I am sick of lying here!"

"It is late. I think they have all gone to bed. I would rest, too, if I could. I cannot sleep—Beatrice seems to cry out to me to kill you, and I am come to do her bidding!"

A ghastly look came over Garth's face, and damp dews started out on his brow.

Once more the gleaming steel flashed between the two men; like wolves at bay they glared into each other's eyes, then there was a dull struggle.

Thrust back on his pillows, with the knife held over him, Garth was almost powerless. The glittering point touched his throat. The slightest upward movement, and he would be a dead man!

He held his breath, every nerve strained in horrible suspense. Then, with a desperate courage, born of a greater fear, he seized the bare blade in his hand, and wrenched it from the Arab's grasp.

A shiver of agony ran through him as the weapon dropped. His hand, cut to the bone, fell heavily on the blood-stained pillow, and he gazed up in silence at Osman, his face quivering with passion.

"You would murder me for her sake!" he gasped. "Fool! She loved me! What is her death to you? Had she lived you would still have lost her! I tell you she loved me! You she only feared and hated!"

Osman stopped the boastful words on Garth's lips with a fierce blow. "You lie!" exclaimed Osman in his teeth. "That you are base enough to have tried to win her from me I know. But that she was false to me, never—never! She was too proud—too scornful—to have turned traitress to me, and to herself! Even I, her husband, was her slave!"

"You! Yes. "With me it was not so!"

The sneer infuriated Osman; he hurled back blow for word, and winding his sinewy arms round Garth, he crushed him in a vice-like grip.

The sick man struggled vainly to break from his hold.

Every moment seemed to rob him of power; and to wrestle with Osman now was like combating with a tiger.

Ere that hot panting struggle ended, the door was flung open, and the innkeeper rushed into the room.

In an instant he had torn Osman from the bedside, and Garth fell back in a half-swoon, blood oozing slowly from his mouth.

The Arab flung him a savage exultant glance, then muttering in his own language, he left the room.

"I think he has nearly done for me," Garth said hoarsely.

"Your hand! Good heaven! how horrible! A surgeon must be sent for——"

"No—no," Garth interrupted, shaking his head; it is not worth while; you can bind it."

The innkeeper called his wife, and they spoke again of summoning a doctor.

Their persistance irritated Garth.

He knew what had to be done, if only someone would carry out his instructions.

The man bound up his wounded hand shudderingly.

Garth did not shrink; he seemed to be numb to pain, and throughout the night he scarcely moved or spoke.

They did not leave him. There was something in his almost torpid calmness that made them anxious for the morning to come.

"I am much better," he said, when they asked him once if he suffered. "I shall get up by-and-by. I think the shaking has done me good."

Notwithstanding, they noticed his voice had grown feebler, more passionless, and the mere effort to breathe seemed to exhaust him.

At daybreak he fell into a heavy sleep, and hours after, when they tried to rouse him, they found that he was dead. There had been poison on the Arab's steel.

Amongst some documents secreted away in a dressing-case which had belonged to Richard Garth, letters were found that awoke a strange interest in those who read them.

They were immediately placed in a lawyer's hands, and Frank Clifton was summoned in a desperate hurry, to hear himself proclaimed innocent; the fraud for which he had been condemned was Richard Garth's crime.

"I always knew the truth would come out one day," Frank said, his boyish face flushed with pride. "Though I never thought that the man who at the time pretended to be my only friend, could have so deeply deceived me."

Gladys was overjoyed when she knew that her brother, for whose sake she had suffered so much, was to take his place in the world, and hold his own with other men.

The shadow was lifted from her life, and the year so stormily commenced seemed suddenly to break into sunshine.

Osman had left Deepwood before the alarm of Garth's death had been set afloat, and he disappeared, no one knew where.

Most likely he had gone back to the East, to join his own tribe. Amongst those in whose fate he had figured he was never seen again, and, remembering what his last act had been, nobody cared to seek him out.

"Did you ever hear anything more of Florence?" Frank asked one day when he called at the Towers, his thoughts going back to the fair pale woman, whose face had sometimes haunted him in Cairo.

Gladys' sweet eyes grew very serious.

"I wrote to tell her of Garth's death," she answered, suppressing a sigh. "My letter was forwarded on to Naples, where she is living with some relatives, and from her reply I imagine she is much better, and has quite got over her mad sorrow. I am glad she is with friends. The news must have been a shock to her, though she does not express any grief."

"Could you expect it?" Frank muttered with a touch of bitterness. "Think what he was to her."

"Her husband; and he is dead," Gladys said gently. "Don't bring up any more wrong against him. What we know is ill enough; we can forgive him all the rest."

"What a true-hearted little woman you are!" Sir Edmund exclaimed, bending down to kiss the soft tender face. "I do not believe you think anyone too bad to have a kind word spoken for them. I hope you are as loyal to me when I am absent."

She pressed his hand warmly against her cheek.

"I do not want you to put me to the test," she answered, smiling; "I never mean to lose sight of you again—not for a single hour."

He laughed a full, rich, happy laugh, and smoothed the shining hair caressingly back from her brow.

They were in one of the small pretty drawing-rooms they liked best to be in when they were without visitors.

Afternoon tea was served on a gipsy-table placed on the hearthrug, and the firelight glowed brightly on them as they sat round in their easy-chairs.

A bunch of early violets scented the room and reminded them spring was approaching, and Sir Edmund was watching for the wild-rose tints to blossom again in Gladys' cheeks.

"Ned, you have never yet told me what became of you during that long disappearance?" she exclaimed quite suddenly. "I am well enough now to hear anything, and there is no reason in the world for you to keep the mystery up. I have heard since that you looked more dead than alive when you came back. What happened?"

An anxious pain darkened his face for a moment. He had rather she had never mentioned this subject—rather she had never asked an explanation. What was he to tell her—how satisfy her with only half the truth?

"You remember the well where you found my gun?" he asked after a pause.

Gladys left her seat, and kneeling down by his side, she linked her arm softly in his.

"How did it come there?" she whispered with a slight shiver.

"It fell from my hand."

"But how? Tell me how it happened."

"I—stumbled over something, and slipped into the well. Fortunately for me there was a ledge about three feet above the water, and by a sheer accident I managed to clutch at it, and to crawl into the recess—a dark, damp hole, that was more like a grave than anything else.

"Heaven knows how long I might have stayed there, hidden away from human sight! I was half dead when a gang of gipsies came to the well for water, and discovered me.

"I was quite insensible, and they had some difficulty in dragging me out, but between them they carried me to one of their caravans, and nursed me through a brain-fever.

"They had not the slightest idea of my identity. In their wandering life they had heard nothing of my disappearance; and I think they hoped, when I recovered, I might repay them by joining their tribe.

"As soon as I was able to make them understand, I begged them to take you word of my safety; but to my despair, I found we had been travelling ever since my rescue, and I was miles from Deepwood!

"I gave them all the money I had about me, and my watch, which had been at their mercy. Then I started on a return journey, and never rested till I was home."

Gladys had grown icy cold, and her eyes were bright with intense feeling.

"I do not know how I lived through that time," she exclaimed, pressing her forehead against his shoulder. "It has taught me how great a part of my life lives in your love. Without you, I was no longer the same."

"Did not the boy make up for my loss?" Sir Edmund asked, putting his arm tenderly round her; "once or twice I have felt inclined to be rather jealous of that baby."

"You are only teasing," she said, her face brightening with a happy smile. "I love baby, but the love I give him is for you. His little life joins our souls; and the fonder I am of him, the nearer I seem to you."

Sir Edmund pressed her closer against his heart. It was sweet to have the whole love of this pure life, and his soul thrilled with silent thanksgiving when he thought of the long years of happiness in store— happiness that would never let life grow dim while he had Gladys.

Gladys! her name seemed to ring with brightness— to ripple with a promise of undying love and fadeless joy.

His pulse throbbed with a stronger pride than he had ever known, and his eyes shone with deeper and more manly passion. His life had reached its perfection.

Gladys wondered what thought was keeping him silent. He had not forgotten her. His firm warm clasp had tightened round her, and as she looked up at him, his lips met hers in a fervent kiss.

"Do you remember our wedding-day?" he asked after a pause.

"It was the most miserable and the most happy day of all my life, Ned."

"Anyhow, I hope you will never have another!" he replied with grim humour. "I found out about those photos the other day. That was more of Richard Garth's work."

"How do you know?" Frank exclaimed, breaking into the conversation with almost fierce energy.

"I came across a copy of the photos in some out-of-the-way studio, and on making enquiries, I learned that the man had been engaged secretly to take a likeness of you both while you were saying good-bye. The fellow was sensible enough to be suspicious," Sir Edmund added, looking earnestly at Gladys; "and thinking they might be useful some day, he managed to get Garth's face without his knowing, and a separate likeness of Frank, whose features were not to be shown in the chief portrait."

"But what could have been his motive?" Gladys asked, indignant and bewildered at the unthought of wrong. "It was heaping injury on injury—crime upon crime. I cannot understand——"

"So much the better, Gladys; it is well to forget it all—that was the last thread to the mystery."

"It is a satisfaction to know you did not find it out before," she said presently. "I like to remember how you took me back, and sheltered Frank, while things were still so dark against us."

"Does this atone for all, Gladys?" he asked, gently lifting her face while he gazed into her shining eyes. "Is the happiness as great as the suffering has been?"

"A thousand times greater! I could never imagine a joy so perfect as what I feel now—I mean at this very moment. And you, Ned," after a long dreamy pause—"are you as much in love with life?"

"In love with you, darling," he corrected laughingly; "the dearest and truest wife in the wide world."

Frank closed an album he had been carelessly turning over, and looked at them with a boyish smile, grateful that at the last all had come right between those two who, for his sake, had been so STRANGELY PARTED.

THE END.

www.ingramcontent.com/pod-product-compliance
Lightning Source LLC
Chambersburg PA
CBHW081146020726
47504CB00009B/2016